THREE WEEKS IN THE SUMMER

Paul Marriner

Bluescale Publishing

www.bluescalepublishing.co.uk

Cover design by Catherine Murray at www.piggledesign.co.uk

Bluescale Publishing

ISBN 978-0-9929648-4-9

For June and Ray – the kindest and
most gentle of souls

THREE WEEKS IN THE SUMMER

Chapter 1
Kon Tum, Vietnam, March 1960
Greguska

The baby in the corner of the shack would not stop crying. Held in his mother's embrace, the baby would not stop crying. The mother sat on the only chair, rocking the baby. Though she had no faith she prayed the baby would settle, and, as they hid in the grounds of the Catholic church in Kon Tum, perhaps her prayers would be heard. Her baby had been changed and fed less than an hour ago, on reaching the hut, and she was so tired the gentle rocking was exhausting. Though she was sore from feeding and doubted her baby was hungry she turned on the chair so the men couldn't see and fumbled with her free hand to unbutton jacket and blouse. She offered her breast to her week old son but with his face pressed into her swollen bosom he cried louder and she was ashamed she could not calm him. Although it was nearly mid-day the small hut's interior was shrouded in greys; with no window the only light came through gaps in the wooden slats forming the walls. The solitary candle on the uneven table was unlit. In another corner were the two men, whispering urgently below the baby's crying. The younger of the two men looked to her and though the light was poor she saw the pleading in his eyes; desperate for her to keep his son quiet. It scared her to see such a face: pleading. He was tall and strong and quick to be sure and gently firm; she had

1

never, in sixteen months of knowing him, seen him afraid, but why else would he plead so with just a glance? And if he was afraid, so too was she. She smiled as best she could, hoping to comfort his fear, and he smiled back. He wiped sweat from his forehead; a futile gesture in the humidity. His shirt stuck to his shoulders and chest and he rolled his sleeves a turn higher but it made no difference. The heat lay heavy on the hut's dried coconut leaf roof and seeped through to the damp air beneath. He turned back to his brother; older and bigger and sweating more, shirt transparent against his paunch. Buttoning her blouse to cover her breast she held her son more tightly and rocked with more urgency. Between the baby's cries she heard their whispers but it meant nothing to her; they spoke Czech, hoping to hide their fears but fuelling her growing dread. The baby cried more loudly.

'Diu.' The baby's father called to her as loud as he dare. 'Please. The boy, hush.'

Diu shook her head. 'I am sorry Greguska. I don't ….. know what to do.' Her English was stilted and rushed.

The older man placed a big hand on his brother's damp shoulder. 'It's all right Greguska. We will be gone soon. Safe.' He turned to Diu and repeated, 'Safe.' He laughed deep and loud as usual but without conviction. It was hard for Diu to laugh back, but she did, for Greguska.

'Yes. Safe.' Greguska patted his brother's hand on his shoulder.

'We can trust the British. They owe us.' The bigger man nodded more than was necessary.

'Will the British go back for my father?' Diu wanted to believe him but looked at her baby, head bowed as she asked the question. Greguska crossed the hut to kneel before her. The baby still cried but Diu was focused on Greguska's voice.

'No.' He spoke kindly but offered no doubt. Diu nodded her understanding but didn't look up, not wanting to show her silent tears. Greguska stroked the baby's head and Diu's hair and stood, decision made. 'But we have another hour or so. I'll go and see.'

His brother shook his head. 'See what?'

'What happened at the house.'

'You know what happened.'

'I didn't see it. There's a chance ....'

'.... he might be ok?' Diu asked but didn't believe her own hope.

'A chance,' Greguska tried to agree.

'No.' The older man spoke with authority.

'But we should find out what the Vietcong learnt.' Greguska was trying to convince himself. 'If they know of us and Diu and the baby it will be difficult to travel.'

His brother pulled him back to the other side of the hut. 'If they have Diu's father, they know,' he whispered, 'and we can only hope the British are here before the search.'

'She deserves to know what happened. We .... I .... owe it.' Greguska motioned back over his shoulder. His brother sighed,

'Okay, but only because it might help us be safe to understand what they know. I will go. You stay until the British come.'

'No. You will be too slow.' Greguska kicked his brother's left ankle lightly and laughed at the resulting curse. 'See. It hurts too much. A man your size shouldn't be throwing himself over fences so much. Besides, Diu and the baby are mine and I should make sure they are safe. And if .... when .... the British do come they will listen to you. You need to make sure they take them. It's like that mess in Estonia in fifty-two. Remember?'

'I remember.' The older man grinned.

'Were we on the right side then?' asked Greguska.

'Are we on the right side now?'

'I don't know.'

'What have I taught you?'

'There is no right or wrong. Just us and them. Like

3

Estonia.'

'Exactly.'

'In Estonia, you went to look. To know it was safe.' Greguska looked up at his big brother, though he was just as tall.

'You were a beginner.'

'You've taught me well. It's my turn and you're hurt.'

It was true. He was struggling just to stand and was scared to take off his boot to see the damage. He felt the ankle and foot swelling inside. As if it gave a degree of control he checked his watch and ordered, 'One hour. If he isn't at the house come straight back. One hour.' He kissed his little brother on both cheeks.

Greguska nodded agreement, kissed Diu and the baby's head and went out into the stifling heat and damp. The baby fell quiet. Diu never saw Greguska again.

Chapter 2
England, June - July 1976
Radio Girl

The bus stop was less than fifty yards from home. Richard took off his blazer and sauntered so as not to catch up with her. She had left the bus at the same stop, as usual, and, as usual, Richard walked ten or twenty yards behind, working through scenarios in which he introduced himself, impressed her with his wit and charm and wasn't a total prat. She (and her family) had moved in seven doors along from Richard three or four months ago and though they didn't take the same bus in the morning, she was often on the same bus home. She wore the uniform of the local comprehensive, so was no older than he and possibly a year or two younger. It was impossible to be sure of girls' ages - some of them were grown and intimidating before their (or his) time and others grown but unaware and unknowing and others still pre-pubescent but nevertheless bold and still others an unapproachable mystery. He placed the girl walking ahead in the last category: tall, pretty, shoulder length dark hair (expertly styled – he didn't know what style, exactly, only that it looked no accident), pale skin (despite the June sun being warmer than usual), emerging breasts just hidden by the blazer and aloof - though the aloofness might be due to the ear-piece in her right ear (always her right) which was hooked into the small, bright blue plastic transistor radio she carried so

5

casually. Occasionally she eased one of the dials on the side back and forth or fussed with the ear-piece. He didn't know to which station she listened (probably Radio One or Luxembourg and he hoped it might be playing Brass Construction - his latest cassette purchase), but she was the only pretty, tall, dark haired girl he knew so confident with her transistor radio. He thought she had dark blue eyes but wasn't sure. Her name was unknown (to him - he assumed others knew it, obviously) and though he was friendly with a few of the girls at her school he hadn't asked after her. He enjoyed the mystery and the secret - he hadn't even told his best friend of his non-romance with Radio Girl - and there was a long summer ahead. And, now he thought of it, she hadn't been carrying books into school these last few days, like he hadn't, so she was probably mid-way through exams. This put her, like him, in fifth form; in which case there was an even longer summer ahead - exams (and school) finished in just two weeks. The exams were going .... okay .... for him but their finale couldn't come soon enough. He thought of asking what subject she'd taken that day and how it went, but where was the subtlety or charm in that? Besides, he had all summer and she was just seven semi-detached, thirties built, suburban doors along - paths were sure to cross. She walked past his front gate and he sped up, anticipating the chocolate Nesquik which waited in the kitchen and he felt he'd earned but Radio Girl had stopped a couple of yards past his gate and he was there before he realised. She turned, tilted her head while extracting the tiny ear-piece, gave her hair a shake to settle it back down and spoke as he stopped at his gate. Her voice was soft and her eyes smiled and they were the deep blue he'd imagined. He didn't hear a word she said. He smiled back at her, the smile he had been practising for weeks, and tried to keep his voice low as he apologised, 'Sorry. I didn't catch that.'

'You're Richard? You're a Rubber Johnny. Right?' She looked from his face to the badge on the blazer he carried.

'Er, yep.' He went to John Le Rugber Independent, but the 'g' was silent (for reasons unknown); 'Rubber Johnny' was inevitable, especially from rival schools. Richard wasn't offended, they were all called that. More importantly, she knew his name. He hoped the spot he'd noticed on his forehead at lunch break wasn't further inflamed with the sweat of the afternoon. Radio Girl smiled sweetly and just wide enough to show how white were her teeth, if not quite even.

'I live a few doors away. Moved in a few months ago.'

'Thought I'd seen you around.'

'Yeah. Mostly on the bus I guess. I heard your friend call you Richard. The guy that gets off two stops before us. He doesn't say much. The other Rubber Johnny. Right?'

'Right.'

'Wass his name?'

'Malcolm.'

'Right. Seems a nice guy.'

'Yep. We go way back.'

'Right.' She looked over Richard's shoulder and back towards from where their bus came, as if she might see Malcolm's stop, at least a mile away. 'Seems a nice guy?' This time it was a question.

It dawned on him why she was asking after Malcolm but he kept his smile. 'Yep we go way back. Nice guy.'

'You always called Richard?'

'Yep.'

'You should try Dick. That's short for Richard right? Dick the Rubber Johnny. That's funny right?' She laughed but there was no malice.

'I guess.' Richard laughed as well, hiding the disappointment it was his friend, rather than he, stood the better chance with Radio Girl. It was not a surprise. Malcolm was tall and athletic and handsome and almost spot-free.

'Gotta go. Revision for tomorrow. You?' Radio Girl turned and was gone before he could agree.

'Right,' Richard said to her back, the practised smile still fixed to his face, and unlatched the gate. Before he could open it an inch he heard the gruff bark from behind the front door, yards up the path. It was a bark of excitement, not anger. Ossie was sitting close behind the door, waiting to hear the latch, probably wondering why it was nearly a minute late (thanks to Radio Girl) and desperate to welcome Richard. Sometimes Richard tried to undo the gate latch and sneak up the path silently so Ossie wouldn't hear, hoping to catch him out: not once.

Ossie barked more frantically as Richard put the key in the front door and eased it open, knowing Ossie would be tight behind it, never learning it would be quicker if he stood back a pace or two. Richard heard his sister's shrill voice scream, 'Ossie! Shut Up!' from inside and his mother's calm voice, asking Ossie to hush - as if it ever made a difference to the happy mongrel. His mother tried to pull Ossie away from the door but though he was not big he was excited and it was difficult for her. Richard squeezed in and dropped to his knees to fuss the dog. His mother let go the dog's collar and went back to the kitchen. Ossie jumped and licked at Richard until satisfied his work was done and went to join Richard's mother when she shook the box of dog biscuits. Richard slipped off his shoes without untying laces.

'Hi mum. What time's dinner?'

'Usual.' She stood up from dropping biscuits into Ossie's bowl and reached up to stroke Richard's cheek. 'Everything oka?' Despite living in England over sixteen years her accent was never lost and some words were still clipped.

'Yep. Everything oka,' Richard mimicked.

'I see you talk to dark hair girl. Pretty.'

'I suppose.'

'I suppose.' It was her turn to mimic his deepening voice. 'Ha ha. She is pretty. And tall.'

'Mum, everyone is, to you.'

'Funny boy. Everything oka?'

'Yep.' He reached over her to take the chocolate Nesquik from the cupboard.

'How did exam go?'

'Okay.'

'Just oka?'

'I suppose ….' He was still thinking of Radio Girl, disappointed she asked after Malcolm and he hadn't even asked her name.

'I suppose.' His mother mimicked him again. 'Why exam only oka?'

'I don't know.'

'I came home early today. I was worried. Tell me, why only oka?'

She was home early. Usually it was just him and his sister at this time of day on a Thursday, when they could bicker, free of parental interruption. His mother worked part-time in a piano showroom (between the ironmongers and a newsagent) in the parade of shops stretching half a mile from the tube station on the corner. She gave demonstrations to prospective customers, mainly on pianos; she didn't fully approve of the electronic keyboards and synthesizers finding their way into the showroom. She was classically trained and a talented pianist but still the manager was asking her to promote the new instruments (Bontempi and Farfisa - he saw the future). In fairness, he didn't push too hard, after all, she was practically working for free - the pittance he paid her - and in reality they both understood she went there three afternoons a week to play the Bechstein. They'd had it over two years but it was a beautiful instrument few customers were able, let alone willing, to afford. Sometimes she steered a customer towards the Bechstein for the excuse to play even when they came in for one of the new Yamaha electric pianos. No-one minded, not even the other sales staff, at least not once they heard the Vietnamese woman play better than they. This might have led to jealousy but the tiny, slight lady with permanent smile, warm eyes, self-deprecating grace and charming accent was easy to like and they were amazed at the power and touch in such small hands (it was astonishing she could cover a full sized grand's keys).

'I know you worried about exam today. More than others. Tell me. How was it?'

'It was all right. I think I did enough. Don't worry.' But he knew she did. Half-way through third form a stiffly kind woman in a formal suit had spent a few English lessons sitting next to him. The lady took him out of school for an entire morning to look at letter tables and word charts and pictures and numbers and geometric patterns and to talk of how he was coping with lessons. Then they invited his mother in 'to chat'. The diagnosis was mild visual dyslexia; the prognosis was vague. The incidence was low and this was the first case ever in John Le Rugber. That last part was, of course, not true, but dyslexia was still a poorly understood condition and it was a rare teacher or doctor who identified a case; generally the sufferers were dismissed as simply not very bright and consigned to the lower sets. Richard was luckier than most dyslexics; his was a mild form and because he was quick-witted with a sharp memory he was able to compensate (to a degree) for what he didn't even know he had. But of course the problems with jumbled letters and difficulty with spelling even simple words was holding him back and he found himself slipping further behind in many subjects when it was generally acknowledged he was as smart as most of his peers. Many teachers assumed it was lack of application on his part but others trusted him to be a conscientious student and one in particular (History) was frustrated enough with his lack of progress to want better for him. For his part, Richard was disappointed with low grades and disheartened so many texts were so, so complicated, but he had no reason to suspect others comprehended anything different - until the stiffly kind lady told him. The diagnosis, whilst a shock in so much as he'd never contemplated such a disadvantage, was also a relief, especially for his mother. She had never understood how her bright, articulate son could speak two languages (he spoke a fair bit of Vietnamese) and play piano to grade four (though mostly by rote, not reading) but struggle to gain a D in English - and she understood how hard he tried. But when she stopped being relieved she was disappointed with herself for not seeing it earlier and angry the school had taken so long. The school (History teacher aside) was less than sympathetic and their primary concern was for their exam results rather than Richard's needs - they had little idea how to help him (independent fee paying school or not). Eventually they decided to carry on as normal but put Richard in for CSEs rather than O Levels, almost unheard of at John Le Rugber. Richard's mother doubted this was the answer but had no other. Richard, for his part, was glad not to be singled out for different lessons and as long as he was allowed to try for maths, physics and music O Level he was happy - the school compromised (the exams were a long way hence at the time) - and now here he was, end of fifth form; CSE and O Level exams for real. And today's exam had gone okay, as he told his mother.

'Good. Everything will be all right,' she confirmed, standing on tip-toe to hug him tightly, which was unusual; he was sixteen and three months. Richard let her squeeze and enjoyed a fleeting memory of years earlier, running from primary school, finding her smile amongst the crowd of mums, throwing himself into her arms and knowing he was loved and sharing her laughter. It no longer mattered he was last pick for the team at playtime or Carol Stratfield called him stupid because .... he didn't know why .... because she could he supposed .... and it didn't matter he couldn't always spell his own surname correctly (as if being undiagnosed dyslexic wasn't enough, his father was Czechoslovakian); it didn't matter he wore a patch over one eye to try and make the other eye stronger or he was one of only two people in the class to wear wire-framed spectacles, though his lenses were thicker. When he was seven none of that mattered as his mother held him tight in the playground after school. He knew none of that mattered because his mother told him so and she told him it would be all right. And it was. Now, at sixteen with the memory flooding as she held him, it was true; none of it had mattered. Yes he still wore spectacles but by now so did many others. He'd finally mastered a surname with only three vowels but two Ks, a J and a Z - possibly his greatest achievement as a dyslexic, though unappreciated by even Malcolm, his closest friend. Yep, things had turned out all right and although Carol Stratfield might still consider him stupid, she was not above holding his hand in the darkness of the Saturday morning cinema club at The Odeon, especially when they re-ran Melody, every other month (it seemed).

So when his mother hugged him on that Thursday in mid-June and told him, 'It will be all right,' he trusted her, despite a sixteen year old's manufactured cynicism and pop-art rebellion. But he didn't know why she told him again that day.

His mother let go as little sister Tina ran down the stairs followed by a school-friend. They rushed past and out into the garden. Ossie barked and followed, keen to be part of whatever excitement they pursued. Richard was pleased Tina had a friend round to tea. Friends meant fish fingers, chips and peas with Birds Eye chocolate mousse for afters.

'I know. It will be all right,' Richard agreed as his mother stopped hugging him and turned to start tea. 'Fish fingers?'

'Of course. And it will be all right,' she repeated, but this time with an edge of desperation.

'Okay. I believe you, but …. er….what will?'

'Everything.'

'Everything? That's good.' He tried to sound convinced but there was a lack of conviction in his mother's voice even a teenage boy couldn't help but notice. 'Anything in particular?' he asked.

'No. Nothing special …. Oh, by way, hospital sent card with date for next test. Next Friday. Eighteenth. Eleven fifteen. Morning.'

'Okay.'

'Oka?'

'Yep.'

'Good. Right, better start tea. You can practise meantime.' She nodded towards the living room where the old upright piano waited.

What his mother didn't mention (perhaps didn't know) was the test consisted of a brain scan which meant jabbing a needle in his arm, pumping in a dye and strapping him to a table to revolve under a machine resembling the death ray from a fifties sci-fi comic strip. It would be a further three weeks, when the consultant called them back in for the results, before Richard realised why his mother had hugged so tight that day and why she so wanted him to believe it would be all right.

Next day Richard told Malcolm of Radio Girl's question (they were best friends) and offered his services as go-between. Malcolm was sensitive in suppressing his excitement (of course he had noticed Radio Girl on the bus) and Richard was grateful but it was still a challenge for him to introduce them later that day, especially without knowing her first name. She told them - Julie - and wasn't fazed by Malcolm's stutter, to Richard's relief. Contact between Malcolm and Julie was restricted to the homeward bus for the next few days as they battled through to the end of exams in the exhausting heat and Richard had to resist trying to engineer it so they didn't sit next to each other - that would be childish. Julie would step on the bus a few stops after the boys and they could see her from the top deck, removing the ear-piece as the bus approached and settling back her hair with a gentle but definite shake. Sometimes Carol Stratfield was on the same bus (she didn't go to the same school as Julie and was on before the boys) and Richard sat with her, leaving Julie and Malcolm alone. Carol talked incessantly and Richard was grateful, even though he didn't follow much of what she said. Carol fell quiet only to light a cigarette (Players No. 10 unless she had been able to lift a couple of Rothmans from her mother's bag). During these brief silences Richard couldn't resist straining to hear Julie and Malcolm's conversation above the general hum of kids' chatter and laughter and rows. Occasionally Carol offered Richard a cigarette (catching his attention by calling him Ritchie Witchy, just as she had in primary school - she never mastered his surname), just to test if he'd changed his mind. He always refused. Since his first hospital appointment to talk about his 'issues', when the consultant had asked him if he was smoking drugs or tobacco and he had lied (he had shared a pack of ten Consulate menthol fags with the guys - though never Malcolm who was serious about his football), he had decided not to smoke.

Now he and Julie were friends, he no longer waited behind her after they left the bus but though they walked together they spoke little and Richard thought she preferred listening to her radio, the way she fiddled with the small transistor's ear-piece. Julie's last exam was two days before Richard's and on the way home, as they strolled in silence from the bus, she stopped and touched his arm. 'Can I ask you something?'

Richard nodded, 'Of course.' He was immediately uncomfortable but didn't know if because of the question or fleeting contact.

'Does Malcolm like me?'

There was a temptation to lie, but Malcolm was his friend, 'Of course.'

'I mean, really …. like me?'

'Yep, really.' This was true and Richard knew because when the guys were talking about girls, Malcolm was quieter than usual and refused to be drawn into juvenile discussion on the order of 'shagability' - when it was obvious Julie topped any list.

'It's just that, well, his stutter is worse when he talks to me than you. Do I make him nervous?'

'Julie, you are so beautiful, you make everyone nervous.' He wanted to say but didn't. Instead: 'Of course, he really likes you, so you make him nervous. It's okay. We're only sixteen and we go to an all boy school.'

'Oh. I see.'

'And well done for not finishing his sentences. He hates that.'

'I thought so. I noticed you never do.'

'Never.'

'You're a good friend.'

Richard shrugged, embarrassed. 'Hey. Did Malcolm mention Saturday night? There's an end of exam party at one of the guy's house. You coming?'

'If Malcolm asks.'

'I'm sure he will. I'll make sure. And there's a long summer ahead,' Richard replied and wondered why he said it with enthusiasm.

After the last exam Richard slipped into the holidays. A high pressure system settled over the south east, drawing hot air from the Mediterranean. There were record high temperatures. These were days of late breakfasts, slow time in the park (very little football being played because of the heat, to Malcolm's disappointment) and lazy nights in friends' gardens. Cans of Carling Black Label and Long Life were pilfered from parents' cabinets; meagre funds were pooled and Party Sevens bought from the obliging off licence on the corner, turning a blind eye to their age. Not a moment was wasted trying to use time productively; no time was lost being other than trivial. Decisions on the coming September were postponed, dependent on exam results which could be ignored until they arrived. Julie often joined their relentlessly unfocused days and Richard was pleased for his friend but couldn't always ignore her blue eyes and had to be careful not to be caught watching, even though Malcolm and Julie were still circling in those first few weeks. Richard's garden became the choice for evenings and Richard would chase his little sister from the patio after tea, put out the deck-chairs and tell his mother and Philip of course they were welcome to join him and Malcolm and Julie and a couple of the other guys; fortunately they always found something on tv to watch (fans of Coronation Street, Emmerdale and Panorama). Richard would set up his small cassette player and much of the evening was spent arguing (often in agreement) on the merits (or otherwise) of the rock or blues or disco or funk (rarely reggae), spilling from the player's tinny mono speaker as they switched cassettes. Melody Maker and New Musical Express articles were repeated almost verbatim in support of one genre and band or another and Malcolm insisted the old order was going to be b .... b .... b .... blown away (hadn't they heard The Ramones first album, released just a couple of months earlier? Didn't they understand the Sex Pistols were n .... n .... now?) but all were united against Radio One's current chart topper: 'I've Got A Brand New Combine Harvester'.

Julie brought her little transistor for use when the boys tired of debating music and instead argued cricket or football or the Soweto uprising or Viking 1 going into orbit round Mars or if The Crown would serve them on a Friday night or if Revell model kits really were more detailed than Airfix (Richard didn't think so but wouldn't bring out any of his own models to prove it while Julie was there).

When they couldn't nick or afford beer they sucked orange Jubblys and Richard's mother sometimes brought out toast and marmite at the end of the evening. On these warm, clear nights in June the drought and forest fires reported in the news were easily ignored and the only shadows on Richard's summer were the 'issues'. His mother had been the first to use that term (sounding very formal despite her accent), trying not to be melodramatic but at the same time not belittling the symptoms. Richard hadn't had an 'issue' since before the exams but a couple of days after Czechoslovakia beat West Germany to win the European Championship (Richard reminding all of his Czech heritage in the days leading up to the game), Malcom goaded Richard into joining the football game that had started over the park - Richard was persuaded he should honour the Czech victory. The park's grass was patchy and brown and it was painful to fall or slide on the compacted and cracked dried mud and the ball bounced high and random. The game (Germany v England/Czechoslovakia mixed) started seven or eight aside but the heat was suffocating, especially for the unfit lads, like Richard, and they gave up when the score reached twelve-ten to Germany. Richard flopped in the shade of one of the trees lining the path bordering the grass and complained bitterly the water fountain had been allowed to fall into arid disuse. He removed his spectacles and wiped the sweat from his eyes and forehead but it reappeared instantly.

Breathing heavily he lay face down, trying to find a cool patch of earth, but there was none, even in shade and when he gave up and turned over the 'issue' hit him. Half the park disappeared - the left half. He sat up. Half the play area was gone - the left half. Half Malcolm's face was gone - the left half. It was not that the missing halves were replaced by anything or even blackness. There simply was nothing there. Wherever he looked the left half was gone - even when he wasn't looking. He was half blind.

The first time it had happened, seven or eight months earlier, he had panicked and every time since the same panic rose in his chest, but with each 'issue' he was understanding more that it would pass and the rising panic gave way to fear for what followed once his sight returned to normal. He needed to be somewhere to feel safe and apologised, though he had no reason to and the words were gibberish. Malcolm had seen it before and guided him home. His mother took him through to a darkened room, reminding him they'd see the consultant soon.

A couple of days later Julie told them she was to spend four weeks with her father in Yorkshire (her parents were separated) but didn't tell them until just before going away. Malcolm shrugged, as if pretending to understand, but Sheffield was a long way north. On Julie's last night he took her to The Odeon for a re-run of The Man Who Fell To Earth (Malcolm was a Bowie fan) without Richard, who later teased it was their first official date. Malcolm insisted they had managed nothing further than holding hands - Richard couldn't tell if he was being coy but his friend was more quiet than usual over the next four weeks: waiting.

They all were: waiting. Malcolm was waiting for Julie to come home. Richard was waiting to see what happened when she did. They were all waiting for their exam results and everyone waited for rain. June slipped into July and although the temperature dipped a degree or two, it was still oppressively hot and there were no clouds. In such heat, waiting dampened expectation and the days ran into one another - except for 2nd July - the only time Richard ever saw his mother crying. That wasn't true. He had seen her cry with happiness many times and with sadness a few times, but this was the first time he had seen her cry with .... he didn't know. She sat at the small table in the kitchen, untouched cold tea in front of her. His step-father knelt beside her. Richard came in just after ten, from Malcolm's, and she was sitting there, crying silently but deeply, from her soul - not numb with pain but paralysed with loss. His step-father stood when he heard Richard come in and took him to the lounge to answer the unspoken question.

'Your mum's upset.'

'Er, yeah. Why?'

'The news. North and South Vietnam are unified. It's now The Socialist Republic of Vietnam. They say it was inevitable, but even so ....'

'Isn't that good? Won't they be one now?'

'I don't know. I don't understand. You should try, one day, to understand. It's your history. But at the moment I don't think your mother cries for the future. It's the past and the suffering they went through to reach today. I don't know if she thinks it's good or not, just she can't forget what happened and doesn't know if it was all worth it. How could it be?'

'What, so she's crying for my dad?' Richard knew very little of the story.

'I suppose. But the others too. Thousands. Hundreds of thousands. Of others. A generation of grief. I don't really understand. I don't know what to do or say.'

Richard saw his step-father's pain at being helpless and patted his shoulder. He went to the kitchen. His mother hadn't moved and he knelt to put an arm around her. 'S'okay mum. Everything will be all right,' and prayed she would believe him as he had her all these years.

The day of Richard's appointment with the consultant (it was put back a week) his mother woke him much earlier than he now expected. She made breakfast for both him and Tina (she still had two weeks of school) and insisted they leave early. Richard's step-father, Philip, took them to the hospital on his way to work - in a brand new, bright yellow Datsun 180b. Philip was Sales Manager in a Datsun showroom and, as he told anyone that would listen, though interest rates were high the country was crawling out of recession and things were looking up - how could they not in the relentless sunshine - and Datsuns were selling well with their reputation for reliability, compared to British Leyland's finest. The dealership where Philip worked was making money and he was proud to be driving one of their latest models, even if it was in the gaudiest shade of yellow, shining defiantly in the summer to embarrass the browns and drab ambers of home-built competition.

Philip and his mother had married shortly after Richard's seventh birthday. Richard didn't remember much but recalled his uncle Dudek being thrilled his mother insist he keep his father's surname; Richard was pleased as he'd almost nailed the spelling. His younger sister Tina was born nearly a year after the wedding and it never struck either of them as strange their surnames differed, though he thought his mother tired of having to explain. His sister appeared more Vietnamese than he, which worked in her favour; she was petite, pretty, dusky, dark eyed, black haired and attractively different from other girls. She was now eight and had just started to be the butt of a few jokes at school as the children started to notice she was part non-English. Richard admired she had already developed a sophisticated way of smiling at such nonsense as if to say I pity your ignorance and celebrate your inability to affect me. Of course, she didn't use those words, but Richard's private education had given him a great vocabulary, even if he didn't always use it properly. That education was one of the two things his father left him; the other was his surname. He was grateful for both. His mother said the education was paid for by the British Government in exchange for whatever it was his father did in Vietnam that killed him and which his mother didn't talk of - but he mostly believed it would be all right in the end; his mother said so.

His mother had brought him to England from Vietnam as a baby, only weeks old, shortly after his father died, serving in British Military Intelligence. Why a Czechoslovakian was in British Military Intelligence was never explained, never mind why he was in Vietnam, and whenever he touched on it his mother would say, 'That, Richard, is other story. And it will be all right.' And change the subject. He never learnt the story but knew he underestimated what must have been a lonely, difficult journey for a young woman on a boat for such a long time, surrounded by strangers and looking towards an uncertain future in a new land without her child's father. Despite the obstacles she settled well in England and when, a few years later, met another man (Philip) and re-married she insisted Richard keep his father's Czechoslovakian surname. That name, his part Vietnamese looks from his mother and an English Christian name made him a source of curiosity. Sometimes, looking back, the curiosity was expressed in terms that might be considered offensive, but, to be honest, no more offensive than the names they called John Edenford when he started ballet or the baiting Simon Rouster suffered for an entire term because his uncle was arrested for soliciting on the heath (they didn't know what soliciting was but the fact their parents changed subject rather than explain made it tease-worthy) or the abuse Adam Nalldan endured because he was the one who turned up first day at John Le Rugber in short trousers. And on those days when, because of his name or features, he felt alone or was treated differently or was mocked, his mother calmly confirmed, 'Everything will be all right,' and it was. Richard could imagine how she, as a rare Vietnamese lady in England must have faced similar situations on a daily basis and probably her new husband, Philip, received ignorant abuse for marrying a foreigner, so she understood mis-trust and bigotry. So did Philip. He was a good man; never seeking to replace Richard's father but always willing to do so when asked. He dropped them off at the hospital with a sincere concern the consultation would go okay.

The core of the hospital had been built at the turn of the century but was now surrounded by a mix of clinics and wards built and expanded in the early sixties as the National Health Service settled. Now, twenty five years later, the buildings were tired and old-fashioned. It was not an easy task for Richard and his mother to find Neurology (even though they had been there only four weeks earlier for the final test), and when they did the receptionist gave the impression they were only just in time for their appointment when they had at least fifteen minutes.

The consultant appeared very old and very small. He wore a three piece suit under a white lab coat and looked cold and pale, despite the late June sun brightening his office. He spoke deliberately, as if Richard and his mother were stupid, and Richard wanted to tell him she spoke three languages fluently, played the piano almost to concert standard and cooked the best fish fingers and chips in the world. They sat in silence while he finished looking at letters from a manila folder and unfolded a long wide roll of paper showing jagged needle thin lines tracing mountains on a grid. Other large sheets of paper showed the outline of a head from differing angles, each with a crude brain shape made of pixelated bars and squares of different shades. He looked back to the folder and took off his spectacles.

'Hello Richard. How are you today?'

The consultant was so polite for one in his position Richard felt obliged to say, 'Fine thank you Sir,' when he was still having the 'issues' that were the reason for starting the tests three or four months ago.

'And how are you Mrs. Cooper? May I call you Diu?'

Richard's mother nodded, even though the pronunciation of her first name was dubious. Richard saw she was holding her breath.

'Good. Diu. Well. Richard and Diu. Good news. The scan did not reveal there to be a brain tumour.'

'Thank God,' Diu blurted out and gulped in air.

'Indeed,' offered the consultant, possibly taking the thanks as being in part for him.

Richard sat in confused silence and it was as if they talked about someone else. At no point in the months of appointments and tests had anyone let slip they thought there was the merest possibility his 'issues' were anything to do with a brain tumour. The consultant spent time explaining the results to Diu and she asked a lot of relevant questions which surprised him.

Richard sat nodding while the words brain and tumour bobbled around his head - then they collided and he said the words out loud, much louder than intended. 'Brain tumour! Who said I've a brain tumour?'

He'd interrupted them and the consultant reacted first. 'No-one. In fact, you don't have one. That's the good news. But the symptoms can be similar so we needed to eliminate the possibility.'

'But you thought I had a brain tumour?' Richard pushed his spectacles higher up his nose. The question was to his mother, who answered simply,

'There. I told you it would be all right. Didn't I?'

And, compared to a brain tumour, he had to admit it was. The consultant leant forward and patted her on the hand as if for a job well done and went on to explain as it wasn't a tumour, the symptoms and other tests indicated Richard was a classic migraine sufferer. He took this to be a compliment; being considered classic. It wasn't until afterwards he learnt it was the migraine defined as classic, not him.

As a reward for not having a brain tumour, they had Chinese takeaway that night and Philip let Richard have a can of Double Diamond. Diu waited until he had finished before suggesting fresh, country air would be good for his migraines (she had found an article in Reader's Digest suggesting as much) and a trip to his Uncle Dudek's might be a good idea (as long as he avoided eating cheese - another Reader's Digest suggestion). Richard was hesitant and his mother didn't press. He had planned to spend the holidays just hanging out with Malcolm and the guys and 'bumping into' Radio Girl, expecting an instant mutual and animal attraction, leading to a feverish summer affair - but that aspiration was blown. Julie had declared for Malcolm and Richard's plan was wasted but he was reluctant to abandon it. Besides, Malcolm's dad ran a fencing business and had offered the boys a couple of weeks labouring work for a fiver a day - too good to refuse.

'And a young man needs a few bob in his pocket.' Philip had helped convince Diu.

Chapter 3
Carol

The fencing business was physically much harder than either Richard or Malcolm imagined, especially in the pitiless sun; digging holes for posts in hard earth was back-breaking and blister-making. But the days went fast and working alongside Malcolm's father's regular guys was an education - they could intimidate and it was impossible to tell their true mood until admonishments, insults and abuse broke into collective laughter (though even that wasn't always natural).

The customers were mostly friendly, providing lemon or orange squash at regular intervals against the sun - even for the men, who thought it amusing. One, Gerry, waited until the customer was back indoors before taking his hip flask from a hidden pocket in his dungarees and topping up the squash with a thin, watery, brown liquid the boys took to be whisky. Gerry didn't bother hiding it from the boys (breaking into the first few lines of Molly Malone as he poured, in an Irish accent that was otherwise absent) and perhaps hadn't realised Malcolm was the boss's son - he was slow on any uptake, but powerful with a spade (though he claimed it was technique) and laughed at the boys when their efforts bounced off the earth. Richard learnt to hold the spade incorrectly so Gerry couldn't resist taking it from him to show how it should be done (again).

The evenings were even slower with their tiredness but the wages paid in cash on Friday made it worthwhile.

Malcolm missed Julie more on the weekends (she was still at her father's). So did Richard, but when Malcolm suggested Richard ask out Carol Stratfield he had no good reason not to (that he could say) and Malcolm knew a guy from football who had her number.

Carol's father or brother answered the call and was relaxed when Richard asked to speak to her - it was as if they didn't hear his heart pounding or sense the tremor in his voice. It wasn't he was nervous of asking her out, they had been friends (sort of) a long while and been out together before, in groups (especially to the cinema); it was just he was out of practise of asking anyone - very out of practise. He rang from home one afternoon while his mother was shopping with Tina and Philip was at work. He prepared a set of opening lines to suit whoever should answer the phone - Carol, her mother, father (or older brother) or little sister - but wasn't prepared for the disinterest shown by her father (or older brother) as he was left hanging longer than expected. Finally, Carol said, 'Yeah?'

'Carol?'

'Yeah.'

'It's Richard.'

'Who?'

'Richard. Ritchie Witchy.'

'Oh. Hi Witchy. Haven't seen you since the bus. Wotchya doing?'

'Nothing much. You?'

'Talking to you? How's Radio Girl?'

'What? Oh, dunno. She's not around much these days. Gone to visit her dad somewhere.' Richard regretting telling Carol he called her that.

'Malcolm okay?' she asked sincerely and Richard was surprised.

'Yep. I suppose.'

'You suppose. Good. Wotchya want?' she asked; direct but not aggressive.

'Do you .... would you .... what you doing Thursday .... night?'

'Thursday?'

'Yep.'

'Tomorrow?'

'Yep.'

'You do know you're famed by the girls on the bus for your witty repartee, don't you?'

'Really?'

'Really. But not just now apparently.'

'Oh.'

'Top of the pops is on.'

'What?'

'Thursday. Top of the pops is on.'

'Yep. Maybe we could .... go out after?'

'Where?'

'A drink? Down The Crown?'

'Will they serve you?'

'Dunno. They say there's more chance on a Thursday. I was paid last week. It's on me.'

'I assumed that.' She laughed. 'Okay. You coming here first?'

'Okay.'

Richard's mother remembered Carol's address (she had taken Richard to tea there when he was six) and didn't tease him too much when he asked. It was a bus ride away, which meant missing Top of the Pops, but that was okay, it was far too lightweight for Richard these days - he was allowed to stay up late for The Old Grey Whistle Test. Carol was ready and didn't let Richard in, ignoring the shout from her father not to 'go walking over the heath, there's been more fires'. The heath was an anomaly in their suburb; several acres of land bombed out during the war, subsequently cleared but not developed. It had reverted to scrubland (not really a heath) with little intervention from the council and was a popular haunt for lovers with nowhere else to go - rumours of devil worshippers were rife but unproven and the recent spate of fires had destroyed much of the gorse, brambles and tall grasses.

The Crown was a Fuller's pub, just on the edge of the heath, a short bus ride from Carol's. It had a reputation for serving underage drinkers, as long as they were able to provide a precise birth date without hesitation. Carol and Richard practised theirs on the bus.

Between the bus stop and The Crown, Carol lit a cigarette, 'It'll help you get served,' she said, offering one to Richard who refused, happy to take his chances with his new birth date. Richard ushered Carol into the saloon bar (despite drinks costing more than in the public bar) and took a second to look round; there were few people inside and no-one he recognised (as if that was likely). The pub's garden backed onto the heath and the warm evening had enticed most customers outside. Richard drew himself to full height and wished for the confidence in his stride to appear natural (it wasn't). Thanks to his father he was tall and he had his mother's slender frame and no puppy fat. He hoped his darker skin and the touch of orient in his eyes made it harder to age him, though there was no reason to believe that and he was still not shaving (not even the slightest wisp feathered his top lip), unlike many of his friends. He wore his best jeans (flares), a pair of Adidas Samba, plain white shirt and denim waistcoat (though he was no Quo fan).

There were two barmaids behind the counter, probably both in their twenties but he wasn't good at ages. They looked at each other and one stepped forward to welcome Richard and Carol to the bar. 'Evening.' Her smile was practised but sincere.

'Hi.'

'What would you like?'

'Can I have a pint of lager please and ....' Richard turned to ask Carol but before she spoke the barmaid said,

'You are over eighteen aren't you?'

'Of course.' Richard spoke slowly, hoping to hide nerves.

'Of course he is,' said Carol and drew on her cigarette. 'I'm no cradle snatcher. Go on, tell her your date of birth.' She nudged Richard.

'Second March, nineteen .... forty eight.'

The barmaid looked to her colleague, 'Looks good for someone .... nearly thirty, doesn't he?'

The other barmaid laughed.

'Idiot. It was fifty eight,' Carol said lightly. Richard blushed. The barmaid leant across the counter and indicated to Richard to come close. She whispered,

'But if you promise to sit quietly in the corner we'll all pretend. Okay?' She stood away. 'So, sir. A pint of lager for you.'

'Er. Yes please.'

'And madam?' She looked to Carol.

'Port and lemonade please.'

'The good port or .... the cheap?'

Carol looked to Richard who confirmed, 'The good stuff.' What else could he say? Regardless of it being drowned in lemonade.

'Good choice sir.'

They sat in a booth in the corner, only partly visible from the bar and when Carol offered him a cigarette (persistent) he shook his head. They sipped from their drinks and Carol thanked him as she put her glass on the table, '.... for the good port.'

'Does it taste better?'

'Of course. I expect.'

They lapsed into silence, which surprised Richard; he had never known Carol quiet more than ten seconds. His own nervousness was also a surprise. He and Carol went back a long way but she was different here. She wore more make-up than usual, with blue eye-shadow and black mascara outlining hazel eyes. She had smooth skin stretched over slightly chubby cheeks and her mouth, which he'd always thought a little small, was perfect when accentuated by red lipstick - not gaudy but rich with colour and shine. Her shoulder length hair was parted in the centre, flicked back at the sides but turned under as it fell to her shoulders. He sipped from his lager, still not sure he enjoyed the taste but it was cold - a good thing in the warm pub; the windows and doors were open but the air was stuffy. He unbuttoned his denim waistcoat and wondered how to compliment Carol on her appearance.

'Music?' She thought of something to say and pointed to the jukebox on the wall.

'Okay. What's it take?'

'Dunno. Oh, hang on, says five pence per play or ten for thirty pence.' She stood and crossed the pub to the machine, searching through her bag on the way. She smiled at the barmaids who smiled back, as if sharing a secret. Richard watched her. The white blouse she wore had large collar and cuffs. The sleeves were baggy and her bust (both bigger and higher, somehow, than Julie's - he couldn't help but compare) filled the body, causing a small gap at the buttons. If the angle was right he could catch a glimpse of the off-white bra beneath. The dark blue skirt's waist was high and the skirt stopped just below her knees; it was tight round her hips - she had curves he hadn't noticed before. The skirt was nowhere near as short as her school uniform but carried far more suggestion.

She studied the jukebox for a few seconds before turning to catch Richard's eye (easy because he was still watching) and mouthing, 'Witchy. Help.'

He joined her, standing close enough to catch her flowery perfume and surprised himself by pulling in a deep breath through his nose, embarrassed in case she noticed. She seemed not to, peering intently at the box on the wall. The choice was extensive and they spent a couple of minutes pretending to argue over the Bowie tracks before feeding in the coins and pushing the buttons carefully -

pressing O26 rather than P26 would bring embarrassment from 'Una Paloma Blanca'.

The few other customers in the pub watched them. Richard didn't care; he was proud to be with Carol.

They were back at their table by the time the opening bars of 'Golden Years' started and a little more relaxed but it was still not the Carol he knew. He refused another cigarette and Carol lit another. 'So. Are Malcolm and Radio Girl doing it?'

Richard sipped deliberately to gain thinking time. 'Doing it?'

'Don't be shy. You know....' she whispered and Richard leant forward to hear her. She stretched toward him and he smelt her fragrance again despite the cigarette, '.... are they fucking yet?'

She touched his hand. He wanted to touch it in return, slowly, but had no idea if it was the right thing to do.

'C'mon, Malcolm would tell you. Have they? Fucked yet?'

Richard didn't think so and didn't like to think about it. That's not to say he didn't like thinking about Julie and fucking. He did. A lot. In the bath and in his bedroom - less so when walking round the shops or having dinner or watching tv or practising piano or digging out an old fence post, but even then it wasn't far from mind. Malcolm was never involved.

'C'mon. You can tell me.' She touched his hand again.

'No.' He laughed to show he wasn't shocked by the question. 'At least not that I know. And she's been away for a few weeks.'

'So Malcolm must be really horny by now.' She sat back in her chair. 'I'm not sure she's the type anyway.'

Richard didn't know what 'type' Julie was. He had assumed there were 'types' of girl that did and 'types' that didn't and it was good to hear it confirmed by a girl. He wondered what type was Carol.

'Play That Funky Music' began. 'Good choice,' Richard acknowledged.

'Thank you. Thought you'd approve, but don't change subject. Is she? The type?'

'I don't know. Honest. Are you?' He looked straight into her hazel eyes, feeling brave for asking.

'Are you?' she asked back.

'I ….'

Carol interrupted, 'Of course you are. You have a prick.' She whispered the last part and giggled. Richard could only nod. Julie had competition for tonight's fantasy. She held Richard's gaze. 'Anyway, if Malcolm and Radio Girl haven't yet, they soon will. My brother reckons it's to do with the weather this summer. Everyone's at it. Here's to summer.' She raised her glass before taking a sip. Richard did likewise and asked,

'Is your brother …. you know ….?'

'Definitely. But he's nearly nineteen. It's why he won't look for a job until autumn. His girlfriend this week is a bit of a slapper but I like her. She says she'll teach me …. stuff.' She paused to give Richard time to think about ….

'…. stuff?'

'Oh yes.' She leant forward and whispered again, 'Stuff.'

'Stuff,' he repeated, smelling her perfume again.

She sat back in her chair. 'Oh, my mum said say hi to your mum. She remembered her from some birthday party or something. When I was kid.'

'I'll tell her. I sort of remember that party. You cried when you opened the present I brought. A toy piano. My mother gave me toy pianos to take to all friends' birthday parties. Weird.'

'Weird,' Carol agreed. 'Hey, been meaning to ask. You don't mind if I call you Witchy sometimes, do you?'

'No. It's much better than Rubber Johnny but you're the only one allowed to call me Witchy.'

'Our secret. Anyway, what you been doing since school finished?'

'Dossing about. Worked for Malcolm's old man for a few days. Earned a few quid …. and …. I had a …. test, in hospital. Otherwise, not much doing.'

'Test? In hospital. What for?'

'It was a brain scan …. and yes, they found one, ha ha. No big deal. Headaches and stuff.' He didn't want to talk about it and was surprised he mentioned it at all; perhaps it was front of mind because he'd been back to the GP earlier that day, for the prescription recommended by the consultant. 'What about you? Doing much?'

'Nope. Dossing about mostly. What you doing September?'

'Dunno. You?'

'Don't know. How about we just take off for a few months? Get a rail card and bum around the continent. I can work on my tan. You can rub in the lotion.'

Her tan looked fine already from where Richard sat but before he could work out how to say so there was a deafening two-tone screech from outside. Carol nearly dropped her glass. The screaming siren continued for a few more seconds but the following silence was little relief, such was the ringing in their heads. One of the barmaids took her hands from her ears and came from behind the bar. As she reached the open door a fireman in heavy black double-breasted tunic and bright yellow over-trousers came through. His face was red but he looked calm and spoke to her quietly, knowing all eyes were on him. The barmaid listened intently. The shock in her face made Richard stand and take Carol's hand. 'Come on, let's see.'

The barmaid went behind the bar and through to the back. The fireman asked for the few customers' attention, politely, and as he spoke Richard caught the smell of burning grass wafting in through the open window. A fire on the heath was almost out of control and the fireman asked everyone to leave - calmly. He went through and repeated the message to the crowded garden. The people there already smelt the burning and reacted. The pub's alarm went off, triggered by the barmaid. Customers filed back into and through the pub. A team of fireman ran a hose from the tender in the car park round to the garden and started to douse a patch of dry earth some twenty yards wide, heathside of the garden. Richard and Carol were among the first out as the smell of burning grew stronger. They edged to the side of the pub to see out back, towards the heath. There were no flames but grey smoke rose from behind the head-high bushes and gorse. Although people in the car park were calm and quiet there was fear in many eyes and those with cars (not many) moved them.

'Your dad was right about the heath.'

Carol looked at Richard with mischief. 'Yeah. Shame. I was gonna suggest we go for a walk there later.'

'That is a shame.' Richard nodded.

'Yeah. And we didn't finish our drinks. And there are still at least three of our songs in the jukebox.'

'What now?'

'Too late for cinema and Wimpy bar's closed. What about the youth club top of my road?'

They both thought for a couple of seconds then simultaneously said, 'Nah,' with a shake of heads.

'My place for a cup of tea. Let's walk.' Carol took Richard's hand. He squeezed to let her know it was a good thing.

They watched the nine o'clock news with Carol's parents (she shared her bedroom with her little sister who was already in bed) and the embarrassing silence was ended by Carol's dad's lament at the breaking news of Southend Pier burning - though not an Essex lad, his family had holidayed there in the late fifties and he vaguely remembered the fire of 'fifty-nine. By the time the news was over Richard was worried Carol's father might cry and checked his watch obviously, saying he'd better be off - bus to catch. He said good night to her parents. Carol showed him to the door and thanked him for the drink.

'No problem. Thanks for coming.' Richard was sincere.

Carol opened the door. Richard went through and she followed, pulling the door to behind her. They stopped in the open porch; it was in shadow though it was not yet night dark. Carol stood on the step so she was nearly his height. 'Should we do this again?'

There was a light breeze which carried Carol's scent.

'I think so. Yes,' Richard answered quickly. 'What do you think?'

'I think I owe you a drink and we can hear the rest of our songs at The Crown.' She leant towards him and kissed him on the cheek. He pecked her back and their cheeks stayed touching. He started to moved his arms, to wrap them around her but so did she and their hands clashed.

'Sorry.'

'No, sorry.'

Oddly their cheeks still touched. Richard's heart beat fast and he ran through options (he had thought Carol would take the lead - she seemed to know .... stuff) but none of the articles he'd read (furtively) in Men Only or Mayfair helped - they tended to start at a point way past his current circumstances. Perhaps making the 'introductory' moves was more Mills and Boon territory, but he had read none of those. He had to do something. He put his hands round Carol's waist (surprisingly small) and pulled her body closer to his. She helped and her smell, flowery before, now took on a more musky hint. He thought (hoped) he felt her breasts graze his chest and took his cheek away from her face to look into her eyes in the manner he remembered Robert Redford looking at

Mia Farrow in his mother's favourite film. Although her face was in shade he saw her smile and moved to kiss her on the lips but she turned her face and he kissed her other cheek instead.

'I've been smoking. I should have cleaned my teeth before ….'

'S'okay. I ….'

She interrupted him by pulling him tight, placing a hand behind his head and turning it into her neck. He nuzzled, not sure if this was for his benefit or hers, but either way she smelt good. His spectacles were awkward and he didn't want the metal frame to hurt her but she pulled his head further into her neck. He sniffed and enjoyed her hips pressing against him.

'Next time ….' she whispered and though he didn't know what she meant, he repeated,'

'Next time.'

'And you can stop smelling me now,' she said kindly, pulling away. Richard forced a laugh and took a step back, adjusting his spectacles.

'I'd better go. I know, what you doing Saturday? There are a few people coming to my place. We're having a Colditz Escape night. Come along.'

'Colditz escape?'

'Board game. You'll love it.'

'Probably not, but I'll come.'

'Good. Sevenish. There'll be a bit to drink, but not much.'

'S'okay. I'll blag a bottle or can of something.

'Good. See you then.' He hesitated, wondering if another peck on the cheek was appropriate but decided not. He backed down the path to the gate, where he called, 'You do smell good though.'

'Thanks. See you Saturday.'

Julie had come home late July. Richard saw her the day after taking out Carol, when his mother asked him to pop round to the bakery for a farmhouse loaf. It was a boring Friday (the fencing business had gone quiet for the summer) and they (Richard, Malcolm and mates) were tiring of hanging round the park. They alternated between tree shade and barren grass to pass the time and though it helped their tan move beyond pink (except for Richard - his half Vietnamese heritage meant he was always darker than the others, but oddly, no darker after the sun), something was lacking. Richard see-sawed between boredom (dulled by both weather and inaction to the point where an hour of piano practise followed by painting the Airfix Hurricane model he'd started back in the Easter break appealed) and excitement (the memory of Carol's touch and smell was still live). The previous night's memories came in short, thrilling waves he couldn't quite capture. He needed to be alone to give them a chance. He left the guys to it (not that 'it' was much) and strolled the ten minutes home, but before he found the small tin of grey-green enamel paint for the model, his mother called him. She needed bread for Philip's sandwiches and asked Richard to go to the shops (giving him fifty pence, stressing change was expected). The bakery was hotter than the street and there was no queue but Richard took his time choosing a loaf from the shelves behind the counter, enjoying the smell. On the way home he noticed the tanned legs and tight shorts a few yards ahead of him, moving away. The rhythm in the girl's walk was familiar and the hypnotic sway of her hips held his attention. He followed for ten yards before taking notice of the dark hair and slender shoulders and realising it was Julie. She wore a white t-shirt, showing off a tan that wasn't there when she left to go to her father's, and when she turned to take the crossing outside the tube station he noticed she looked a cup size bigger, though still small (not that he fully understood what a 'cup' was but he appreciated the difference); the t-shirt was tight. She wore sunglasses and looked straight ahead, serious but not imperious, thoughtful but approachable. He hadn't noticed her nose in profile before but it was straight and exactly the right size and her cheekbones were fine though her face wasn't thin. Richard slowed so as not to catch her and watched as she crossed. She had been gone just over four weeks and had grown - no, he thought again, not grown - matured, no, still not right - evolved. That was the word: evolved. Surprising himself, he called to her across the road. She turned, lowered her sunglasses and her frown dissolved into her smile. She took the ear-piece from her head with a familiar shake of her hair and waited for him to catch up.

'You're back.' Richard stated the obvious.

'Couple of days. Did I miss much?'

Richard pretended to think hard before, 'Er, no. Does Malcolm know?'

'What?'

'You're back. He didn't say.'

'No.' Julie looked to her radio and fiddled with the tuning dial.

'Oh. Should I tell him?'

'I don't know.'

'Oh.' Richard didn't know what to say. He was scared of the answer to the question he wanted to ask; scared for both Malcolm and himself. Julie started walking again, Richard by her side. After fifteen yards she broke the silence.

'I don't know.'

Richard nodded, as if he understood what or why she didn't know until she asked, 'Do you?'

'I don't, but I think the most likely answer is no.' He had no idea what she talked of.

More silence. Another fifteen yards.

'He didn't telephone me. At my father's.'

'Oh,' Richard answered vaguely. 'Should he?'

'I gave him the number.'

'Did he say he'd ring?'

'Not as such.'

'Did you ask him to?'

'Not as such.'

'Would have been nice if he did though?'

'Yes.'

Richard was pleased with his deduction and offered comfort. 'You do know he hates, really, really hates, talking on the telephone? Don't you? That's why he didn't call. Because of the stutter. He hates phones.'

'But I don't mind the stammer. Doesn't he realise by now?'

'Maybe. But he reckons he didn't stammer until his dad had the phone put in. Something about sharing the line and when his father worked away his mother made Malcolm ring him but he couldn't always get a line and when he did he didn't know what to say. And when he did his father didn't.'

'Didn't what?'

'Know what to say. So he really hates phones.'

'Really?'

'So he says. I don't know. It was before I met him.'

'Oh,' said Julie and it was clear she wanted to believe this explanation. They walked in silence until just short of Julie's house when Richard asked,

'Do you want me to tell him you're back?'

'I still don't know.'

'Better from you than me.'

'Yes. Maybe I'll ring him later.' She stopped at her gate and pressed the ear-piece into her right ear but still held her sunglasses.

'Good,' said Richard and nearly meant it. He half-turned, but stopped and raised a hand to catch her attention again. 'Hey, what station you listening to?' He pointed to the blue transistor radio she held.

Julie smiled. 'For me to know and you to ....'

'.... find out.' He finished the sentence and laughed and tried to catch and hold her gaze - her eyes were bluer than ever against her newly tanned face - but she turned and walked up the path to her front door and he was left staring at her hips in tight denim.

He turned away to walk the few yards home as a bus pulled away from the stop, fifty yards further on. The girl that had just left the bus span around and walked away, fast. Richard saw and called after her, 'Carol,' but she didn't turn. He called again but she kept walking and he thought he must have been mistaken; no reason for Carol to be there or not to turn.

Richard gave the bread to his mother and wasted half an hour in his bedroom, caught between thoughts of the colour scheme for the Hurricane (pre or post 1940?), replaying events on Carol's porch (had he been cool? had she expected something else?) and whether he should tell Malcolm about Julie, even though he'd told Julie it was better coming from her. He went back to the park (Malcolm and the guys were still there), and told him - saying he should ring her at home that evening.

'Ph .... phone? Julie?'

'Yep. Trust me.' And Richard wanted to add Malcolm really, really should trust him - he was surrendering his own chances with the girl who, literally, made his heart beat faster. But he couldn't say that, not even to his best friend.

'Phone? I .... d .... d.... don't like ph .... phones.'

'Fuck the phone. Do you like Julie?'

Malcolm nodded.

'Enough to make a phone call?'

Malcolm nodded again.

'Ring her. If you don't I will,' Richard joked, though he didn't find it funny. 'And why not ask her round to my place tomorrow. We need more players for the Escape From Colditz night.'

No-one escaped from Colditz that Saturday night. As host, Richard played the role of Camp Commandant, with the others playing English, Polish, French or Dutch prisoners, desperate to escape; Malcolm opted to play the Dutch - the orange pieces matching the embroidery on Julie's cheesecloth blouse. Richard had enjoyed setting the table on the patio and imagining scenarios in which he and Carol found themselves alone at the bottom of the garden at the end of the evening. He talked Philip (not hard) into buying a Party Seven and a bottle of cheap white wine (German) and they opened the beer first, pouring conservatively, conscious it needed to last.

Richard's mother called from the kitchen that someone else was at the door and Richard went round the side of the house and out through the back-gate, hoping to find Carol.

'Julie. Good timing. We're just setting up. Come round. Malcolm's here.'

'Here.' She offered Richard a half full bottle of spirit and a Corona lemonade she had brought.

'S'okay. I think you can hold on to those. I doubt others will be drinking Dubonnet.'

'Okay, oh, and thanks for getting Malcolm to ring me.' She pecked him on the cheek.

'No problem.' Richard led her to the patio, hoping she didn't see his blush.

Julie sat by Malcolm. She didn't mind she didn't follow the rules and didn't expect Malcolm to explain them. Richard let the guys choose the music for the cassette player and Malcolm's argument for p .... p .... punk was over-ruled in favour of a poor copy of a copy of 'The Dark Side Of The Moon', despite Julie's half-hearted complaint.

41

'Escape From Colditz' was not a quick game, and Pink Floyd had been replaced by Yes and Led Zeppelin and Genesis by the time they wanted to give up (Richard was a good Camp Commandant and the game took his mind from wondering why Carol hadn't come). Richard insisted they try for a further twenty minutes before someone went Do or Die - they did, and died. The Party Seven was almost empty and the wine had been opened; the Dubonnet was gone, even though it was drunk only by Julie. The sunlight was almost faded and the patio was darkening despite the overspill light from the kitchen. It was still warm and they were happy to let the game drift to a close while the alcohol mellowed them further. Genesis faded to silence and Julie stood unsteadily, took a cassette from her bag and tottered over to where the player sat on the floor, an extension lead draping through the open kitchen window. Richard watched her (without being noticed, he hoped) as she leant against the wall for support while bending to take off her sandals. He called something about watching her feet (her perfect feet, though he didn't say) on the uneven patio paving and Julie waved nonchalantly as she struggled to put her cassette in the player. Richard crossed the patio to help.

'What is it?' one of the others asked.

'Donna Summer,' Julie mumbled.

Richard took the cassette from her. 'I prefer my funk heavier and my soul sweeter. But, for you ....' He hoped it wasn't as pretentious as it sounded (it was, but Julie was drunk) and helped her find the PLAY button. A couple of seconds later Donna Summer started to moan and a couple of the guys at the table groaned. Julie shrugged her shoulders to show she didn't care. She was moving side to side, but only just and was just behind the rhythm which seeped into her. Richard sat back in his chair and watched, no longer caring if Malcolm saw him (Malcolm also watched Julie). She was almost a silhouette. Richard's Radio Girl was never sexier than when swaying to 'Love To Love You Baby', out on Malcolm's patio at the end of a steaming day towards the end of a steaming July. She was overcome with rhythm and lived the music for her own sake, oblivious of the boys - never more desirable and even more so when effortless and naïve. Richard forgot he was disappointed Carol hadn't come.

The gathering broke up soon afterwards and Malcolm walked Julie home.

Next morning Richard told his mother a few days in the countryside at Uncle Dudek's was a good idea after all.

Three Weeks In The Summer

Chapter 4
August 1976
Uncle Dudek

The Monday after no one escaped from Colditz, Richard spent the morning in the garden, painting a base coat on the model Hurricane at the table on the patio. Tina came outside occasionally to annoy him, and his mother brought glasses of squash, reminding him not to spend too long in the sun. After lunch his mother went to work in the piano shop and Richard commandeered the lounge where the new Toshiba music centre took pride of place (or at least second place, behind the tv). This afternoon he was going to experiment with copying tracks (from both cassette and vinyl) to produce a personalised tape to take to Uncle Dudek's. The first task was to choose the right tracks. He looked at the blank piece of paper in front of him. Dyslexia was a hurdle but the bigger problem was mood - swinging between disappointment Carol hadn't come to the Colditz night, envy that Malcolm had walked Julie home and fleeting excitement she had remarked what a good friend he was (with peck on cheek). There was no reason to suppose the vision of her swaying to Donna Summer was not intended for him as much as anyone else. Or maybe she hadn't intended it for anyone? Maybe that simply was her, free, and if she didn't mind being so free when Malcolm was there and he was such a good friend well, maybe …. what did that mean? And, again, why hadn't Carol come? He missed her. He wanted to smell her perfume and wanted her to tell him it was a good thing; she knew …. stuff.

There was too much to consider. The whiteness of the paper in front of him brightened the longer it stayed blank.

He opened his cassette carry case, found James Brown (easily, it was in alpha order, by artist, ignoring the word 'The') and copied 'Get Up Offa That Thing' to the C90 tape in his portable player. He played it back and it was okay; bit muffled, but good enough. The second track he copied was 'Golden Years' and the third 'Play That Funky Music'. When it finished he phoned Carol. Her little sister picked up the phone and answered formally, 'Hello. Can I help you?'

'Hi. Is Carol there?'

'Can I tell her who's calling?' The tone was falsely officious.

'Richard.'

'I'll see.'

There was a 'clunk' as she put the phone down and Richard heard her shout, 'Oi! Carol, your two-timing git is on the phone.'

Richard replaced his receiver and erased the C90 in his portable cassette player to start again.

Diu came in from work just after five and called for help from the door; the box she carried was almost as long as she was tall.

'Mum, you carried this from the shops?' Richard was incredulous as he pulled Ossie out the way and took the box off her in the hall.

'Not heavy.'

'What is it?'

'Electronic organ. Bontempi.'

'You hate these things.'

'It's not for me. You. Take to Uncle Dudek's so you keep practising. Not like real piano, I know. But me and Philip think it a good idea, to keep you practising. Philip paid. You thank him when he comes home.'

'How good is that ....' Richard split the cardboard box extracting the beige plastic instrument with black and white keys. In less than five minutes the organ's thin, reedy sound filled the lounge. Diu winced at the noise but smiled at the tune (Richard had been working on 'Summer Breeze' for weeks) and joined in on the upright piano, careful not to drown the organ. They played a couple of duets (grade 4) before Diu had chores to do and Richard revamped the mental playlist for his mix tape to include songs he could now play along to at Uncle Dudek's.

He finished copying the tracks to his portable player before Philip came home from work and made sure to welcome him with thanks for the Bontempi.

That evening Carol rang but Richard missed her, he was round Malcolm's.

The journey to his uncle Dudek's took nearly three hours; Philip driving the bright yellow Datsun, having taken the day from work. The Datsun had a built-in cassette player and Richard insisted on playing his new mix tape. Tina moaned at each track, out of tradition, and Richard complained of their singing along (even Philip) to 'Here Comes The Sun'.

Dudek lived in Oakjack Ford, in the south-west corner of The New Forest. They took the new M3 as far as they could to Popham and from there a succession of A and B roads to and through the New Forest. Diu was good with the road map and they found a quiet place to park from where Tina could see a few ponies, huddled under a small copse for shade. The ponies didn't graze but stood heads lowered, as if waiting to be chastised. Tina 'aahhed' while Diu 'oohed' and said she was reminded of the ponies used for work in Kon Tum, where she grew up. But before Tina could ask even one question the ponies started, as one, and a half-second later the harsh and abrupt clang of an alarm bell made Diu jump. An old Land Rover in fire engine configuration trundled past (probably as fast as it could), honking a warning as it neared the parked yellow Datsun. Richard watched it pass back from where they'd come, back into the heart of The New Forest. The road was straight and the light resting over it in the distance shimmered with the heat. A haze of light-grey smoke hung in the air on the horizon. Richard couldn't tell how far it was and there was no smell of burning but the urgency (if not speed) in the fire engine was unsettling and Philip called them back to the car.

Dudek's house was on the edge of the village: Oakjack Ford. The Edwardian house had four bedrooms, large gardens front and back, and was welcoming in the sunshine though it needed care and attention. There was a row of five similar houses, laying back from the main road into the village and Dudek's was first as they approached. The driveway to the house was in shadow from summer overgrowth and Philip parked next to a dirty black Citroen DS, three or four years old. The gravel crunched under foot as Richard dragged a big (but mostly empty) suitcase from the Datsun's boot to the doorway. Philip carried the Bontempi. Diu knocked loudly and they waited longer than was comfortable until hearing the argument.

'Nag, nag, nag. If I want wife I will buy one.' Dudek's deep voice carried round the corner of the house.

'You have not money …. enough to buy me,' a woman replied; a voice Richard didn't recognise.

'Just help me not fall over.'

'You should have brought sticks. You want I carry you? Quicker you crawl.'

'Weak woman. Your Grandmother would do better.'

'My Grandmother is too much woman for you and too smart to come here and be your …. slave.'

'Ha, what do you know about me and your Grandmother? What do you know about anything? Just a girl. You should …. ah! Here!' Dudek shouted as he turned the corner and saw Diu and family at his front door. 'So good to see you. So good.' He released the girl's grip from his arm and shuffled the last couple of yards.

'Now he walks okay,' the young woman muttered, just loud enough for Dudek to hear. He waved a hand dismissively and hugged his visitors one by one, leaving Diu until last for a prolonged embrace. When finished he leant on Diu for support and turned back to the girl,

'This is Anika. She is …. looking after me. While I heal.' He half raised his left leg to show the bandages round his ankle.

Anika nodded and smiled; bottom teeth slightly crooked and nose slightly crooked too, but you had to look closely to tell, which Richard did.

'Hello. Yes. I am Anika.' Her eastern European accent was staccato but gentle and she spoke as if wanting her English to be precise. She wore a pair of flared jeans and a simple blue t-shirt with a yellow circle tie-dye pattern exploding in the middle. She was braless, Richard noticed. After a chorus of hellos Anika helped Diu help Dudek back round the side of the house. There was a wooden table and chairs and Anika left them to sit while she went to the kitchen. Diu and Dudek held hands and talked, totally relaxed, catching up. Philip and Richard mostly listened and Tina was soon bored and drifted off to explore the lush garden, Dudek shouting after her to 'be careful near the pond' and explaining to Diu,

'It has shrunk in the last year and the drought is killing it, but there's enough water left to swim.'

'I'll make sure she doesn't go in.' Richard followed Tina. Philip took the suitcase and Bontempi indoors.

The garden was a hundred feet or more long and overgrown from half way, hiding the pond which formed the bottom boundary. The pond lay across the back of the row of houses and, though called a pond, back in Richard's suburb they'd consider it a lake. Richard pushed through the high grasses and confusion of untended flowers and ducked under some apple trees. There was a short area of more untended grass leading to the pond's edge. The dense reeds which normally grew from the water stood in dried mud and the water had retreated four or five feet from how he remembered. This bank was more exposed and the sun was hot. The bank on the other side was in tree shade, particularly from the willow, and to Richard's left the water stretched out behind the other houses. The surface was calm save occasional ripples from a fish breaking surface. It was quiet and Richard took a minute to tune in to the gentle insect buzz resting on the still air. He wondered if it was a scene better suited to Carol or Julie and enjoyed not having to decide one way or the other. It was easy to imagine Julie sitting at the water's edge, doing nothing, and just as easy imagining Carol slipping off her shoes and taking a few steps in to the cooling water. There was allure to both.

'Richard! Fish!' Tina interrupted. She was a few yards to the right, lying over the grass edging the dried mud, leaning out to swish a small branch in the water. Richard knelt beside her and they spent a few minutes watching. The water was shallow but reflections were a distraction and Tina saw no more fish though she tried to convince Richard there had been at least three, each at least six inches long.

Philip called them back to the house as Anika brought a tray with tea and pastries. Richard and Tina sat at the table and Anika pulled up another chair to join them, squeezing next to Richard. He smelt a soapy fragrance and hoped it was her perfume but may have been washing up liquid.

'Help yourselves to cake, kolache,' Dudek instructed.

'Kolache,' repeated Philip enthusiastically.

'No, kolache,' Diu laughed and pointed to the pastries. 'Homemade?' she asked Anika, 'Smell lovely.' There was a plate of round pillows of dough each with spoonfuls of fruit in the middle: apricot, raspberry and blackcurrant.

'Thank you,' acknowledged Anika, 'I use jam for the middle. We had no …. real fruit.'

'She cooks well. Like home,' Dudek said with a hint of pride. Diu took over tea pouring duties and Anika passed round the plate of kolaches. There was a short silence while first mouthfuls were taken, followed by appreciative murmurs. Dudek shifted in his chair, wincing.

'Are you okay Dudek?' Anika noticed his discomfort.

'Yes, but more tablets?'

Anika looked at her watch and did a quick calculation. 'Three hours passed. Not time yet. Sorry,' she said sympathetically.

'An aspirin …. or two? Not one of my special pills. Save that for later.' Dudek touched Anika's arm and she sighed.

'Aspirin.' She went to the kitchen.

'Does it hurt much?' asked Diu, indicating to his ankle.

'No. Not much. I have known worse. But the older I am ….'

'What happened uncle Dudek?' Tina asked.

'I had operation, last week, to take out pieces of bone that have been …. floating round my ankle. They were there for many years, since it was broken, but lately causing pain. The doctor was keen to dig them out before causing more.'

'When did you break your ankle?' Tina asked.

Dudek looked at Diu, Richard noticed.

'Many years ago. Before you were born. When I was younger and thought I could jump fences,' Dudek answered Tina but kept his eyes on Diu.

'How long ago?' Richard wanted to know but Diu interrupted,

'Long, long time. Never mind. Anika, how long are you staying?' Diu asked as Anika came back outside with a couple of small white tablets and a glass of water. 'Your English is very good.'

'Thank you. So is yours,' she said sincerely. 'I study long time back home in Pilsen and came here few weeks ago when we hear Dudek needed someone.'

'My angel,' Dudek patted Anika's arm, 'and a happy reminder of home.'

Richard watched Dudek. His uncle was not as big as he remembered and there was something wistful in his tone.

The morning passed into afternoon and Anika prepared a late lunch while Richard and Tina explored the pond further, lazily in the sun. Diu asked Anika to help her remember the Czechoslovakian she had learnt so many years ago and Anika said she'd like to learn some Vietnamese. Philip and Dudek argued gently over whether or not the Czech victory in the European Championships a few weeks earlier was deserved. By early evening Dudek tired and Diu hinted they should leave but Dudek insisted they have one last cup of tea before the long drive home; Philip was convinced by the promise of another kolache. They sat in comfortable silence until Philip tapped Diu on the arm, suggesting, 'We should make a move, it's a drive home.'

'No. Can I stay here? With Richard?' Tina's disappointment was real.

'Don't you want to go the drama summer school next week?' Diu reminded her.

'Oh. I forgot'

'Don't worry little one. You can come back when that's finished. Can't she?' asked Dudek

'We'll see. It's a long summer,' Philip offered both kindly and vaguely and stood to hasten the exit.

The evening sun glowed orange and shade crept over the garden. Philip started to speak but was interrupted by the resonant timbre of a saxophone's slow, plaintive notes. They couldn't tell from where it came but Dudek pointed to the garden to his right. 'Young Samuel. He likes to play outside in the garden in the summer. I don't mind. I don't know the songs but I think they're in tune. He's playing early this evening.'

Philip sat and they listened as Young Samuel coaxed a gentle melody from his saxophone, holding the notes long. The songs were not known to them and were slow and melancholy for a summer's evening.

'His wife will be under the tree,' Anika said, 'at end of garden. She lies in .... swinging bed .... hammock. Yes. Hammock. He plays. She lies. She is dying.' There was sympathy in her voice though her words were terse.

'True,' Dudek confirmed and they listened to the saxophone more closely. No-one asked further about Young Samuel's wife, which Richard thought strange, but realised later it didn't matter what she was dying of or why. As a song faltered to a close Philip stood again and Diu collected her things.

The goodbyes weren't laboured; they'd be back in just a few weeks to pick up Richard. Anika brought two walking sticks for Dudek and he hobbled behind as they went round the house to see them off. The front of the house was in shadow and Richard waved discreetly, wondering briefly if it was the right thing to be staying but there was no chance to change minds. As the bright yellow Datsun left the drive Anika caught Richard's arm. 'Your room. I'll show you. Bring your case.' She led him back round the house as the saxophone playing started again.

The house had three storeys and Richard was staying at the top in a large room under the eaves. Anika went through first and gave a twirl as if to say 'ta da!'

'Dudek wanted to paint it, but there was no time, sorry.'

'S'okay. Looks all right.' Richard hoisted the case on to the bed, trying to hide the effort.

'Yes, of course.' Anika's sarcasm was subtle and it was a few seconds before Richard laughed,

'No, really, it's okay.'

There was a single bed, single wardrobe and dressing table with no mirror. The walls were bare plaster, save for the odd patch of wallpaper still waiting to be scraped. The skirting boards and architrave were painted pale powder blue (but flaking) and the ceiling plain white with an ornate rose above the hanging light. 'I guess it was a nursery once,' said Richard.

'Maybe. I was sleeping here but as it's the best bedroom, after Dudek's, he wanted you should have it.'

'You moved out for me?'

'Maybe,' Anika was coy. 'Maybe I have come all the way from Pilsen, a visitor to your land, but still I give up my room. Maybe. Ah, there goes Young Samuel again.' She went to the window.

The bedroom was to the rear of the house. It had a large window with bench underneath, running the width. The window looked over the back gardens. Anika knelt on the bench to see. Richard knelt beside her. In the next garden sat Young Samuel in an old striped canvas deck chair. It was in the mottled shade of a small orchard of six or seven apple trees and a couple of them were close enough together for a hammock to be slung. That's where Young Samuel's wife lay. Anika and Richard couldn't see her because of the densely leafed branches but there was a tall, slim oxygen tank on a trolley next to the tree with a tube running to the hammock. Young Samuel played gently and slowly, without music but with passion. Anika and Richard watched in silence, as if afraid of discovery though Young Samuel had to know the music was loud enough to attract attention. After a few minutes Richard was bored but didn't move. Young Samuel was an excuse to stay there, next to Anika, until she remembered Dudek's tablets and went downstairs. She offered to come back up afterwards to help him unpack but he remembered the Airfix model (Hurricane mk1) sitting on the top of the packed case and said he could handle it okay.

Three Weeks In The Summer

Chapter 5
Anika

Through his semi-waking confusion Richard heard Anika call and knock on his bedroom door, lightly at first, then loudly. When he didn't respond she entered. He had slept heavily, lying on top of the sheets, window opened wide; the night had been airless and there was no breeze in the morning.

'Hello Richard. Time to be up.' Anika shook him, encouraging his confusion: the room was new; the wake-up call was unexpected and it was awkward to be laying in Y fronts on a strange bed. 'You dress. Breakfast ready.' Anika left him. He remembered where he was and wondered if his embarrassment showed.

'Okay. Be right there.' He called to her back and rolled off the bed, searching for his spectacles.

'Here.' Anika came back in and threw a towel. 'Bathroom downstairs. Bath first. Water is hot.'

After bathing, Richard joined Anika and Dudek in the kitchen. They sat at a small table. The back door was open and the sun already high. 'Hi. What's time?' Richard asked, scanning the walls for a clock. He found five. They hung vertically on the wall next to the back door and each showed a different time.

'Fifteen past nine,' said Anika before explaining, 'London top, then Washington, Moscow, Istanbul and Kon Tum bottom. We like to know the time.'

'Kon Tum. Vietnam. Where mum comes from?' Richard asked. Dudek nodded.

Anika offered, 'Cornflakes, toast or porridge?'

'Porridge? In August?'

'My favourite,' said Dudek. 'Rain or shine. Best thing from Scotland. Try.' He looked over the top of the Daily Telegraph.

'Uh, cornflakes please.'

'Children today. No sense of adventure. Sleep okay?'

'Yeah, thanks.'

'Good. Not so late up tonight eh?' Dudek smiled and retreated behind the paper. The previous night they had played chess on the patio (Dudek's new colour television having blown a valve already) and were late to bed - Richard had insisted they keep playing until he won at least a game, though he suspected Dudek had let him win that last one.

Anika pushed the box of cornflakes and bottle of milk towards Richard and poured herself a coffee. 'Tea?' she asked.

Richard looked up from tipping the milk. Anika wore the same jeans as yesterday but a skimpier vest today; bright yellow with a sunflower shaped motif on the front with dark blue petals. 'Could I have coffee? Black please.'

'Of course.' Anika poured and lit a black cigarette with a strong smell that Richard thought might be liquorice.

Dudek lowered his paper, gave an obvious sniff and caught Richard's eye. 'Instead of breakfast. No wonder she is skinny,' and to Anika, 'You said you'd give them up, when Richard came.'

'No, but only three left. I'm waiting for mama to send over another pack. I have two a day.'

'Packs?' asked Richard.

'Ha ha, funny boy. Two black smokes a day.'

'I admire your restraint.' Dudek put down the paper to take a cigarette from the pack in front of him - Rothmans. Richard wondered if Carol was still nicking them from her mum's bag.

'Don't tell your mother. I'm supposed to have given up. Good for my ankle, but bad for my heart,' Dudek whispered to Richard who smiled.

'Ah, reminds me. You need more tablets,' said Anika.

'For the pain?' Dudek was hopeful.

'No. Heart. Do you have pre …. pres …. paper from doctor?'

Dudek nodded towards a small pile of papers on the windowsill, near the back door. Anika found the form. 'I will take to shop today.'

'Chemist,' Dudek said.

'Chemist,' Anika repeated.

Richard turned in his chair to reach his back pocket and pulled out a crumpled piece of paper. 'Reminds me. I need to pick up my tablets. We forgot them last week.' He dropped the prescription on the table. 'Can I come with you?'

'Of course.'

Richard helped Anika clear the table and dried up while she washed. Dudek hobbled to his study to, '…. ring some people.' When he left the room Anika leant towards Richard and whispered,

'Every morning. He has to ring people.'

'Who?'

'Who knows? I think he's forgotten they retired him.'

'Oh, is he …. sad, about retiring? Is he bored?'

'Maybe.' Anika shrugged.

'Maybe sad or maybe bored?'

'Maybe.'

'Maybe?'

'Does it matter?' she asked.

'Maybe.'

'Your English is funny. I don't know. Anyway, we go to …. chemist. Come.'

Anika finished tidying the kitchen, slipped on a pair of plimsolls and waited for Richard to find his trainers before shouting, 'Goodbye!' to Dudek and leading Richard outside. They passed Dudek's black Citroen and crossed the brown earth (which had been lawn), turning right at the end of the drive to walk into the village, less than a mile away. The road was bordered by houses, cottages and bungalows, all set back from the road. The pavement was intermittent and much of the time they walked on patchy dried grass and loose earth and stones. Few cars passed and Richard was reminded of Sundays back in his suburb, except here it was Wednesday.

'Sleepy eh?' said Richard.

'No. I had a good night.'

'I meant the village, this place. Not much happening?'

'Oh. Yes. I see. Sleepy yes.' Anika nodded.

'What's your home town like?'

'Pilsen? Not so …. sleepy. Bigger but not big like London. You come from London?'

'Not really. A few miles outside but on the underground.'

'Underground?'

'I mean the tube. Underground trains. We have a station for the underground railway.'

'You have a station?'

'Er, no, I mean we live near one, a station, on the underground.'

'Oh. I haven't been there yet. But perhaps before I go home ….'

'You can stay with us. I'll take you into town.'

'Stay with you?'

'You are family right?'

'Hmmmm. Dudek's family and mine come from same village, long ago. Though he has not been back there for a very long time. He and my grandmother write. I think once they were .... lovers. But only because when I ask she says to .... mind my business. Is that right? Mind my business?'

'Yes. That's right. You could ask Dudek?'

'Dudek doesn't say much about those days. It is a long time since he left there.'

'Does he talk about my father? Greguska?'

'No. But maybe you get him drunk one night. He talks more drunk but it's not good for his heart, I think.'

'What, talking or drinking?'

'See. You do talk English funny.' She took the prescription from her purse and indicated they should cross the road. They had reached what Richard supposed was the heart of the village: Oakjack Ford. On their side of the road, as they came to the village, was a pub, 'The Blue And The Gorse,' Richard read out loud slowly, adding, 'strange name.'

'Many of your pub names are strange. There's another in the village called Devil's Peat. What does it mean?'

'I don't know,' admitted Richard, 'is the devil called Peter?'

Anika looked at him, confused.

Next to The Blue And The Gorse was a terrace of three shops: butcher; bakery; tea shop. Across the street, to where they walked, was a greengrocer, souvenir shop, newsagent and their destination, a post office combined with pharmacy. Beyond that, heading out of the other end of the village, Richard saw another pub and what looked like a blacksmith, displaying wrought iron gates on its forecourt.

Anika pointed Richard to the post office/pharmacy. It looked more like a double-fronted house than a shop,

despite the sign. A bell over the door inside clanged as
they pushed it open.

'Hello Elizabeth,' called Anika to no-one in
particular.

'Hello dear,' came a response but Richard couldn't
see from where. The shop was crowded with aisles of
shelving - to the right was a mini-market of food and
household goods and to the left a tidy display of cosmetics
and medicines. Other shelves held an odd mix of
souvenirs, greetings cards, toys and books - mostly old
stock or, oddly, apparently secondhand. At the back of the
shop were two tall counters. There were three people
queuing at one of them, the post office. They turned to see
who had entered and smiled and nodded on recognising
Anika.

A woman in a pale blue jacket and formal white
blouse stood up from behind the post office counter to
hand over a strip of stamps to a customer. The woman
smiled past her customer to Anika who gave a quick wave
and ushered Richard to the other counter at the back of
the shop, under the sign: pharmacy.

'Hello Anika. Time to renew your uncle's
prescription already? Is he taking them properly?' said a
young man in a white lab coat. He reached over the
counter to take the prescription and (Richard suspected)
let his fingers linger on her small (very small, now that
Richard noticed) hand longer than was necessary (and
anyway, Richard thought, what a stupid question – how
can you not take tablets properly?).

'Yes. He is okay, thank you Peter.' She took from
her purse the cash Dudek had given and counted it out
again before handing over. The pharmacist paid the cash
into the till asking, 'Will you wait?'

'Yes please. And also ....' Anika turned to Richard.
He passed over his crumpled prescription and the young
man took much longer to read it than he had Dudek's.

'We've not had this in before. Maybe it's a new drug. I'll have to order in. Is it urgent?'

'I suppose not.' Richard shrugged his shoulders.

'It might take a four or five days.' The pharmacist frowned.

'It's more urgent than that,' said Anika, unsmiling.

'Two days?' The pharmacist tried again.

'Much better. Thank you.' Her smile returned.

'Thank you,' echoed Richard to the pharmacist's back as he went through a door and out the back to fill Dudek's prescription.

Anika wasted time browsing the shampoos, face creams, plasters, lipsticks, nail polishes and toothpastes. In the other half of the shop Richard found a shelf with board games in faded, dusty boxes (but no 'Escape from Colditz') and, more interestingly, some Airfix model warships.

The pharmacist came back with two boxes of tablets and handed them over to Anika, saying, 'See you Friday for the other prescription.'

Anika took the tablets, waved over her shoulder and went to find Richard, calling him to the post office side of the shop. The other customers had gone and Anika went straight to the counter. 'Hello Elizabeth. Two first class stamps please.'

'Hello Anika. How's your uncle?'

'Okay.'

'Is his ankle better?'

'Not yet, but he says he will take you dancing as soon as he can.'

'I don't dance well,' Elizabeth said and turned to Richard. 'Hello.'

'This is Richard. Dudek is his uncle,' Anika answered for him.

'Hello,' Richard said.

'Nice to meet you. Richard. You're uncle speaks of you often. He is very proud.' She spoke formally but sincerely.

'He's from London. Not home.' And by home Anika meant Czechoslovakia.

'Nearly.' Richard explained.

'Nearly?'

'London. Nearly London.'

'Oh. Welcome anyway.' Elizabeth smiled warmly.

'Thank you. And two type C batteries please? Evereadys?' Richard pointed to a shelf behind Elizabeth.

Richard paid for the batteries and Anika the stamps, saying goodbye and adding, 'Shall I tell my uncle you'll bring him round a cake for tea?'

'Perhaps. When his ankle is better.'

Anika laughed and left the shop, Richard close behind. Two steps out of the shop and into the sunshine Richard said, 'I didn't think Dudek was your uncle.'

'Perhaps ....'

'But ....'

'You don't know everything about me. For example, did you know my name is Anna?'

'Not Anika?'

'But everyone calls me that, so I suppose it is my name, isn't it?'

'And is Dudek your uncle?'

'No. Of course not.'

'Then why ....'

'You English like an explanation for everything. It is easier.'

'Oh. 'cos that would make us .... cousins .... or something.'

'Is that bad?' Anika stopped and looked at Richard. In flat plimsolls she was three or four inches shorter than him. Her look of mischievous defiance was hard for Richard to hold.

'No, but ....'

'Good. Anyway, cousins look after each other. I look after you. Your tablets will be here Friday, not next week.'

'Thanks.'

'I know. But he ....' she threw a look of disdain back to the shop, '.... thinks I owe him a favour.'

'I'm sorry. Next week would've been okay.'

'S'okay, it's a game. Come.' She crossed the road, not waiting for Richard.

The bakery smelt good to Richard, like the bakery near home, and he lingered just inside the door while Anika bought a loaf. 'Bloomer please Erica.'

Erica retrieved the bread from under the counter. 'I put one by. Hello.' She looked to Richard.

'Hi.' He edged further inside.

Erica looked to be similar in age to Anika; more curves, blonde and with more colour (Anika looked pale in comparison) but they both had a glow of relaxed energy and confidence.

'And you are?' asked Erica.

'Richard,' said Anika. 'He might be my .... cousin .... but hasn't decided yet.' She took the loaf.

'I think he should decide not, and he doesn't look Czech,' said Erica, evidently understanding Anika, when Richard didn't.

'Handsome, isn't he? His mother is from Vietnam,' said Anika, not looking at Richard.

'Careful Richard. Anika can be a man-eater, I hear,' Erica half whispered at Richard who hoped it was at least partly true and Anika didn't deny it.

'Ha. Come Richard,' Anika called as she left the shop but stopped half way out to ask Erica, 'Will you be down the pub Friday?'

'Where else?' Erica sighed. 'Say hello to Dudek.'

Anika gave the paper bag with bread inside to Richard. He sniffed at it and they turned right from the bakery, heading out the other end of the village. It was just a few yards to the other pub: Devil's Peat. A blackboard hung by the door, advertising live music - Rocknow Station was playing there soon. The word music was an easy one for him so he took a few seconds to bother reading the rest. The font was challenging but there was no hurry.

'Is that the pub you and Erica are going to on Friday?' Richard pointed as he asked.

'No. We go in the B and G. It's better for Dudek. Less noisy.'

'B and G?'

'The Blue and Gorse. Other end of the village. Though sometimes we come here for bands. A new man is owner and they have more music.'

Richard made a mental note of the band - Rocknow Station. He liked the name and wondered if they were ever reviewed in Melody Maker. They wandered on past the Blacksmith's shop. Just outside the village was a wooden bench at a bus stop and two elderly men sat in silence, one reading a newspaper. The other, on seeing Anika, touched an imaginary cap on his head, saying, 'Mornin'.' The other man looked up from his paper and repeated the welcome, adding,

'When will your uncle be well enough to play skittles? We've a big match next week, against The Red Lion.'

'I'll tell him.'

'Good. Who's this?' The first man waved a stick at Richard.

'Richard.'

'Ah. The nephew. Can you play skittles?'

'I don't know.'

'Don't forget. Red Lion, next week. Tell him.'

'I will,' Anika said as they passed.

'How long have you been here? Do you know everyone in the village?' asked Richard.

'Not long, but it is small village and Dudek they know, not me. Also, I do work in the B and G sometimes, now Megan can't work there. I need the money. Lucky for me, not so much for Megan.'

'Megan?'

'The lady in the hammock. Dying.'

'Of course.'

'Of course she's dying?' Anika asked, sounding confused.

'No I just meant ….'

'No matter. You play skittles?'

'No, but how hard can it be?'

'We'll learn, though I don't think they like girls in the team.'

In less than ten yards they were out of the village. The road narrowed and was bordered with low hedges, parched in the sun. Beyond the hedges the land was sparse meadow with few trees.

'This isn't the way back, is it?' asked Richard.

'Just different. I show you different way. You live here now.'

Anika turned right, off the road and onto a track Richard would not have seen. The track doubled back through the meadow and into heathland south of the village, towards the row of houses that included Dudek's. They walked slowly, picking their way through the gorse, Anika humming songs Richard didn't recognise. It was mid-morning and hot and the gorse offered no shade. He hoped he appeared as cool in his Montreal Olympics t-shirt as Anika did in her vest-top, but doubted it. After a couple of hundred yards Richard had lost his sense of direction and the gorse was high enough to create a maze but Anika knew the way. A track from the right merged with theirs just before a sharp left turn and the gorse gave way to a small oasis of trees and tall grass.

'This is the other end of our pond.' Anika pushed through the grass to the reeds at the water's edge. Richard could now see, to his right, the back of the row of houses, of which Dudek's was the furthest. Anika led him to the left, clock-wise round the pond to the back of Dudek's.

'Time for coffee?' Dudek called as they emerged from the apple trees half way down his garden. He sat at the table on the patio. The shirt and tie he had worn at breakfast were gone and he wore a white sleeveless vest with heavy dark brown trousers. A folded broadsheet lay in his lap.

'Yes thank you,' said Anika.

'Richard?'

'Yes please.' For the second time he found himself asking for the bitter drink he never touched at home. An ice cold cola or Corona lemonade would have been preferable.

Dudek made a show of how difficult it was to stand on his strapped ankle and Anika pushed him gently back to the seat. 'I'll make it. You rest. Has been a busy morning for you.'

'Of course. Richard will help you.'

Anika supervised Richard making coffee and sorting biscuits and they joined Dudek at the patio table.

'Elizabeth asked after you. Again,' said Anika as she sat. 'I said you will take her dancing when your leg is better.'

'I asked her once. She said no.' He waved a hand dismissively.

'You will ask again.'

'I did ask again. She said no again.'

'I think this time she will say yes. Maybe to dinner.'

'Perhaps ....' Dudek looked into his coffee cup but his musings were interrupted by the barking of a dog from the bottom of the garden. A big black and brown mongrel bounded up the lawn, stopping every few yards to shake furiously; he was sopping wet.

'He's been in the pond again. Stupid dog.'

The dog barked louder on hearing Dudek's voice, and trotted the last few yards to sniff happily at their legs, tail wagging frantically.

'Bluey. He's from four houses along,' Anika explained to Richard. 'He swims in the pond and gets out at wrong house. Sometimes comes here. Not that Dudek cares.' She rolled her eyes as Dudek broke a Rich Tea in half and offered it to the dog. Dudek shrugged his shoulders.

The dog moved round to Richard who fussed him despite the wet fur.

'He likes you,' said Dudek. 'You have a dog at home yes? They can tell.'

'Yes. Ossie.'

'Good name. After our great centre forward?'

'What? No, after our great forward …. until he left Chelsea for Southampton. I should give Ossie a new name. He's a has-been.'

'Ha. Has-been? He won the cup with us this year, didn't he? Ha. Ossie. Good name for a dog. We should call this one Ossie too.'

'You're a Southampton supporter?'

'Of course. All my life. At least, all my life since I have lived here.'

'Which is?' Richard asked, fairly sure the answer was not long.

'Never mind. Long enough.'

'Five years,' said Anika.

'Ha. Children today. No respect for poetic licence. How long have you supported Chelsea?' Dudek took another half biscuit and the dog went to him at the sound of the biscuit being broken.

'Since I can remember.'

'Not so long then. Ha! Do you play?'

'Not well. Did you?'

'No. When I was young it was not the right time or place.'

'What about my father?'

'Greguska?' Dudek said the name slowly. 'No. There was never time. We were always .... moving and .... well, moving. And then he met your mother and there was even less .... time. Anyway .... you should finish your coffee and practise.' He pointed at the open French doors to the dining room where the Bontempi lay on a dark wood table. 'I promised your mother to remind you. Half an hour every day, before lunch. You know how good your mother is and Greguska loved to hear her play. So you must practise. Anika will help me take the dog home.'

Anika left her chair to take the two sticks from the back of Dudek's and help him stand. He took a biscuit from the plate on the table and called the dog who seemed to understand and trailed them round the side of the house, stopping to piss on a gutter downpipe.

Richard went through the French doors and into the dining room, enjoying the cool shade though there was no breeze from the garden. He practised scales and wondered if his mother had practised them for his father.

Later, as afternoon shadows welcomed dusk, they heard Young Samuel's saxophone sing to Megan as she lay in her hammock.

Richard was last down again. He ate breakfast alone while Dudek made calls in the study. Anika flitted in and out of the kitchen, looking busy, wearing a pinny and yellow rubber gloves, carrying cloths and a bottle of bleach. Richard burnt some bread, claimed it to be proper toast when Anika complained of the smell, and made coffee but was disappointed when Anika said, 'Later,' she had lots to do; Thursday was cleaning day. He looked at the stub of the black cigarette in the ashtray on the table that Anika had smoked, presumably with coffee, for breakfast and pondered how much different it might taste compared to the menthol fags he had tried. He missed Ossie and thought about the dog from the pond and if it might come to the garden today. He looked for a newspaper to browse but there was none on the table and he guessed Dudek took it to his study while 'ringing some people'. There was a radio on the windowsill; he tried to re-tune it but the only station with a listenable quality of signal was Radio 4. It was too early for Bontempi practise. He worked out the time differences between London, Washington, Moscow, Istanbul and Kon Tum from the clocks on the wall. Anika flitted in and out some more. He resisted the temptation to flit in and out behind her. Finally he went back to his room to collect the Airfix model, paints and cassette player and settled at the table on the patio. The light was good for painting.

'Ah. Hurricane. Mark one or two?' asked Dudek. Richard had been concentrating hard on fine brush work and didn't hear him come into the garden, despite the sticks. Dudek sat beside him and laid the sticks on the floor.

'Mark one. I'm going to paint it with colours of three ten squadron in nineteen forty. A Czech squadron.'

'Excellent choice. Brave young men. Great pilots.' Dudek sat beside Richard. 'Very young. Not much older than you.'

'Were you …. did you ….' Richard faltered on the question.

'Fight in that war? Not fight, as such. Your father and I escaped here through Poland, Germany and France in late thirty nine but we weren't involved much until the end of the war ….'

'Did my father ….'

'He was too young really. But very brave ….'

Richard waited, unsure which of the many questions he should ask. Dudek was quiet.

'Uncle?' Richard tried to prompt.

71

Dudek picked up the model plane and held it high. 'So many brave young Czechs. I didn't meet them but we knew their names. We read they were heroes. Where will you put the lion?'

'Lion?'

'Yes. I believe they painted lions on their planes.'

'I don't know.'

'We'll go to the library in Christchurch. Find a book about those days. It is not so long ago. Do you read much?'

'Not enough.' Richard wondered if his mother had mentioned his dyslexia to his uncle. Dudek gave the plane back to Richard.

'Good model. I like it.'

Richard started to speak but Dudek interrupted suggesting he might like to make his uncle a tea. Before Richard could agree Anika came from the kitchen carrying a mug.

'Coffee. No sugar.' She put the mug on the table.

'Thank you, but Richard would have put in sugar.'

'Richard doesn't know you're not to have sugar.' She bent to peck his cheek.

She wore a gingham blue and white check bikini. Richard had seen neither Julie nor Carol back home in a bikini but imagined (easily) Anika's breasts were somewhere in between in size and, despite being slender, Anika's gentle belly swell was closer to Carol's than Julie's (he imagined). Anika was paler than both the other girls but her hair darker and shorter, cut into a bob that was curly towards the ends. Richard fixed on her face and, to his own surprise said, 'Hot, isn't it?'

'Why else do I wear this?' said Anika and shrugged her shoulders.

Richard waited for her to laugh or smile but instead she leant over the table, close to Richard (she smelt soapy again) and pressed PLAY on the cassette player Richard had brought. The introduction to 'Summer Breeze' was just audible and Anika turned up the volume, which Richard took to be a sign of approval. He tried not to watch as she took a sun lounger from the shed and laid on it in the shade of the apple trees. She was cool in the heat but not the sun and precisely as pale as she should be.

The mix tape was finished by the time Richard was satisfied with the paint job. He was thinking about the Hurricane's transfers when Dudek called to Anika and asked her to go into town that afternoon to pay the electricity bill. The red reminder had been delivered.

'Of course,' said Anika and sat up on the sun bed to check her watch. She climbed gracefully from the lounger. Richard kept his head lowered, concentrating on the sheet of transfers for the model and jumped as she ruffled his hair on passing. 'You need a haircut. I'll do it for you. Now we make lunch. Come on.' She went into the kitchen, stopping just inside to check her watch against the clocks on the wall by the door. Richard joined her in the kitchen, standing as close as he dare, and she threw him the remains of the bloomer they had bought the previous day, telling him to cut and butter six slices while she put on clothes.

Lunch was a simple cheese sandwich eaten in relaxed silence - Dudek glanced through the newspaper and Anika flicked through Titbits magazine, explaining she had started Pride and Prejudice but Dudek thought Titbits much better for learning about the English. As they cleared the table Dudek reminded Anika about paying the electricity bill and she rummaged through a drawer next to the sink which was full of keys, pens and half-used Sellotape rolls before finding a cheque book. She passed it to Dudek along with a ballpoint. Dudek wrote a cheque in precise, neat block capitals and signed with a flourish. He passed it back to Anika who copied the amount and payee onto the cheque stub and ripped the cheque from the book, putting it in the torn envelope with the red reminder.

'Coming?' asked Anika when the kitchen was tidied.
'To?'

'To pay the electric bill.' Anika waved the envelope.
'Okay.'

'Good. I'll drive.' She took the keys from a row of hooks near the front door and shouted goodbye to Dudek. Richard did likewise and followed her to the Citroen sitting on the driveway.

'Uncle Dudek's?' asked Richard.

'Of course. He worked in Paris for a while.'

'And?'

'And liked them I suppose. Careful. Hot inside.' She opened the driver's door and leant across to open the passenger door but then stood outside waiting for the car's interior to cool a little. Although the front garden and drive were bordered by trees, the sun was high and the car exposed. They waited a short while before Anika started the car, opened the vents, wound down the front windows and indicated to Richard to get in. Anika let out the clutch, twirled the steering wheel and the Citroen lurched forward. They turned left out of the drive, heading away from Oakjack Ford and Richard was grateful for the cooling air, rushing in noisily. Except it wasn't fresh.

'What's that smell?' He had to almost shout.

Anika tilted her head towards the open window at her side and breathed in. 'Fire.'

'Fire?'

'Gorse fire. There have been a few already.'

Richard breathed in again. Though he couldn't see any smoke the smell of acrid burning could be tasted. It wasn't strong but bitter enough that he would have closed the window if not for the heat. He wound it up half-way. 'Are they bad? The fires?'

'The people trying to stop them think so. They are hard to put out and the sun is so hot.'

'Where are they?

'I don't know. There have been many. There is so much gorse and heathland. Some have come close to Oakjack and sometimes we see the smoke.'

'We saw on the way here. And there was a fire engine.'

Anika nodded in understanding. Richard scanned the heathland left and right but there was no sign of fire. 'Where are we going?'

'Town,' said Anika and turned left again. 'It's okay. They don't have fire in town today.' She took her hand from the Citroen's steering wheel to pat his leg.

Christchurch was ten minutes away and Richard had to admit Anika drove well. The town was quiet and she found a place to park near the High Street from where they walked to the Electricity Board showroom. Strolling side by side, Richard caught their reflection in a shop window and wondered if others thought they might be a couple. Anika saw him looking. 'See, your hair needs cut.'

'What? Oh, yes.'

'I'll do it for you.'

'No, it's all right. I'll get it done back home.' He looked again in the shop window and it was true it was needed. His black hair had always been thick, losing any style the barber cut.

'You don't trust me. It's okay. I can cut hair. My sister is a hair cutter back home. I have seen her do it hundreds.'

'Watching is one thing, but doing ....?' Richard let the question tail away.

'Trust me. It is a .... mess.' Anika ruffled his hair and he flinched. 'Ah. Sorry. You're too big for that. I understand. But your hair makes you look too young. Trust me. I will cut it and you will look older. And new spectacles. Those are too .... round.'

'I suppose.'

'And you will look less sad. Often you look sad.'

'Do I?' He looked again at his reflection and pushed his spectacles higher on his nose.

'Yes. Are you? Sad?'

'No.'

'For home?'

'No.'

'Friends?'

'Maybe a little.'

'Girls?'

Hesitation.

'Ah. Girl.' Anika smiled and nodded, as if discovering a secret.

'No.'

'I don't believe you. Now that I look at you I see it in your eyes. A little lost. A little lonely.'

'No …. I came because I wanted to get away from them.' Richard defended himself but was disappointed to sound defensive.

'Them?'

'Girls.'

'Ah …. them. You are trying escape. But you should understand that's when you will miss them more. I know.' Her voice diminished to a whisper and she gazed theatrically to the sky. Richard saw a chance to turn the conversation away from him.

'Are you missing someone?'

'Ha! No. Of course not. But I'm sure someone is missing me. That's the difference. Don't you think?'

'I suppose.' Richard had to agree. She wore a plain white blouse, thin cotton, almost transparent, and jeans low and tight at the hip but very wide at the bottom where they hid a pair of black court shoes. Already, if she were to go away he would miss her, he knew; though he didn't know if more than Julie or Carol.

'And do you go to school with these girls?'

'Er, no. Rubber Johnny is just for boys.'

'Rubberjohnny? I have heard that word. I don't think it meant school.'

Richard looked away, embarrassed.

'Ah. So what does it mean?'

'Nothing, it's just a nickname for our school.'

'Really?'

'Really. The school is called John Le Rugber. With a silent 'g'.' He explained pointlessly.

'Is it a good school?'

'I suppose.'

'Are you a good student?'

'Not especially. I have …. a problem …. with reading.'

'The school doesn't teach reading?'

'No. I mean, yes. The problem is I'm not good …. at reading.'

'Oh. The school must teach more. Your uncle says it is a good school and you are a great student.'

'He said that?'

'Yes, but he also said you are tall and handsome and clever, so who knows?' she said mischievously and started to walk ahead. When Richard caught her up he started to ask what else his uncle had said but she interrupted, 'John Le Rugber? How do you write that?'

Richard spelt it.

'I have seen that written. On an envelope. Perhaps Dudek was writing to tell them what a good student you are. Last month. Dudek asked me to post it.'

'John Le Rugber.'

'Yes. I am very good with words. After all I am Czech.'

Richard didn't understand the connection but agreed. 'I'm sure.'

'I'm sure too. Dudek asked me to make sure to post it, he wrote a cheque for the letter.'

'Why?'

'I don't know …. maybe ….'

'Anika!'

Anika was interrupted by her name, called from over the road. They looked over to see Erica, from the bakery. She was with a tall, thin young man. He was blonde like Erica and wore a striped collarless shirt with buttons half way down and flared jeans. His face and neck were red from the sun. They crossed the road to Anika and Richard.

Richard and the young man stood awkwardly while the girls chatted, complimenting each other's clothes (Erica wore a denim dress buttoned at the front from bust to knee) and, again, confirmed they'd be in the pub on Friday. They said goodbyes and the young man nodded farewell to Richard who nodded back. Anika led Richard to the Electricity Board showroom to pay Dudek's bill over the counter at the back of the shop. Richard waited outside and counted the money he'd brought with him. When Anika came out he offered to buy her an ice cream and she pointed further up the high street to a tea shop with a swinging advertising board on the pavement offering Mr Whippy. They both had ninety-nines and stood in the shade of the tea shop's canopy to eat them before melting. When they were down to cone they started the stroll back to the car, passing a barber's where Anika pointed to a sun-faded picture of Robert Redford from All The President's Men.

'I'll cut your hair that way.'

'Robert Redford? I'm not blond.'

'No, but it wouldn't cost you. You'd be even more handsome.'

'I don't know. It does need a cut. Maybe I should just go here.'

'You don't trust me? Or maybe you need …. something else …. from here.' She pointed to an advert for Durex. 'Oh, I know where I hear rubberjohnny now. They call your school that? Ha ha.'

'Some do. It's a piss-take.'

'Piss-take?'

'When someone makes a joke of you. Sometimes funny, sometimes cruel.'

'Ah. Piss-take. Like when Erica says I am a man-eater? What does that mean?'

'You don't know?'

'No. Should I?' Anika finished her cone and looked at Richard, almost daring him to answer.

'Have you had any boy-friends since you've been here?'

'No. Not really.'

'What does that mean?'

Anika took the little piece of cone Richard had left. 'Anyway, what if Erica is the man-eater? You should be careful. Do you think she is pretty?'

'Not as pretty as you,' Richard said without thinking, though he was pleased to say it.

'Ha. You're just saying that. And she is more ....' Anika made an hour-glass shape with her hands.

'No, I .... I ....'

'It's true. I am too .... skinny. You prefer Erica.'

'No. I like .... skinny.' Richard used her word, though she wasn't skinny, just less curvy.

'Thank you.'

'And you are younger?' He thought it might be another compliment.

'True. But not much. She is twenty one soon. I have nine months to go.'

'And anyway, what about that guy with her? Boyfriend?'

'Why do you care?' she teased.

'I don't, but ....'

'It's okay. He's her brother, Larry. And they say he likes men, not girls. Did you not see how he looked at you?'

Richard couldn't tell if she joked or not and before he could ask she said, 'Anyway. What do you think of Erica? Nice?'

'She's too old for me. Isn't she?'

'What? We are nearly the same years. Am I too old?' She smiled broadly and before Richard could respond she was walking back towards the car.

The smell of burning gorse was stronger on the way home and Dudek was waiting for them when they pulled into the drive.

'Everything okay?' Dudek asked.

'Of course.' Anika pecked his cheek.

'Good. I smelt the fire and worried.'

'Is the fire close?' Richard asked.

'I don't know. I don't think so. They wouldn't let it get this close to the village, surely. But I didn't know if you saw it on the way to town.'

'No. But I saw the fire engine on the way here, on Tuesday. It wasn't …. big. Can it handle a proper fire?'

'We have to trust.' Dudek leant on Richard who helped him back into the cool of the house.

'If the fire gets …. close what will you do?' asked Richard.

'I will take my most precious things and go, I suppose.'

'Which are?'

Dudek thought for a few seconds before laughing. 'You and Anika. What else is there to worry for? Anyway, I have been in worse situations.'

'What about your papers?' Anika asked. 'All those words you have written? All you have done?'

'Hmmmm. True. They'll never let me publish but still …. it would be sad to lose them. Okay, I will save my papers. Anika will save Richard and Richard will save me.

We are covered. Meantime, Anika, is it time for afternoon tea? Would you?'

'Of course, uncle.'

Richard spent half an hour playing the Bontempi along to 'You're My Best Friend' but was bored before it was learnt. He wandered down to the pond, hoping the dog four houses along might come to the garden but there was no sign and he was going back to the house when he heard a voice from the garden next door. It was followed by a few halting notes from a saxophone; Young Samuel was playing to Megan. Anika joined Richard in the garden and motioned to him to follow her. She went to the pond and dropped to her knees to creep along the edge, to the back of Young Samuel's garden, stopping every couple of yards to turn and check Richard was close and press her finger to her lips. Richard returned the gesture to show he understood but it was hard to crawl with the sharp grass tickling and the disturbed insects buzzing his face and itching his bare arms. The saxophone was quieter here as they crawled through long grass. Anika lowered to her stomach and slithered a couple of yards until she reached a concrete bunker a little way up Young Samuel's garden, mostly submerged in the ground and overgrown with weeds and tall grasses. It was about six foot square and the thick roof was only three or four foot above ground level. They crept in; a rusting iron door lay to one side. The smell of damp was strong and Richard shivered after the heat of the afternoon. Anika whispered, 'Shhh,' unnecessarily and edged to the far wall where a couple of slits were cut into the concrete. Although the grass growing outside was tall enough to cover these windows, they were able to see out, further into Young Samuel's garden. Just ten yards away was the small orchard and they saw the hammock in which Megan lay. There was a tiny bulge in the cloth, a cocoon for her small frame. As before, there was an oxygen tank on a trolley next to the tree and a tube disappearing into the hammock. Young

Samuel sat in a deckchair, playing the saxophone and sipping directly from a bottle of wine between melodies, occasionally talking to Megan, though they couldn't make out what he said.

It was not so dark in the bunker they couldn't see and Anika brushed the dust from a piece of flat earth (though it made no difference to the dirt) and sat cross legged. She took a pack of cigarettes from a back pocket and a brass zippo lighter from the other. From the pack she took one of her black cigarettes for herself and a Rothmans which she offered to Richard and which he declined. She lit her liquorice smelling stick and drew on it as Young Samuel started another melody. 'Are they real songs or is he making them up?' she whispered.

'I don't know. I don't recognise them. Aren't you scared he will see smoke coming from here?' Richard tried to make the question sound casual.

Anika blew a lungful towards the door. 'No. He never takes his eyes off her. See?'

Richard looked and nodded, asking, 'Have you ever seen her face?'

'Never. I have seen him carry her from the house to the hammock but always she wore a mask.'

'Really?'

'Ha, no, of course not. I have seen her often. Sometimes I go and look after her, if Samuel goes out. But she does not look well. She is thin and white. Whiter than me even.' She tried to joke. 'I like the music. I should learn to play the saxophone. Do you think when Megan is …. gone, he will teach me?'

'I could teach you piano.'

'Can it speak of lost love like that?' She waved her cigarette at the small window. 'Can it tell a story in a few notes of a man losing his soul mate and his fear of the loneliness he knows to come? Poor Samuel.' She drew on the cigarette.

'I don't think I could ever make the piano say that.'

'Because you are young. But that's okay. Maybe when your heart is breaking ....' she leant forward and patted his cheek gently. She sucked on the cigarette and her pale cheeks appeared to flush as the ash glowed. 'But yes, you can teach me piano. And maybe I'll teach you to play as if your heart was broken.'

Richard looked away to peek through the slit and, to change the subject, asked, 'Why do they call him Young Samuel? He's not young.'

'I don't know. Perhaps Dudek does. Or maybe you come to the pub tomorrow night. Dudek and Young Samuel drink together on a Friday. You can ask him.'

They listened a little longer until Young Samuel stopped playing and watched as he laid down the saxophone and drank from the bottle of wine. The sun was slipping down, towards dusk, and the shadows made the bunker feel cold. They crept out, back to the pond and along to Dudek's garden. Young Samuel started to play again.

'Remember, you will teach me piano. And I will cut your hair,' Anika reminded Richard as they came out from under the apple trees.

'Of course, to the piano. Not sure about the hair. Do you play any instrument?'

'No. My school did not have any except for, what you call it ....? Little drum with tin .... circles, for shaking and hitting. Tamber ....'

'Tambourine?'

'Tambourine. Yes. It was not a big school like your Rubber Johnny. They really call it that? Ha. Do they teach piano there? I bet they have piano there. Dudek says it is a good school. He doesn't know you call it Rubber Johnny.'

'I don't call it that. Others do. It's not funny.' Richard regretted letting the school nickname slip earlier.

'Okay. I won't tell Dudek.'

Dinner was sausage and mash, with Dudek supervising Anika's cooking. She complained the sausage was nothing like sausage from home and Dudek agreed, but with enough gravy it was good enough to eat (he joked). After, they settled in the back room. Anika read and Dudek asked if Richard wanted to learn backgammon. Richard offered to make them a cup of tea while Dudek set up the board. The kitchen wasn't visible from the back room and Richard filled and switched on the kettle before opening the drawer next to the sink and searching for the cheque book he had seen Anika find there earlier. He had worried the tremble in his voice on offering to make tea betrayed him and now there was a tremble in his hand as he rummaged through the drawer, though the sound of the kettle was louder. He was more scared of Anika coming out than his uncle, though he was sure his excuse of looking for a pen was credible. The kettle boiled as he found the cheque book and slipped it into his back pocket, fear being replaced by guilt at his deception.

The evening passed slowly. Anika complained regularly at the lack of television and Dudek regularly promised to call a repair man in the morning, though when Dudek mentioned how disappointed he was to be missing Dad's Army, Anika said he needn't ring for her benefit. By ten o'clock the sun had been down an hour but though the garden was dark the French doors were open and it was still warm. An occasional breeze brought a hint of the smell of burning from earlier in the day but it was faint enough Richard thought it might be imagined. He was genuinely tired enough to want to go to bed and said his goodnights.

In the bathroom he flicked through the cheque book. It was the first cheque book he had ever bothered to look at but understood the stubs were a record of payees and it was easy to find the stub from a few weeks earlier showing a payment to John Le Rugber. It was just short of seven hundred pounds, a large amount. He went back through the stubs and found another payment to the school for a similar amount six months earlier, in January, and a smaller payment in October the previous year. He put the cheque book in his underwear drawer for the night and struggled to sleep, partly because he was concerned his uncle was making the payments but more because he was worried he didn't know how to find out. He could ask Dudek or his mother, but as they hadn't told him he supposed they didn't want him to know. He missed Malcolm. Malcolm's thoughts would have been helpful; he was usually a voice of reason, perhaps because for him, if it was worth the trouble to say it, it was worth thinking about. He missed Julie and Carol. Not that he could have asked them; he just missed them. He listened to Anika, on the floor below, getting ready for bed.

He slept fitfully without a plan.

Three Weeks In The Summer

Chapter 6
Jennifer

The drawer had a squeak in the morning that hadn't been there the previous evening, but Richard was first to the kitchen and took just seconds to replace the cheque book. He ate breakfast wondering how to broach the subject of the school cheques with his uncle and by the time Dudek and Anika were down he was washing his bowl and spoon. Anika opened the back door to another cloudless day, took a few seconds to breathe in and nodded with satisfaction, commenting there was no smell of burning in the air. Dudek was half way through his porridge when the Daily Telegraph and Titbits magazine were forced through the door; Richard flinched at the harsh clank as the letterbox sprang back violently.

'He'll lose a finger one day.' Dudek started to stand. Anika placed a hand on his shoulder and went to the door.

'Late today and no Make a Medley?' said Dudek as Anika passed the broadsheet to him.

'No what?' asked Anika.

'Make Medley. For Richard. His mother said he likes to read it. I asked Bill in the newsagent for it to be delivered.' Dudek was proud of his thoughtfulness and pleased at Richard's broad grin as he said,

'Oh. You mean Melody Maker.'

'Didn't I say that?' Dudek asked Anika.

'Nearly,' she half agreed.

'I thought it would be here yesterday. Bill said Thursdays, I'm sure. Sorry it's not here today either,' he said sincerely.

'No problem uncle. It's kind of you to order it for me.' Richard was just as sincere but had to hide concern at expectations. It was true he liked Melody Maker but sometimes pages were not printed clearly and the dyslexia made it hard to read. He hated when that happened on important articles. Only a few weeks previously he had reluctantly asked Philip to read a few lines of a review of Stanley Clarke's latest album, School Days, and disagreed with some of the review even though he had yet to hear the album.

Having already eaten, breakfast passed slowly for Richard while he waited to be alone with his uncle to ask about the cheques. It didn't seem right to ask while Anika was there but she always was and when Dudek went into his study to 'ring some people' she stood and ruffled Richard's hair. 'We have to get your tablets from the .... chemist. It's Friday. I forgot. I need to change.'

She left Richard at the table and was back in a minute, having swapped the plain white blouse she had been wearing for her sunflower vest. She explained, 'Peter, the chemist, likes the sunflower, I think.'

Richard nodded his agreement, 'Who wouldn't?'

Anika and Richard walked to Oakjack Ford. When they left the house the air was clean but as they neared the village they walked into the smell of burning gorse. The smell did not drift to them on a breeze but hung in the air; they recognised it immediately. Beyond the village they saw grey smoke but couldn't tell how far.

The post office was busy but the pharmacy quiet and the counter unmanned. Anika called for Peter but he was not there; an older lady came from out back. Anika let Richard ask for his tablets and the pharmacist remarked on Richard's address not being local, almost with suspicion. She passed him a paper bag with a box of tablets inside and asked if they were the right ones. Richard saw the letters on the side of the box but it was not a word he knew and the letters and form held no pattern he recognised. The pharmacist spoke over his hesitation, 'Effergot.'

'I think so,' said Richard, 'I haven't had them before,' and nodded as the pharmacist took a school-matronly approach to insisting he read the dosage instructions when home. Perhaps he would ask uncle Dudek, rather than Anika, to read them. He thanked the lady in the white lab coat and joined Anika in the queue for the post office. At the counter Elizabeth was pleased to see them, but before she spoke the bell over the door clanged and a man in a heavy black coat and bright yellow over-trousers, tucked in to heavy boots, entered. Richard recognised Larry - Erica's brother - from the previous day in town, despite the coat swamping his thin frame and dirt-caked face and hands. The smell of burning gorse was on him. His entrance was dramatic because of the attire but his demeanour was calm though serious and he barely acknowledged Anika and Richard as he reached the counter.

'Elizabeth. Bad news I'm afraid. The fire on the heath a couple of miles off to the north-east is bad. The peat is burning and as fast as we get one fire under control another breaks out. It's about two miles away at the moment. Two miles.' He repeated the distance and Elizabeth's eyes widened with fear.

'Two miles?'

'Yep.' Larry pointed off to his right, as if that made it visible. It was the other direction to Dudek's house.

'What does that mean?' Elizabeth asked.

89

'No need to panic. We're just telling people to be ready to leave if the fire gets within half a mile. But I'll be back well before if necessary and you're probably okay anyway. You have clear space out back that might be a fire-break. And you're not thatched roof. Truth be told we're more worried about Hinton. More thatch. Don't worry but be ready.' Larry spoke with an authority at odds with the nervous young man Richard had seen the previous day. The words he spoke didn't sound his own, but were well delivered.

'And are you going to tell Bill at the newsagent?'

'Yes. And the others. I'm doing the rounds.'

'Ask him to tell Jennifer she should come back here straight-away please? Straight-away.'

'Of course.' The door-bell clanged again as Larry left but the smell of burning lingered.

Elizabeth took a slow breath. 'Well, that's more excitement than I need,' but within another two breaths she was back to post mistress. 'Now, what can I do for you?' she asked Anika and Richard but Richard was talking to Anika,

'Where's Hinton?'

Elizabeth answered. 'Next village along. About three miles. A little bigger than us, well, they got the railway didn't they? Anyway, what would you like?'

'Shouldn't we be going back home to tell uncle?' Richard asked Anika.

'There's time. Isn't there Elizabeth.' Anika calmed him.

'Of course. Nothing to worry about yet. Larry said.'

'I didn't know he was in the fire …. service?' Anika said.

'Oh he's not. They've asked for volunteers. I've never known anything like it. Still, not to worry yet.'

'Good. I was wondering if you had a parcel for me. From home. I'm expecting something from mama.'

'Nothing that hasn't already gone out on the round I'm afraid. If it wasn't delivered this morning we've not had it yet. Sorry. Maybe tomorrow?' Elizabeth offered practised optimism.

'Are you open tomorrow?'

'In the morning.'

'So you could come for tea in the afternoon? You said you'd think about it,' Anika asked.

'Did I? Is this just so I can bring your parcel if it turns up?' Elizabeth tried a joke.

Anika laughed, 'Maybe, but also because I think my uncle would like to see you for tea.'

'He said that?'

'Oh, and bring a cake and he will be very pleased. Homemade.'

'Homemade?'

'I don't suppose you know any Czech recipes do you?'

'No, not really.' Elizabeth laughed.

'So will you come? To tea? Uncle would like that.'

'Is your uncle expecting me?'

'No. But he wouldn't turn you away. Especially with homemade cake.'

'Maybe.' Elizabeth looked at the large wall clock behind her. 'Anyway, I better pack up a few things, just in case Larry comes back. Would you pop into the newsagent to see if Jennifer is there and remind her to come back, now?'

'Of course. See you tomorrow.'

Richard followed Anika out, sniffed the air to make sure he wasn't imagining the smell and caught Anika's arm. 'Don't we need to tell uncle Dudek?' He was surprised to see only two other people wandering the village; he had expected signs of growing fear and panic but all was preternaturally calm.

'We will. Don't worry. Yet.' Anika patted his shoulder.

'When should we start?'

'To worry? When we can do something about it, which might be never, so don't worry. And if we can do something, we will. So even when we can worry, we won't.'

Richard was worried he didn't understand. 'As long as you're sure?'

'Sure? Of what? Never mind. Come, we need cigarettes.' The newsagent was two doors along and as they neared Larry came out and crossed the road without looking their way.

The newsagent's window was crowded with adverts and posters and the interior crowded with shelves of papers and magazines, leading to a counter at the back. A big man stood behind the counter, almost hiding the rows of colourful cigarette packs behind him. Off to one side was a trestle table covered with magazines being sorted and sifted by a girl, around Richard's age. The big man was leafing hurriedly through a ledger book, looking worried, but he smiled to acknowledge Anika and Richard. 'Morning Anika.'

'Hello Bill. Heard about the fire?' she asked, already knowing the answer.

'Yep. Sounds bad. We're tidying up ready to leave if we have to. Just need to make sure the cat's close by.'

'And I thought I'd better stock up on cigarettes for uncle Dudek. Eighty Rothmans please. And ....' she took a purse from her denim handbag, frowning at the lack of cash, '.... twenty Players Ten for me.' Bill turned to the cigarettes behind him and Anika turned to the girl. 'Hi Jennifer. Elizabeth says to go to her now.'

'I know. Larry said. I'm nearly finished.' She didn't look up from her task.

Anika asked Bill, 'Oh, and Dudek asked if that magazine he wanted was here ....' she looked at Richard who said,

'Melody Maker?'

Jennifer looked up.

'Tell Dudek I'm sorry but it hasn't come yet. Should have been here on Thursday,' said Bill.

'You could try NME. That's always on time,' Jennifer added. Richard looked at her and she looked back. She was shorter than Anika with a pixie cut to dark brown hair and wore black, thick framed spectacles. The reflections of the glass almost obscured grey eyes and her face was a light summer bronze.

'NME?' asked Anika.

'New Musical Express,' Richard told her before asking Jennifer, 'Do you have it? It's okay.'

'We only get a couple in and they've gone. I've got this week's but it's in my room, above the post office. You can have it when I've read it. I prefer Melody Maker too.'

'Thanks. I'm Richard. Dudek's ....'

'.... nephew. Townie. I know. We heard you were coming to visit. I thought you'd be taller. Some say.'

'Oh. Sorry.' Richard didn't know why he apologised, especially as he was much taller than her and only just shorter than Bill.

'That's okay,' said Jennifer.

Richard nodded, though he knew his approval was irrelevant.

'You should go Jennifer. Elizabeth is waiting,' Anika reminded her.

Jennifer shrugged her shoulders and looked to Bill who nodded, saying, 'We can sort those out tomorrow, before your paper round.'

'If we're all still here.' She tried to make a joke.

'And can you remind Elizabeth about coming to tea tomorrow?' Anika asked.

'Did she say she would?'

'I thought so.'

'Hmmm. Might see you tomorrow.' She answered Anika but spoke to Richard. 'They said you'd be darker than you are. What's your mum? Chinese?'

'Vietnamese.'

'Close eh?'

'Not really.'

'Oh. Anyway, I'll let you have that NME when I'm finished with it.'

'Thanks.'

Richard watched her leave. Anika paid for the cigarettes and lit one of Dudek's Rothmans when she was outside the shop, offering one to Richard. He refused, as usual. Richard looked over to the post office asking, 'Is Jennifer Elizabeth's daughter?'

'No. Too young. Elizabeth is her mother's mother, but Jennifer calls her Elizabeth. I don't know why. You can ask her if she comes to tea tomorrow.'

'Why are you so keen for Elizabeth to have tea with uncle?'

'Keen? What does it mean?'

'Er, want it a lot, excited to make it happen. Keen.'

'Oh. I don't know why. They'd be good friends. Once, maybe five years ago, just after your uncle came here, I think they went out together but my grandmother came to visit and something happened. They went out again last summer, but …. Your uncle doesn't say much but he says Oakjack Ford is like the village he grew up in Czechoslovakia, with warm rain. He says he can't go back.'

'Why?'

'I don't know. But if he is going to stay here it would be good if Elizabeth and he are …. friends.'

'Will you tell him Elizabeth might come for tea?'

'No. She might not and he might be disappointed. The fire smell is not so strong now. Good, but we should tell Dudek.'

Chapter 7
Larry

Anika recounted Larry's news of the fire to Dudek. He had smelt the burning but would try not to be concerned until the fire engine's bell could be heard close by, though he went to his study to 'ring some people'.

Anika and Richard lazed in the garden for a while (Anika on the lounger under the apple trees) then Richard practised on the Bontempi but it was hard to concentrate - he was still working through ways to ask his uncle about the payments to his school. Anika was a welcome distraction when she came in through the French doors and asked if it was time for her first piano lesson. She wore a baggy white t-shirt over her bikini and Richard refrained from pointing out it was an electronic organ, not a piano. The organ sat on the dining table and Anika pulled a chair next to Richard's. She had to sit close (the organ had only thirty two keys) and she smelt a little of sweat, from the day's heat; Richard didn't mind (he liked it) but kept his own arms close to his side (just in case), making it difficult to show how to use the keyboard. He explained octaves and middle C but Anika was mainly interested in learning how to play 'Chopsticks' - so Richard taught her and Dudek came to listen. Anika learnt fast and Richard thought they duetted well (shoulders bumping frequently and fingers occasionally touching) until Dudek tapped them both and put a finger to his lips to indicate they should be quiet. As the Bontempi's last note faded they heard a faint bark.

'Did you hear? Or am I imagining?' Dudek asked. 'Bluey?'

Anika and Richard nodded. The barking was quiet but insistent. They went into the garden expecting to see the curious mongrel trotting up the lawn but he was not there. The barking continued but became quieter and it was hard to tell from where. They listened harder. The barking stopped - then another muted bark from the bottom of the garden but still no sign of Bluey. They waited until they heard another weak bark and walked on to the small orchard half way down. They waited again. Another bark - louder. They ducked under the trees. Dudek waved Anika and Richard to go on without him, he was still slow with sticks, and they pushed on through the tall grasses to the pond. Another bark. They reached the brown reeds at the pond's dried mudside and waited. The trees on the other side of the pond cast shade but this side was open apart from the tall grasses and reeds. There was no barking but a succession of noisy splashes. Then silence save a bee's hum. Then another splash. Anika stepped forward. The sun was high and hot. White, blue and yellow flowers dotted the grass and it should have been idyllic but the occasional splashes breaking the silence were unnatural and the water, instead of offering welcome, was black and the reflections confusing. Another splash then a weak bark. Anika's foot broke through the mud crust and she sank a little into the softer earth beneath. She took another step and waved Richard to join her and he took off his trainers to stand by her side. Another splash. They saw from where this came - a clump of green reeds emerging from the water. Movement. Something big and brown, wriggling to be free. Another bark.

'Bluey!' Anika shouted, and ran along the pond's edge to the reeds where the dog from four houses along was struggling to keep its head above water. Richard splashed behind her and they were with the dog in seconds. Anika held Bluey's head, there was fear in his eyes, and Richard waded up to his waist. The pond's bottom was cold sludge. His feet sank in and he was scared he couldn't see where he stood and how deep it might be but Bluey barked a welcome. Richard grabbed him round the chest and tried to pick him up but he couldn't be raised. Richard scrabbled under the water. Weed was wrapped round Bluey's legs but came free as Richard pulled and Bluey kicked. Water crashed and cascaded as the three of them thrashed their way to the pond's edge, seeking the grass beyond the dried mud. They were soaked through. Richard's spectacles were dotted with beads of water and more ran from his hair into his eyes. He lay next to Anika for a second or two but Bluey was immediately into a vigorous head to tail shake. The water flew from his fur, showering his rescuers and when he slowed the shaking to bark it was easy to believe he was giving thanks. A couple of seconds later he was sniffing and jumping at them and it was just as easy to believe he had already forgotten the drama of a minute earlier.

'You looked scared.' Anika stood and held out a hand to help up Richard.

'No I didn't. I was just worried. For Bluey. He was afraid.' Richard took off his spectacles and tried to wipe them on his t-shirt but they smeared, making it even harder to see.

'I had his head. He would have been okay.'

'But I was up to my waist. Look at my legs.'

They looked down to the mud covering Richard's feet and legs as far as his knees.

'Good job you're tall.' Dudek joined them. He laughed, almost losing his balance on his sticks and trying to grab Bluey's collar to calm him. Richard's shirt and jeans were sodden, his black hair matted to his head. Despite the sun the water was cold. Anika peeled off her white t-shirt and shivered.

'Come, I'll get towels,' said Dudek, giving up on Bluey who was now back to exploring the pond edge as if for the first time.

Anika reached up to tousle Richard's wet hair. He removed his spectacles and shook his mop of hair, throwing more drips onto her. She stepped back into the pond to splash water back at him in revenge. Richard retaliated by kicking water until it was a full water fight. Bluey joined in, barking excitedly. The heavy drops of water thrown into the air were broken by the sunlight and tiny rainbows sparkled. Richard tried to grab Anika but she was too quick for him and he fell headfirst into the pond. Bluey barked ever more joyfully and Anika laughed loud. Richard emerged slowly, water plastering his clothes to his skin, smiling broadly and with no spite. Ripples flowed across the surface of the water, lily pads bobbed and reeds swayed. Anika held out a hand to steady him as he stepped across the mud. He put back on his spectacles but took them off, they were impossible to see through.

'Your eyes are nearly black. I didn't notice before.' Anika looked directly at his face.

'I've never tried contact lenses,' Richard said, as if it was an explanation.

'Oh. And now you smell.'

Richard sniffed at his hands. It was true. The pond water might not have been as clean as it looked. 'So do you.'

'And it's cold. And your hair's a mess.'

'Like yours is fine,' said Richard, but actually he thought it was. Her hair was black with wetness and the bob-cut straggly in places and spikey in others but, always, with some imagined rebellious, innocent charm.

'Come, let's wash and take Bluey home.'

Anika planned on having dinner ready for six (a fish and chip supper) and Dudek planned on going down the pub afterwards with Young Samuel from next door, as had become their Friday (and Sunday) night routine. But their plans were disturbed when, at just gone four, the Landlord from The Blue And The Gorse rang and asked if Anika wanted an extra shift from half-five, someone had called in sick. Anika needed the money and Dudek said he and Richard could fry a few chips and piece of fish, so Anika went to work and Dudek and Richard ruined the meal. By seven they were still hungry and the house was quiet without Anika. Richard struggled with how to ask his uncle about the payments to school, but just when he thought he had a credible opening to the subject, Dudek suggested the pub, knocking for Young Samuel on the way, to grab a beer and a sandwich adding, 'But don't tell your mother I took you there.'

'S'okay. I go to the pub all the time at home,' Richard assured him.

'And Diu knows?'

'I'm not sure. Perhaps you're right. Better keep it secret.'

'I'm good at those.'

'How you gonna get there? You can't walk all that way.'

'Can't you drive?' said Dudek, throwing the Citroen's keys at Richard as they talked in the hallway, on their way out. Richard caught them and threw them back,

'I don't know how. Sorry.'

'It's not difficult. I taught your father to drive when he was about your age. Though, to be fair, it took a couple of days.'

'Sorry uncle. I can help you walk though.'

'Hmmm. Problem, but ....' he looked up from tying laces and saw, through the front door's glass, the figure approaching, '.... help is at hand.' He opened the door before the figure knocked and introduced, 'Young Samuel, this is my nephew, Richard. Richard, this is Young Samuel.

My neighbour, good friend and best saxophone player in the village.'

Young Samuel and Richard exchanged greetings and Young Samuel asked Dudek, 'Where have you been? I've been waiting. It's Friday.'

'I know. I'm sorry. Problem. Can you drive us there, in the Citroen? Anika had to go early, they need her behind the bar.'

'Of course, but I won't be staying late. Just a couple of drinks. Megan's .... not well, this evening.'

'That's okay, we'll worry about getting home when the time comes. Lead on!' Dudek called, throwing the keys at Young Samuel and taking only one stick to help as he limped to the car.

Young Samuel parked the Citroen in The Blue And The Gorse car park and waited while Richard helped Dudek from the passenger seat. It was still light but, for the first time in weeks, there was an occasional gust of wind stronger than a breeze. Richard stood to face and enjoy it but as he did four young men walked past and into the pub, dishevelled and flush-faced. Larry was among them and though Richard tried a nod of acknowledgment, it seemed Larry looked straight through him, to Dudek. Dudek appeared not to notice and before anything could be said one of the young men drew Larry's attention, observing, 'Bit of wind tonight. Not a good thing. Busy day on the fires tomorrow.' Larry and the others murmured agreement and walked on to the pub.

The bar was crowded. Richard and Dudek went to find a table while Young Samuel jostled for space at the counter. Anika was there, serving with an air of efficiency and maturity Richard hadn't seen before. She wore a red dress with a white floral pattern and half sleeves. It was, to Richard's eyes, a fifties style (like he knew), but the important thing for the customers (predominately male) was the hint of cleavage in the low v-neck collar. Richard tried but failed to catch her eye. Customers moved aside politely to let Dudek and his walking stick pass, most with a welcoming comment, and Dudek introduced Richard, often with an affectionate ruffle of his hair. Richard wondered what it was about his mop of black hair that people thought it okay to touch, perhaps he really should have a cut, and was glad when they found a table near a half open window. Dudek settled in a chair and lit a cigarette, nodding 'hello' at other drinkers. Richard waited until the greetings finished before asking, 'Why is Samuel called Young Samuel? He's not .... young, is he?'

'Not compared to you. And he's not even the youngest Samuel here.' He pointed with his cigarette hand to a group sitting at the other end of the bar. 'See that man with the green shirt? That's Old Samuel. He's lived in the village since birth. Nearly forty years, I hear.'

'And your friend Samuel?'

'Maybe four years. About a year less than me. Came here when the city was too much for him, he's in his mid-forties I think. The city hurt his heart, in many ways.'

'Which makes him .... older than Old Samuel in the green shirt?'

'Yes. But Old Samuel was here first. New Samuel became Young Samuel even though ....'

'.... he's older.'

'Of course.'

'Does he mind?'

'Who? Old or Young Samuel?'

'Either.'

'I don't think so. Besides, it wouldn't do any good. Names stick, don't they? And Young Samuel's not such a bad one, is it? .... Young Samuel.' Dudek asked Young Samuel who was now at their table, tray of drinks in hand.

'Not so bad. I've been called much worse. Your uncle is often called a Czech Mate, as if it was original.' Samuel rested the tray on the table, gave a vodka and tonic to Dudek, half a lager shandy to Richard (who was embarrassed it was a shandy and a half at that) and placed a pint of bitter in front of an empty chair for himself.

'Czech Mate. Ha. They started using that when I came to England, back in the war. Few things change.' Dudek shrugged his shoulders. 'Anika okay?' he asked Samuel.

'I think so. I was served by the new guy.' Young Samuel pulled a packet of peanuts from his pocket and dropped it on the table as he sat. He lifted his glass, 'Cheers,' though there was little enthusiasm in his voice. Richard raised his glass but they were interrupted before the first sip.

'A young man who's been a hero today can have a proper drink,' Anika said quietly, 'but don't let the boss see, just in case.' She took Richard's glass and gave him a pint of bitter. Richard tried not to let his gratitude show too much.

'Oh, of course. Sorry. I didn't know,' said Young Samuel, though it wasn't clear if he apologised for buying only a half or not knowing of the pond incident earlier.

'That's okay.' Anika placed a hand on his shoulder, asking, 'How's Megan?' and nodding as Young Samuel gave a sad smile, a slight shrug and shook his head.

There was nothing for Anika to say and Richard was relieved when a customer called to her from the bar for another round. It was one of the young men that had walked in just ahead of them.

'Ah, the fire fighters,' said Anika and added loudly, 'More heroes. Coming boys.' They cheered or jeered or offered crude suggestions, apart from Larry who looked from Dudek to his glass.

Dudek, Samuel and Richard drank; Richard pretended to like the dark brown watery bitter. Dudek broke the silence. 'Yes. A hero. Richard. Tell Samuel what happened at the pond today.' Dudek turned to Samuel, 'You know Bluey? The stupid dog a few houses along. He was in the pond again and stuck in the reeds. Richard had to go in up to his neck to save him.'

'Not quite neck. And Anika was there too,' said Richard.

'You're both heroes. Nazdravee!' Dudek raised his glass again.

'Nazdravee?' Richard repeated.

'It means cheers. In Czech,' explained Samuel. 'I've known your uncle for …. four years but that's the only Czech he's taught me.'

'That's all you need. You can go a long way in Prague with that word. But you,' he pointed at Richard, 'should know a bit more. We will teach you some before you go home. Make your father proud. Maybe go visit the old country one day.'

'I'd like to. Would you come?'

'Hmmm. No. Too much has happened. They would not welcome me and there is no blood family left. But you should go.'

A question burst into Richard's mind so funda-mental he was shocked he didn't already know the answer. 'Is my father there?'

'What do you mean?'

'I know he died in Vietnam, just after I was born, but I just realised, I don't know what happened to him.'

'To him?'

'I suppose I mean his body. Did you take it back to Czechoslovakia? How come I don't know?' Richard was surprised at himself.

Dudek took a long sip from his glass, almost emptying it, then spoke slowly. 'No. I didn't take it home.'

'Did mum bury him in Vietnam?' Richard asked quickly, anxious for an answer.

'Sort of …. this is something we should talk of when Diu is here. Yes, that would be better.'

'Why?'

'It was long ago. I …. It's better for Diu to tell you. Perhaps.'

'Perhaps I should learn more Vietnamese than Czech and go back to that home country?' Richard said and immediately regretted the bitter tone. Samuel looked away. Dudek shrugged his big shoulders.

'Perhaps. I'm sorry.' He finished his drink. 'My round,' and started to stand but Samuel was quicker.

'I'll go. You can't carry drinks with a stick. You can pay though.'

'Of course.' Dudek struggled to pull his wallet from a pocket sitting down and gave Samuel the money.

They sat in awkward silence until Dudek said, 'I'm sorry,' to Richard when Samuel was on his way back from the bar with a repeat round.

'No. I'm sorry uncle. I just …. mum and me haven't really talked about it, you know. And when I try she just tells me it will be all right.'

'And it will. She is a wise lady, your mother. You must listen to her.' Dudek neatly side-stepped the issue. 'And she is a great pianist. So you must practise and be good and make your father proud. Music is a great friend. Isn't it Samuel?'

'Eh?'

'Music is a great friend.'

'Ha, you mean my saxophone?' He placed the drinks on the table and sat. 'I'm not sure all agree with you.' He turned to Richard. 'Long time ago, I played sax well. When I was about your age I suppose. I studied hard and loved to play. By the time I was about eighteen, which was …. nineteen-fifty, I had a jazz band thing going, trying to copy what the Americans were doing and there were a few clubs in London to play. Not that we made any money. But you know how good it is to play right? I hear you practising. Sounding good. Need to keep it going.' He stopped to take a drink. Dudek and Richard copied, though Richard was still only half-way through the first pint. 'Your uncle is right. Music is a great friend. I forgot that for a while. Too wrapped up in making money. Stopped the band. Lost my friends. I put away the sax and didn't find it until I came here.'

'Which is our good fortune.' Dudek tried to lighten the tone. 'Remember? You had not played for so long when you started practising again I had to come round and ask you to stop. It sounded so bad.'

'Ha. True.' Samuel talked to Richard. 'First time we met. I'd just moved in next door and the removal men came across my old saxophone in the van and asked where I wanted it. I said leave it in the kitchen, picked it up that night, nearly forgotten which end to blow, and made such a bad noise your uncle knocked on the door to complain. My first night here. But I'm glad he did. And I got better, didn't I?' he asked Dudek.

Dudek looked thoughtful, as if weighing a risk, and said, 'Especially when Megan came along. All of a sudden you were playing beautiful. It's what love can do, yes?'

'Yes,' said Samuel and patted Dudek's leg. 'What love can do. Speaking of which, I should go. Make sure Megan's all right.'

'Of course. Say hello from us. Shall we have a drink on Sunday?'

Samuel stood and downed his pint. 'I expect we can have a quick one. Just the one mind. I'll let you know,' and nodded a goodbye to Dudek and Richard.

When Samuel was through the door Richard asked, 'Does Megan have any chance?'

Dudek shook his head. 'I don't think so. But Young Samuel still says he is lucky they met. It's true you know, from when he met Megan he played much better. Perhaps music can still be a great friend for him after .... you know.' Dudek looked up and forced a smile. 'Let's hope so, I have to listen to him practise. They say my name means bagpipe player. I should learn. Music could be my friend too. Ha. Samuel and I could play together.'

They sat in silence again, Richard regretting what he'd said about his father. He sipped at the pint of bitter, liking it better with each taste. Dudek lit another cigarette and offered one to Richard, who shook his head.

'Good,' said Dudek. 'It's probably what's killing Megan. Probably kill me too. We should stop Anika while she's still young. Those horrible sticks her grandmother sends her to smoke arrived yesterday but I've hidden the parcel. Don't tell her. Our secret.'

'Our secret.' Richard was grateful for something they could share. He relaxed further as the bitter warmed him. It was hot in the pub, despite open windows. Anika came round to collect glasses and Dudek asked her for another vodka and tonic (double this time) and another bitter for Richard who wasn't going to refuse. Cigarette and pipe smoke hung at the ceiling and noise levels increased as alcohol took effect. Richard tried to tune in to the chatter. It was a constant stream of stories, opinions, invective, jokes, argument and indulgent sentimentalism, overlaid on an ever changing sea of topics and debate. But one subject cropped up more often than others as more and more drinkers feted the young men at the bar for their bravery in volunteering to help fight the fires on the heath.

Anika brought drinks to Dudek and Richard. Richard thanked her (slurring a little) and wondered what Julie and Malcolm were doing this Friday evening. The drink was relaxing and he said to Dudek, 'The people here all know each other. Back home it took me months just to say hello to the new girl that moved close.'

'Months?'

'Yep.'

'Ha, but that's because she is pretty, right?'

'No …. I mean yes, she's pretty enough, but that's not why.'

'Why then?'

'I don't know.'

'Ha. So she is very pretty.'

'I suppose. Thing is, everyone here knows each other. I met a girl in the newsagent who knew who I was and I've only been here a week.'

'That's because I told everyone about you. I'm sorry. I'm very proud. You are so like my little brother. Darker, of course, and more handsome, thanks to your mother. But, tell me. This girl at home. How pretty?'

Richard laughed. 'Okay. Very.'

'I knew it …. but ….?'

'But what?'

'You are here. She is there. So there is a but ….'

'No …. yes …. but …. she's my best friend's girlfriend.'

'Oh. Did you ask her first?'

'No.'

'Does she know you like her?'

'No.'

'Does your best friend know you like her?'

'No.'

'Hmmm. You're not as smart as you first appear are you?' Dudek reached over and tousled Richard's hair, again. 'Oh well. What of the girl you met here? Is she pretty?'

'I suppose.' Richard smoothed his hair.

'Ha. Of course she is. All young women are pretty. Trust me. So ask her out.'

'Who?'

'The girl you met here.'

'Elizabeth's granddaughter?'

'Oh.'

'You know her.'

'Of course. And she is pretty.'

'See. Everyone here knows everyone else.'

'They …. we …. do, I suppose. Perhaps I'll never be one of them but they are mostly good to me and I like them. They are good people. Mostly. Some have lived their whole lives here. Met their wives, had families, grown old and died without leaving the village. Perhaps they are the really lucky ones. Others, like me and Samuel, came here and they almost accept us and Samuel was lucky enough to find Megan. She came here from town. To escape. Like me and Samuel. They were lucky to find each other. Not so lucky now.' Dudek sipped from his drink. 'Richard. Earlier. About your father. You should understand, whatever else, Greguska and Diu were lucky to have found each other. They didn't have long but it mattered and, after all, they had you. They were lucky. They loved each other so much. I should have …. I should …. I should be so lucky ….' Dudek's voice tailed off. The opportunity to question was open again but before Richard could find the right one a glass of vodka was slammed in front of them, the clear liquid splashing on to the table.

'For you. Old man.' Larry spat the words and mustered all the sarcasm he could to slowly add, 'Naz …. dra …. vee. Cheers.' His face was more red than usual and the threat in his tone scared Richard. Dudek smiled but it was not sincere. His eyes narrowed as his mouth widened.

'Thank you Larry. That's kind. If you go back to your friends I'd like to buy you all a drink.'

'Friends? I thought you were my …..'

Before the sentence was finished Anika was next to him. 'Larry. Larry. I need your help ….'

'What?'

'Help. You can help me. It's Erica's birthday soon isn't it?' Anika placed one hand on Larry's arm and another on his back and gently turned him as she talked and leant forward, causing him to take a couple of steps towards the door.

'What?'

'Your sister. Erica. It's her birthday soon. What does she want? You know her well. Of course. What does she like? Clothes? What size is she? What's her favourite colour? What are you getting her? How old will she be? Twenty one isn't it? An important date ….' Anika eased him towards the door, talking incessantly. Dudek began to rise but Richard stopped him,

'It's okay. I'll go,' and was out of his chair before Dudek could say otherwise. By the time Richard caught up with them through the crowd, Anika had guided him to the door. She laughed with the other customers as they assumed she was helping him and she made sure not to be insulting to Larry and kept speaking; her accent was still clipped but she kept smiling. Richard went past them to open the door and Anika ushered Larry into the car park. The fresh air hit him and through his drunken confusion he realised what Anika had done. He shouted, 'No!' and tried to turn back to the pub but Anika's slender frame stood firm in his way.

'Larry. You should go home. You are …. tired.'

'No!' Larry shouted again and tried to push Anika aside.

For Richard, the next few seconds slipped into slow motion. He saw Anika's eyes widen with fear and he heard the anger in Larry's voice. His own heart rate leapt and he took a couple of short breaths. Larry's hands were on Anika's shoulders and he pushed her to one side. She lost her balance and started to fall. Richard was behind Larry and took a step to reach him and spin him round more violently than he intended. He may have shouted something (later, he didn't remember) and he was taller than Larry and just as strong. Larry was off balance. Richard shoved him hard in the chest with two hands but he didn't fall and after two steps back caught his balance and launched himself at Richard, shrieking, flailing his arms and lashing out with his feet. There was no co-ordination in the attack but Richard had no defence and took three or four (he didn't know how many) hits to the side of the head and kicks to his shins. Although they shocked him there was no pain (yet) and he knew he had to stay on his feet as his spectacles were knocked to the ground. Anika was back up and screaming and jumped on

Larry's back but he shrugged her off before she could grip round his neck. Richard lowered his hands from protecting his head and swung a punch. Larry didn't see it but the aim was poor and it caught him high on the temple. He was drunk and hardly felt it but before he launched another attack Dudek was at the door and his big voice was enough to freeze the moment,

'Lawrence! Enough!' He stepped out from the pub.

Larry turned to Dudek, took two strides and threw a punch but Dudek neatly side-stepped, caught the swinging fist and used the momentum to pull. Dudek tripped him as he came forward and when Larry hit the ground Dudek was instantly on him, knee in his back, weight far too much for Larry to move. Dudek leaned forward and spoke quietly into Larry's ear, a whisper. Larry stopped writhing. Dudek whispered more. Larry nodded and Dudek stood up carefully, looking for support now his ankle was hurting as the adrenaline subsided. A couple of men were watching from the pub's doorway but were pushed aside by Erica. She hadn't seen the short fight but Larry was still on the floor and Dudek stood large over him. She shouted her brother's name and went to help him as he rolled to one side. He stood, shook Erica away and almost ran from the car park, not looking at either Anika or Richard. Erica looked to Anika, questions in her eyes but Anika simply said, 'Sorry.'

'Later,' said Erica, and made it sound a threat, before trotting awkwardly in high heels after her brother. Dudek leant on Anika and said something but Richard didn't hear. His heart was pounding. There was a surge of relief and a sudden flood of euphoria. But in seconds it was gone as his peripheral vision shrank and the left side of his sight vanished. The few lights from the pub were confusing to his remaining vision and he couldn't understand Dudek's speech. He tried to speak but could not form words. Neither Anika nor Dudek knew he had a problem until he was able to mutter, 'Head. Bad.' And,

with a huge effort in concentration, a pleading, 'Home ....
Please.'

Three Weeks In The Summer

Chapter 8
Lesson Four, Part One

Saturday morning was slow. Dudek was up but moving slowly; Richard was slow out of bed. He didn't appear until gone ten, having spent at least five minutes searching unsuccessfully for his spectacles. He sipped at the tea Dudek poured for him. Richard had worried there might be a difficult atmosphere following the previous night's fight outside the pub but the opposite felt true; there was a sense of having shared a challenge, faced a fear together and conquered it - with, and for, each other. Dudek insisted Richard have a bowl of porridge and eat out on the patio, taking shade under the umbrella and enjoying the warm air. Richard was hungry (he'd noticed he usually was, coming out the other side of a migraine) and relaxed, even though his thoughts were still haphazard; irrelevancies and oddities kept springing to mind and just as quickly disappearing. He was unable to fix on any one idea. But the porridge tasted good. As he scraped the last spoonful from the bowl, Anika came from the kitchen with a cheery, 'Hello.' She sat next to him and turned him to face her so she could slip his spectacles on his face.

He winced as she accidently brushed the bruise high on his left cheek.

'When we got back home last night Dudek realised you didn't have them. We had a look in the car but guessed you must have lost them at the pub. Larry is such a …. prat. I went back this morning. They were by the door. Lucky no one stood on them. Are they okay?'

Richard took them off to examine and nodded. One of the arms was bent but the lenses looked okay. 'Thanks. I didn't realise I lost them last night.'

'No. After …. you know …. you were a bit ….' She twirled an index finger next to her temple. 'Does that hurt?'

Richard had winced again when replacing his spectacles. 'A bit. You okay?'

'Fine. It was a bit …. crazy.'

'Is Dudek okay?'

'He hasn't said much about it but he's proud of you for coming to help me.'

'Hmmm. It was me needed help at the end. Are you sure you're okay?' Richard asked and pointed to Anika's elbow.

'A …. graze. Right word?'

'Yep.'

'Graze. And Larry is such a ….'

'…. prat. Yep. Why did he ….'

'Who knows?' Anika interrupted before Richard could finish his question. Dudek joined them, limping more heavily than he had the previous day. He had taken off his shirt but still wore a vest. Braces held his trousers and he often pulled at them, as if they chafed his shoulders.

'Better after my breakfast?' he asked Richard.

'Yes, thanks. Tasted better than last time I tried.'

'Extra honey. Anika found your eye-glasses. Good. Is your head better? Diu told me you were having headaches. Last night was …. strange.'

Richard was embarrassed at being asked (even so subtly) to explain, 'It's okay. It's not the headache that's worse. It's the other stuff. When I can't see. The doctor says not to worry. Hey, it's not like it's a brain tumour or something.'

'Tumour? Who said that? Diu didn't say anything.'
There was panic in Dudek's tone - the first time Richard
had known it.

'Sorry, joke. It's a joke. Bad one. Sorry. The doctors
thought it might have been, but it isn't so, all in all, it's
okay.'

'But what about the lights?' Dudek leant forward
and touched Richard's arm. 'When Anika drove us home
you kept muttering about the lights.'

'Did I? Sorry. I just .... after the half blindness I see
flashing lights. Neon. Zig-zag. They flash and I can't see
through them and they make me feel sick. But it's all right.
They go away pretty quick and then my head hurts. Bad.'

'And this has happened before?' Anika asked.

'Yep.'

'Good .... I mean, good it's not because you were
hit on the head.' Anika smiled at him and he noticed her
bottom lip was swollen and wanted to touch it, which was
ridiculous for so many reasons and he realised but was
happy at having had the idea; his post migraine mind was a
mess.

'Yes. That's good,' agreed Dudek.

'Will the tablets work?' Anika asked.

'It's okay. It's not a big deal.'

'How do you feel now?'

'Okay. It'll just take a day or two before it'll clear
properly, my head I mean. It's no big deal. It's not like it's
a tumour or anything.'

'You said that already,' said Anika.

'Did I?'

'It's still not funny.'

'Sorry.'

'No matter,' said Dudek. 'Did you take your
tablets?'

'Honestly. It's not a big deal.'

'Okay. But did you take your tablets?'

'I .... I haven't read the dosage yet. I'll do it later.'

'And then take them.' Dudek tried to be firm. 'And now, I will make you special coffee and then teach you to fight. Last night you were brave. Very. But you hit like a girl. After coffee. Anika, help me?'

Dudek limped back into the kitchen; Anika followed. Richard heard Dudek giving instructions and the boiling of water and the clinking of cutlery and china. Five minutes or so later Anika brought out a tray with three small cups and a china coffee pot, steaming. They sat at the table and Dudek poured from the pot to the cups and gave instructions they should all drink together, but carefully, it was very hot. Anika counted to three and on four they sipped. Dudek laughed at Richard and Anika's faces as the hot, dark brown liquid was immediately painfully sweet and, seconds after, unbearably bitter.

'I know,' said Dudek, 'disgusting. But in a few seconds delicious. Trust.' He lit a Rothmans and waited. He was right. After a short while the taste was subtle caramel and soothing cream and they enjoyed, amazed at the transformation. And though the coffee had been hot and the sun was high, the drink was refreshing, as if cold.

When their cups were empty Dudek spoke. 'So. Now, lessons in how to survive, how to not be hit, how to hit and when to run. Both of you.'

'Do I need to change into shorts or something?' asked Richard.

'Next time you are in a fight will you be wearing shorts?'

'I don't suppose.'

'Will you have time to change?'

'Er, I suppose not.'

'Exactly.'

'But ….'

'But what?' Dudek interrupted.

'Should we wait until your ankle is better?'

'Was it better last night?'

'No.'

116

'Will the next person wait for my ankle to be better?'

'I suppose not.'

'Exactly. Now stop interrupting. I am getting angry.'

'No you're not.' Anika laughed.

'Yes I am. First lesson. Don't believe you will always know when someone is angry.'

'Are you angry with me?' she asked.

'No. I am angry with myself. Yesterday was a bad day. Two times I let you be in danger, your mothers would be very angry. And I am angry. With myself. It was stupid. First the dog and then the pub. Stupid of me.' He looked at Richard. 'You are my little brother's son and nothing means more to me.'

'What about me?' asked Anika with exaggerated umbrage.

'You are my .... childhood sweetheart's .... grand-daughter and nothing means more to me.'

'But I thought he ....'

'Enough questions. Second lesson. Don't be so brave, both of you. Smart is always better than brave. Your father understood that.' He patted Richard's arm. 'He was the smartest and bravest man I ever knew.'

Richard saw the sincerity in his uncle's eyes but before he could ask a question Dudek said, 'And now you want to know why I say that about your father. That is for another time. Third lesson. Don't get drunk if not at home, always know who is around you or moving to you, sit with your back to a wall and be able to see the door. Yes, I know, everything I did wrong last night. Stupid old man that I am. Did you know your father's name, Greguska, means watchful? It was a good name for him.'

He took a break to pour more coffee.

'Lesson four. Don't have people close who you ....' he looked from Richard to Anika, '.... who you would die for,' he swallowed and forced a smile, 'and the rest is easy.

Duck when you see a punch coming, run if you can and if not kick them in the balls and run.

'That's not what you did last night,' said Anika.

'Ah, well I couldn't run, so I had to use the last resort. Sit on him. But that only works if you're fat, like me.'

'Uncle Dudek. Come on, how did you know how to …. sort out Larry when he came at you?'

'Long, long time ago I was good at it and had to do it more than once. That's the only way to be good at it. Do it. Not in the gym. For real. That's why I tell you to run if you can. You will never have to fight often enough to be good at it, I pray.'

'What would my father have done?'

'He wouldn't have let you and Anika be in that position. He would have been watching. I think he still is. Everything turned out okay so yes, Greguska is still watching. All of us.'

'Watchful? Greguska really means watchful?' Richard asked.

'Yes. But he knew when to act. Sometimes you have to act. You cannot be a watcher all your life.'

'What was he watching for?'

'Oh, all sorts of things. It was our job. To watch and tell. To understand why things happened and predict actions. Your father was good because he was a good watcher but even better at knowing people. Here.' Dudek leant forward and placed a hand over Richard's chest. 'To know people here is a gift. Good and bad. Remember, the heart is not always good. If someone lets you see their heart easily, ask what they are hiding. Greguska knew.'

As always when talk was of his father, a hundred questions jumbled through Richard's head, but without focus. All he asked was, 'Why?'

'Why what?'

'Okay. First. Why was it your job?'

'Long story. We'll need more coffee.' Dudek tried to make light of the question but when Richard didn't smile or laugh he asked, 'How much has Diu told you of me and your father?'

'Not much. You had something to do with military intelligence and, whatever happened in Vietnam, my father never came back.'

'The most important thing happened in Vietnam was Greguska and Diu fell in love and you were born. And your father was very brave, and that's why the British looked after you and your mother and made sure to bring you back here safe. A …. reward, for being brave.'

'What, instead of a medal?' Richard asked sarcastically.

'What use is a medal? Better for them to bring you here safe.'

'Mum says he was a hero.'

'Yes.'

'And that's why they pay for my school.'

'Yes. And you make your father proud by doing well at school.'

Richard went quiet, thinking of the cheques Dudek had written to his school, and asked, 'So you and mum don't pay anything to the school?'

'No. Of course not. The British government pays. More use than a medal.'

Richard looked at Anika, wondering if she might make the connection with the letter to John Le Rugber she had seen but she poured the last of the coffee from the pot into their cups and laughed when they all sipped together and winced at the sweet and bitter taste. Dudek drained his cup in two then checked his watch, saying, 'Excuse me, I have to ring some people.' He limped back into the house. Anika and Richard sat for a while and it became uncomfortable when Richard thought Anika was looking at him. Eventually she said,

'So your father was a hero and you don't know why.'

'I suppose.'

'That's okay. I never knew my father either. And at least yours was a hero. And you were my hero last night.'

Richard couldn't tell if she teased and offered a meek, 'You're welcome.'

'Prosim. In my town we say prosim for you are welcome.'

'Prosim.'

'Does your head still hurt?'

'A little. Why?'

'It is …. dark …. round your eyes. You look tired. It is getting hotter. You should sleep. I'm going on the low chair for a while.' Anika didn't wait for an answer but removed her favourite white baggy t-shirt (wearing her favourite blue gingham bikini underneath) as she sauntered to the lounger under the apple tree. Richard went to his room, hoping to nap and resisted the temptation to watch Anika out the window.

Richard missed lunch. When he finally came downstairs Dudek said they hadn't wanted to wake him, he slept so soundly. Richard felt child-like but in a good way; it was settling to think Dudek and Anika were looking after him - perhaps he was missing his mother more than he would admit. He poured a glass of water, sat at the Bontempi and twenty five minutes of practise flashed by while playing along to his cassette player. The door-bell rang and Anika shouted from the kitchen, 'Uncle, put on a shirt, we have visitors.'

Dudek came in from the patio to search for his shirt and had just finished buttoning when Anika walked into the dining room and introduced, 'Elizabeth and Jenny ….'

'Jennifer,' said Jennifer.

'Hello Dudek. Haven't seen you in the village for a while, thought we'd pop round to catch up.' Elizabeth handed a cake to Anika.

'Elizabeth, so good to see you,' said Dudek.

'Look what Elizabeth brought.' Anika lifted the cake, trophy-like. Elizabeth added,

'It's home-made. Called medovnik. I found the idea in the library, in town. It's a Czech recipe,' Elizabeth explained.

'Medovnik? Yes. Honey cake. Excellent. Thank you very much. That's kind. And to look up a home recipe. Thank you.' Dudek was both surprised Elizabeth was visiting and humbled she had taken trouble to bake a Czech recipe. Anika caught Richard's eye; she looked a little smug.

'I hope it tastes okay,' Elizabeth sounded nervous. 'To be honest I'm not sure what it should taste like.'

'I'm sure it will be light and sweet, just like my grandmother's. It looks perfect.'

'Even with the sunken top?' Elizabeth asked.

'That shows it's perfectly home-made. Let's taste.'

Anika took the cake to the kitchen and Dudek ushered Elizabeth out to the patio to sit in the umbrella's shade. Jennifer passed to Richard the newspaper she carried: Melody Maker. 'It came in this morning. Thought you'd want it.'

Richard scanned the cover. It had a picture of The Sex Pistols. He thought how pleased Malcolm must be. 'Er, yeah. Thanks. I'll read it later. I'll give you the money for it.'

'Nah, that's okay, don't worry.'

'But ....'

'No problem.' Jennifer stood by the fireplace. 'Wotchya doing?'

'Practising.'

'For what?'

'Just practising. To be better I suppose.'

Jennifer looked out to the garden where Dudek, Elizabeth and Anika chatted. She looked back to Richard. 'I heard about the fight last night. At the pub. That's a nice look.' She pointed to his face.

'Wow, that was quick. Everyone here really does know everything that happens.'

'My nan is postmistress. And I help out in the newsagent. Remember?' She left the fireplace to peer more closely at his bruised cheek. She wasn't wearing her spectacles and squinted as she put her face close to his. Richard resisted the urge to look away, which was easy, she was pretty, as Dudek had predicted. She said, 'You have long eye lashes for a boy. Like a girl's. Very dark too. Is that a Malaysian thing?'

'Vietnamese. Half,' Richard reminded her but her directness was disarming and peculiarly matter-of-fact.

'Does it hurt?' She reached to touch the bruise on his cheek. He drew back.

'Not much.'

'I heard you were brave. Going to Anika's rescue.'

'Not really. It wasn't like that. But if that's the word on the street then, hey, who am I to deny it ….'

'….on the street? Ha. This is Oakjack. So the other story's the truth. Your old uncle had to rescue both of you from a skinny drunk farmhand.'

'I guess the truth is somewhere in the middle.'

'It usually is, some say. Why did Larry have a go at you?'

'He had a go at Dudek and Anika tried to help and I got involved and, it got out of hand. Larry's a prat.'

'Why?'

'Because he was drunk and wanted to fight.'

'I meant why did he have a go at your uncle?'

'Oh. I don't know. We haven't talked about it since.'

'Shame. I was hoping for the gossip. People keep asking me …. as a postmistress's granddaughter I am expected to know. Anyway, the bruise suits you. So, what are you practising for? Apart from getting better, obviously.' She sat next to him at the keyboard but not so close as Anika the previous day. 'You gonna be the next Rick Wakeman? Personally I prefer Jon Lord. Purple has that more heavy blues thing going in the rock.'

'You heard those guys?' Richard was impressed.

'Of course. Who's on here?' She pressed PLAY on Richard's cassette player. The tape was half way through 'Harvest For The World'. 'Bit disco, isn't it?'

'No. Not disco at all. Proper new soul. Off the album. Great album.' Richard was defensive.

'Hmmmmm. You'll be playing along to 'Summer Breeze' next.' Jennifer was not convinced but Richard knew better than to protest further.

'It's on here. You don't like The Isley Brothers? Great soul and funk.'

'Not rocky enough for me. I expect you're the type of boy thinks playing 'Tonight's The Night' is how to seduce a girl.' She played a couple of discordant notes on the Bontempi. Richard was again irritated at how easily he was embarrassed.

'So come on. Play something,' Jennifer urged.

Richard was saved by Anika. She came in to ask if they wanted a cold drink, offering a squash or Top Deck shandy. They chose the Top Deck though Jennifer remarked it was, 'Weak as piss after what I heard you drunk last night. Or so some say. The landlord in the B and G isn't as strict as the new guy down Devil's Peat. How old are you?'

Richard ignored the question.

Anika brought them a can each and indicated to the Bontempi as she asked Jennifer, 'Do you play?'

'No.'

'We do, don't we?' she said to Richard and leant over him to turn off the cassette player and start 'Chopsticks'. Richard joined in further up the register and they played it through twice without mistakes. Jennifer clapped with a hint of sarcasm.

'Thank you. Tomorrow, Beethoven's fifth,' Anika said and went back out into the garden through the French doors.

'Is she your cousin or something?' asked Jennifer.

'No.'

'Why does she call your uncle uncle?

'He just sort of …. is.'

'Some say ….'

'What?'

'What?'

'What do some say?'

'They just do. S'okay, don't be touchy. I'm sure she'd make a good cousin. C'mon, try Elizabeth's cake.'

Richard followed her out into the garden and they sat next to Anika, Dudek and Elizabeth who said, 'Ah, the hero of the hour,' with no sarcasm. 'How are you settling in to our village?'

'It's very …. hot. And everyone knows everyone else, which is odd. But I like it. Oh, and it smells of fire, a lot.' There was a hint of burning in the air.

'We don't usually have so many fires on the heath. I heard they got yesterday's under control and that ….' Elizabeth pointed vaguely in the air, '…. doesn't smell too close. It's usually far more dull round here, which is a good thing.'

'Yeah, right,' said Jennifer. 'Last night doesn't sound dull. What was it about, uncle Dudek?' She called him uncle and he appeared to take it as a sign of respect. Richard wondered how old she was; she was as much a mystery as any of the girls back home. He thought her a year or two younger than him, but then maybe a year or two older as he watched her chat with his uncle. She had a boyish figure but her face was older. She lacked Julie's (supposed) sophistication, Carol's knowing and Anika's alluring confidence and independence, so why did she so easily embarrass him? He wanted to discuss it with Malcolm - perhaps he could write to him, not that writing was easy for him and anyway, Malcolm might show Julie. Richard's thoughts drifted until he heard Jennifer say his name, '.... and Richard said Larry was a dick.'

'Jennifer,' Elizabeth cautioned as Dudek laughed and Anika added,

'Yep, a prat.'

'It was nothing.' Dudek played it down. 'A young man had too much to drink and a simple disagreement got out of hand and the young man acted foolishly,' he paused, 'and that was just me.' He waited for the laugh. It came but subsided into silence. A wasp buzzed close to Jennifer's can of Top Deck. She brushed it away. Elizabeth asked,

'So why was Larry angry?'

Dudek shrugged.

Anika spoke, 'We asked Larry to do a small job here, repairing the fence at the back. Uncle thought we had a price agreed and it seems we didn't. He is too trusting. Please, don't say anything to others.'

'Yes,' Dudek interrupted, 'I know. Stupid to argue over money. Now, women, they are worth arguing over, eh Richard?' he asked Richard but looked at Elizabeth. Richard thought she might be blushing but it was hard to tell, her face was already red from the summer sun.

'We are a great mystery,' agreed Anika and looked to Elizabeth and Jennifer who nodded support as if they understood. Elizabeth cut the cake and handed out plates. Dudek's praise for the taste was sincere; he was sure his grandmother would approve. Elizabeth was modest.

Anika finished her tea. 'Come Jenny. Come and see our pond. It's not so big as it was, every day it is less, but it is a good pond.'

'Jennifer,' Jennifer said quietly.

'Yes. Jennifer,' repeated Anika, 'come see.'

Anika stood, motioned to Richard he should also stand and they left the shade of the umbrella, waiting a few yards down the garden for Jennifer to join them. Dudek shouted after them not to go in the pond even if, '…. that stupid dog is there.'

They ducked under the apple trees and wandered to the pond. Apart from insect buzz and hum it was quiet and still and though the shadows were starting to lengthen as the afternoon drifted by, it was still hot.

'What stupid dog?' asked Jennifer as they sat on the grass by the dried mud at the pond's edge.

'Bluey. From a few doors along,' Richard explained. 'We had to save him yesterday. He was caught in the reeds. Stupid dog. Likes to swim, to cool down I suppose, and sometimes comes to see us in the garden.'

'Bluey. Good name,' said Jennifer. 'If I had a dog I'd call him Geddy.'

'Geddy?' Richard asked.

'You know, Geddy. Bass player with Rush. You heard of them right?'

'Of course. Just didn't know the bass player's name. I've a dog at home. Ossie.'

'After the Black Sabbath singer?'

'No, after Osgood. Used to play for Chelsea. My team.'

'Good name,' said Anika.

'Could've been, if named after the Black Sabbath guy,' said Jennifer.

'You can pretend, if it helps,' said Anika.

'I may not have to. A friend has a bitch that gave birth to six puppies a couple of weeks ago. I just need to talk Elizabeth into letting me have one. We should go see them.'

'Would uncle let you have a dog?' Richard asked Anika.

'Probably, but I won't be here much longer. I suppose I'll be going back and then what happens? Would Dudek want it? I asked him once and he said they had a dog when he was a child but since …. I don't know how long …. he's never stayed in one place long enough.'

'This is a great place for a dog.' Jennifer gestured to the overgrown flora round the pond. 'And you have a big garden. We should take your uncle with us to see the puppies,' Jennifer suggested.

They settled into a silence. Richard thought about a dog for his uncle but not for long, it was too warm and slow an afternoon for serious thought. He saw a ripple disturb the pond's surface and crawled closer to the water's edge to find its cause but saw only the occasional pond skater, skitting across the water but leaving no trace. He crawled back when Young Samuel next door's saxophone started.

'He's even earlier this afternoon,' said Anika.

They listened for a few moments to the random scales (Richard assumed Samuel was warming up) before Jennifer asked, 'Who is that?'

'Young Samuel next door,' Anika answered. 'He likes to play in the evening.'

'Play?'

'Saxophone,' said Anika.

'He's good when he warms up,' added Richard.

'What music does he play?' Jennifer asked.

'Anything he wants. His lover is dying,' Anika said.

'Oh, that Samuel. Megan's Samuel,' Jennifer nodded. There was a question in Anika and Richard's silence which Jennifer answered, 'My nan's postmistress, remember? And anyway, Samuel is often in the pharmacy. Sometimes for his heart tablets but mostly her pain tablets.'

'You really do know everything,' said Richard.

'You're such a townie.'

'Townie?' Anika asked.

'Er, from the town. Doesn't understand village. Don't forget, Elizabeth and the chemist share the shop. Mostly it's dull and few customers. Lots of time to chat.'

'You mean gossip,' said Richard.

'See. A townie. It's chat and it's good 'cos it means we look out for each other. You must hear it all ….' Jennifer looked to Anika, '…. working in the pub.'

Anika nodded, 'I suppose.'

'Ironic isn't it?' Jennifer said, 'Samuel came to Oakjack Ford for his health and hooked up with someone who's dying.'

'Did he know?' asked Richard.

'I don't know. I guess not. Would you hook up with someone dying?' Jennifer asked. Richard shrugged his shoulders. Anika simply said,

'Love.'

They sat in silence while Samuel played his usual selection of melodies until Jennifer asked, 'Is Megan out there with him? I heard she was bed-bound.'

'She's in a hammock. Samuel carries her out. Come.' Anika stood, stretched and walked a few yards towards Samuel's garden before crouching to crawl through the undergrowth to the bunker. Richard told Jennifer to do likewise and followed her. Anika was squatting by the entrance to the bunker and ushered Jennifer and Richard into the cool darkness. Jennifer started to speak, Anika 'shshushed' and they sat peeping through the letterbox windows at Samuel and Megan. As before, although they saw part of Megan's hammock they couldn't see her face. The oxygen tank lay against one of the trees with a tube running up to the hammock. Samuel's playing was loosening up with notes sustained longer and their timbre warmer. After a few minutes Anika sat with her back against the wall, lit a cigarette (Players No. 10) and offered the pack to Richard, who refused, and Jennifer, who accepted. Richard started to ask how old she was, as if it mattered, but checked himself. To ask was to highlight how juvenile it was they should be spying on Samuel and Megan in such fashion, though it had seemed anything but juvenile when he and Anika had done the same thing before.

Anika took a few deep drags from the cigarette and whispered, 'Listen. Love.'

As usual, Samuel played lingering notes and slow runs, swirling round central melodies that were sometimes recognised but more often not. Anika started to ask Jennifer a question but Samuel stopped playing and Anika put a finger to her lips, waiting for another tune to start before continuing, 'So, Jennifer, what happened between Dudek and Elizabeth last summer?'

'Last summer? I don't know. They met up for a drink in the pub a few times, but Elizabeth stopped going.'

'So my uncle and your mum were .... sort of together?' Richard whispered.

'Elizabeth is my nan.'

'Oh, sorry, forgot. Where's your mum?'

'She's dead.'

'Oh, I didn't know.'

'You don't say.'

'Sorry.'

'Sorry she's dead or sorry you didn't know.'

'Both.'

'It's okay. Long, long time ago.'

'My father's dead too.'

'I know. I heard.'

There was an awkward silence which Anika settled. 'So why did Elizabeth stop gong to the pub with Dudek?'

'I don't know. I think she was a little scared.'

'Scared?'

'The last time she had a boyfriend was thirty years ago or something. I told her to keep going but she's spent so long being my nan maybe she can't be anything else. What did your uncle say?'

'He's not really her uncle,' Richard interrupted.

'I know.'

'Not much. But a lot. He doesn't say much about Elizabeth, but often says a little. I think he still likes her,' said Anika.

'And she makes great cake,' Richard added, without turning away from the bunker's window. The two girls looked at him and Jennifer stifled a laugh. Samuel's saxophone playing stopped abruptly mid-note. Richard ducked from the letterbox window. The girls froze. They heard a low moan and muted conversation and waited, expecting to be confronted. There were two distinct voices but the conversation didn't increase in volume; Samuel and Megan were talking; Samuel's tones were anxious. Richard wondered if Jennifer and Anika's heart rates had soared like his and raised his head to see out the window again. Anika edged next to him. Samuel had placed the saxophone on the ground and was hunched over the hammock, talking with Megan. From the bunker they saw only as high as his waist because of the low hanging branches of the apple trees that also hid the hammock. Though the words were indistinct, the anxiety in Samuel's tone became urgent and he turned away from the hammock to disconnect the tube to the oxygen tank and wheel it back to the house. Jennifer squeezed next to Anika and Richard to see just as they heard the sobbing. It started slowly and quietly but within a few seconds was faster and louder, a gasping sob of breathlessness and sorrow and fear.

'You go now,' Anika whispered, 'this is not for you to hear.'

Richard nodded, pleased to be leaving. The sobbing was frightening and he was glad for Anika's direction, it salved his conscience at offering no assistance to Megan and he wanted to be gone before Samuel came back. They left the bunker less cautiously than they entered and worked their way back to Dudek's garden, not stopping at the pond. By the time they emerged from the back of the garden Samuel was again playing the saxophone, though the melodies were more fractured and faster.

At the patio Dudek was sitting forward in his chair but the low sun crept under the umbrella. He heard Anika call 'hello' and took his hand from Elizabeth's to shelter his eyes against the glare. Richard wondered if Jennifer had seen the touching hands. As they reached the table Elizabeth stood, saying, 'We need to make a move. I took fish from the freezer earlier and Jennifer is going to cook it with new potatoes and veg. It's important they should be independent, don't you think?'

'Yes. Of course. They're a soft lot. Not like our generation eh?' Dudek agreed. Elizabeth said to keep what was left of the cake and bring back the plate when finished and Dudek said it wouldn't last long and he hoped she might bake another one for him. They went round the side of the house to the front, saying their goodbyes. Dudek left his stick on the patio and made an effort not to limp too heavily. As Elizabeth and Jennifer walked away down the drive Anika took Dudek's arm to help him back round to the garden, saying,

'Uncle, be careful with Elizabeth. Don't be too forward.'

'I understand. You are right. But I'm not getting younger. And the village is not so full of single ladies as it could be.' He tried to joke.

'If you are sometimes lonely perhaps you should move back to London.'

'No. There I was lonely. Here I am just sometimes living on my own. Besides, no-one wants me back in London. But you are right. I will try to be more …. subtle. Like Richard with Jennifer perhaps. Ha ha.'

'Oh, I think he has come here to get away from …. girls. He says.'

'Ah yes, the pretty girl back home, with his best friend. Come, tell me again, how did it go wrong? Is it a tale of sacrifice or conquest?'

Richard pretended he hadn't heard his uncle and followed them back round to the patio. Young Samuel had stopped playing again. Anika sighed heavily, with sadness, not frustration, 'I'm going round to see if Samuel or Megan need anything.'

'She's a good girl,' Dudek said to Richard, loud enough for Anika to hear, 'but don't tell her I said so.'

'Our secret,' said Richard, also loud enough for her to hear.

'Now, tell me again about this girl trouble.' Dudek patted the seat next to him and Richard sat, embarrassed at the question but glad for the reason not to be going with Anika.

Chapter 9
Fire

Mid-afternoon. Richard sat on the bench under the window in his bedroom, leafing through Melody Maker and picking out those articles worth his effort of reading. The open window allowed what little breeze there was and he heard a dog bark; he guessed Bluey was out exploring but couldn't see past the trees to the pond or the other gardens stretching to his left as he looked out. He went back to Melody Maker, turning to the classified ads, hoping to find a band based in a West London suburb needing a keyboard player - ideally bi-lingual (second language: Vietnamese), with a Bontempi (but classically trained to a maximum of grade 4) and a desire to start a heavy funk band that dabbled in prog rock and was looking to be signed and whose first name was Richard (the keyboard player, not the band - hopefully they didn't have a band name yet; he had plenty of suggestions to offer). He read through the wanted ads slowly and with difficulty. There was nothing quite specific enough for him and he wondered what he would do if he ever saw the ad he imagined every week and went back to day-dreaming out the window, feeling guilty for not using the time to practise, but not enough to do any.

Movement on the patio caught Richard's eye. Anika put down the Titbits magazine and went into the kitchen, just as the faint phone ring caught his ear. He went to the open door of his bedroom, just in case the call was from his mother, but Anika didn't shout up for him. Instead he heard Dudek telling Anika to put on clothes as he needed her to drive him. Although his voice was calm, it carried authority and he heard Anika trot up the stairs to the floor below him and close the bedroom door after her. He waited a short while until he heard her door open and went down the stairs to bump into her, asking, 'Everything okay?'

'I don't know. Elizabeth just called. One of her friends lives the other side of Hinton and asks if she can come over. There are fires close to her cottage and she is scared and the fireman said she should move out and take what she can. Elizabeth is going over there in her car to help out and asked Dudek for help. Elizabeth's Mini doesn't have much room. So, we have a …. mission. Good. I hate boring Sundays. Back home I go to church on Sundays but here …. I tried to take Dudek but he says it's too late for him.' She looked at Richard's feet. 'Better put on shoes or something. C'mon. Your uncle can't lift anything heavy.'

Richard slipped on trainers, changed his Montreal Olympic t-shirt for something older and ran down the stairs. Anika and Dudek were waiting for him in the Citroen, sweating in the car's heat, and at the top of the drive was Elizabeth in her old, bright red Mini, sliding windows wide open. Jennifer was in the passenger seat. Elizabeth pulled away as the Citroen reached the end of the drive and the cars drove in convoy.

Elizabeth's friend, Maisie, lived in a cottage a mile or two the other side of Hinton, and as they drove closer the smell of burning gorse was stronger. They went through Hinton, it was barely bigger than Oakjack Ford, and a mile or two past saw heavy black smoke, just beyond the hedgerows. Despite the heat of the afternoon Richard wound up the Citroen's window. Dudek and Anika did the same as they turned off the main road and onto a gravel lane, little more than a track, uneven and hedged. A couple of hundred yards up the lane was the row of four detached cottages, all with thatched roofs, but before they could get close they were stopped by a young man in jeans and heavy jumper with a bright yellow band round his upper right arm. He waved a fire beater in the shape of a broad, flat witch's broom above his head. The lane was narrow and crowded with cars parked both sides and Elizabeth stopped just short of the young man. From the Citroen behind, Richard saw him speaking with Elizabeth. Dudek asked him to go and find out what was said. Richard stood from the Citroen and saw the top of the cottages further down the lane. They were engulfed in a white shroud. It didn't rise above or from the thatched roofs but flowed through and around them, swamping them in a blanket of destruction, eating down and into the cottages. An occasional breeze brought him a burst of heat and the sound of crackling and he watched as a flame exploded through the smoke and escaped into the air above. He heard shouted voices and a heavy diesel engine clattering and the rush of water as it was pumped through hoses up to the roofs and beyond. Nearer the cottages was an old fire tender, feeding the hoses, and a smaller red Land Rover. Firemen in heavy black coats, yellow helmets, yellow trousers and black boots, swarmed in and around the cottages, pulling and pointing hoses, screaming instructions and setting and tearing down sets of ladders. If there was a plan to their actions they all appeared to understand it and acted seamlessly, instinctively - or they had no plan and their action was a hopeful confusion. Standing next to the Land Rover was a handful of watchers, some crying. They were middle-aged or elderly and two carried cats tightly, their own fears reflected in the cats' widened stares and frequent scrabbling to be free. Richard remembered the evacuation from The Crown, back home. This was so much more immediate and real and he jumped when an explosion cracked through the air and a light shockwave brushed him. One of the men near the Land Rover shouted something about a gas canister and the firemen withdrew further, angling their hoses higher to compensate. Gallon after gallon of water surged at the cottages but Richard couldn't tell if the dousing had any effect. Three of the firemen stood at the nearest cottage's front gate, talking and pointing. The hoses were trying to saturate all four cottages but the smoke wasn't diminishing; the nearest looked to be suffering most. Richard watched as one of the roof joists cracked and the heavy central section of thatching collapsed into the top floor with a roar; fresh oxygen was sucked and burst into flame and the rush of hot air forced the firemen to take steps back in unison. Whatever burnt in the cottage was now giving off black smoke and it swirled skyward, mixing with the white to a noxious grey. Flakes of burning thatch, paper and blackened embers floated gently in the air, in contrast to the violence of the blaze. There was indistinct shouting. The hoses showering the first house were turned away to concentrate on the second. An elderly woman at the Land Rover screamed in anguish and Richard saw what she had just understood; they had not enough water to save all four cottages and the first was already out of control. The sacrifice ripped through her core. She dropped to her knees. The man next to her stepped away, shaking his head. Richard hoped the distraught woman wasn't Elizabeth's friend, though he knew that was selfish. Elizabeth left the Mini, pushing the beater aside to run as best she could to her friend, kneeling and sobbing by the Land Rover. Jennifer stood from the Mini and walked back to stand next to Richard. There was nothing to be said. Anika and Dudek left the Citroen to go to Elizabeth and Maisie.

Elizabeth and Anika helped Maisie back to the Mini while Dudek limped to the Leading Firefighter, standing by the tender. Richard went with him. Dudek asked if he thought Maisie would be able to retrieve anything from her cottage but the Leading Firefighter was doubtful the fire would be dead for hours and even then the summer's dry conditions meant fires they thought were out could spring up days later unexpectedly. He was sympathetic but not optimistic and there was nothing Maisie could accomplish by being there.

It was Dudek's suggestion they go back to his house and no-one had a better idea or the energy to disagree. Though the air was clearer at Oakjack Ford and it was still warm, they preferred to sit inside, in the relative dark of the sitting room at the front of the house. Elizabeth and Anika flanked Maisie on the sagging settee, the room's bay window behind causing them to be almost silhouetted. Dudek sat in his armchair opposite. Richard and Jennifer went to the kitchen and made tea (Jennifer asked why there were so many clocks on the wall - Richard told her, 'We like to know the time.'). He was grateful to be out of the sitting room. Some of Elizabeth's home-made medovnik cake was left over from yesterday but when Jennifer popped her head back in the room to ask if any was wanted, all shook their heads. Richard carried in the tray and Jennifer poured while he went back out to the kitchen for a can of Top Deck. Richard and Jennifer sat on the rug in front of the fireplace, sharing the shandy. The fireplace held a small two bar electric fire with plastic logs for effect. The rug was threadbare, its tiredness matching the fading wallpaper and brown ceiling. Richard didn't think his uncle had bothered decorating this room since he'd moved here and, more likely, it hadn't been touched since the fifties. And now it smelt of the smoke clinging to their clothes. The adults sipped at their tea. Richard wished they'd brought in the cake.

'So, Maisie, how do you and Elizabeth know each other?' Dudek felt the need to speak but Maisie appeared not to hear. Her head was lowered. She looked blankly into her tea cup. It seemed to Richard she shrank as he watched, overwhelmed by the scale and depth of her loss and unable to comprehend a way forward. A fleeting memory of the night he watched the news of Southend pier burning with Carol Stratfield and her father's lament crossed his mind but was so trivial he was embarrassed to let the thought grow.

Elizabeth answered for Maisie, 'We went to school together. Maisie is one of my oldest friends, though we lost touch when I moved to Kent, during the war, but later, when I came home, we got back in touch. Long story.' Elizabeth looked to Maisie for confirmation but she didn't stir. 'I should take her home?' Elizabeth spoke more to Anika than Dudek and made it a question.

'Home?' Dudek asked.

'I meant my place,' said Elizabeth, 'she can have my room, I'll sleep with Jennifer for a while until things are …. sorted.'

'We have a spare room,' said Dudek. 'It needs a tidy but won't take a minute. And we can move the bed from Richard's room and Richard can have the camp bed.' Dudek was keen to be offering solutions.

'Better still,' said Richard, 'We can put the camp bed in the other room for me and …. Maisie …. can have my …. Anika's …. room.'

'Excellent idea. What do you think Anika?'

Anika looked to Maisie but there was no reaction. Anika took a few seconds before speaking, choosing her words carefully. 'It is kind but Maisie might prefer to be with Elizabeth, for a few days at least. We are strangers.'

'Of course. But the offer stands.'

Elizabeth smiled at Dudek who asked, 'Does Maisie have any relatives nearby?'

Maisie looked up from her tea to Elizabeth. Elizabeth spoke haltingly, 'Not any more. Her parents …. passed away …. a long time ago …. and ….'

'….and I haven't seen my brother for …. years. Since the war,' Maisie added.

'Should we contact him?' asked Dudek.

Maisie looked to Elizabeth and said, 'We don't know where he is.'

'I could ring some people. I still have a few contacts. With a name and an old address we ....'

'.... thank you, but no. It's been too long,' Maisie interrupted.

'Yes, too long,' added Elizabeth, quickly.

'It's no trouble,' Dudek continued, 'I can try ....'

'Perhaps later, uncle,' said Anika, shaking her head.

'Yes, of course. Later. Just let me know.'

'Thank you,' said Maisie and went back to staring at her untouched cup of tea. Though the light from the window behind put her face in shade, Richard saw her eyes wet with tears. Dudek fidgeted in his chair. Jennifer offered more tea but it was, of course, too soon; no-one had finished as much as half the first cup. Richard was uncomfortable on the floor.

'Something stronger?' Dudek suggested. Elizabeth and Anika shook their heads. Maisie didn't react.

The heavy knock on the door was a relief. Anika went. It was Samuel. Anika showed him into the sitting room. He needed no introduction and nodded hello before apologising, 'Dudek, sorry to interrupt. I just wanted to let you know I won't be going for a pint tonight. Megan isn't good today and I should keep an eye on her this evening.'

'Of course. No problem. But you must let me know if you want me to do anything or pop round for a glass of .... anything.'

'I will. Thanks.'

'Elizabeth made us cake and there's some left. I could bring it round ....'

'Give Megan our love,' said Anika and Richard thought Samuel might cry. He nodded and pretended a smile.

'Yes. Say hello to Megan,' said Dudek and even Richard understood it was unnecessary.

Samuel mumbled, 'Thanks.'

Anika showed him to the front door and when she was back in the room Elizabeth asked her, 'Will Samuel be all right?'

'I don't know.'

'So sad,' said Elizabeth. 'I remember when Megan first moved to Oakjack and did a few hours with us, serving in the pharmacy. That's where she met Samuel, he was always coming in for his tablets. He didn't care about her .... background.'

There was silence and a few nods.

'Background?' asked Richard, before realising they all seemed to know and were not discussing, so perhaps the question was inappropriate.

'She's .... divorced.' Elizabeth almost whispered the 'd' word. 'She wanted to start again in Oakjack, away from the whispers and rumours. Though even here there was gossip, when she moved in with Samuel.'

'Samuel came for a new life too. She is his first love. Sad. And for Megan, even more sad. To find love second time but to not .... keep it. Awful. We need to make much of every day and give and take kindnesses when we can. They were right to ignore the gossip and be with each other.' Dudek spoke to Elizabeth.

Richard saw Maisie looked up from her tea; this was not a day of which she could make much. 'Can we go now? I've so many things to think about and tomorrow I have so much to do,' she asked Anika who nodded,

'Of course. Whenever you and Elizabeth want to.'

Anika took Maisie's cup. Richard watched as she took control of another situation; seamlessly and with no discernible effort other than a kindly smile and a knack for stopping conversations at the right time. He helped her collect cups, making sure their arms brushed - he might have felt juvenile if she weren't older and so sure; surely she wouldn't allow even the slightest contact by accident. He took the tray to the kitchen while Anika and Dudek saw their guests to the door. Maisie was first out and thanked Dudek as he repeated his offer of a room, but her thanks were automated, her thoughts elsewhere. Elizabeth helped Maisie into the Mini's back seat before going back to the front door.

Jennifer was talking to Richard, '…. Wednesday night. That band is on at Devil's Peat. We should go. Check 'em out. I hear they're coming from London.'

'From London? To play Oakjack Ford?'

'Exactly. We shouldn't miss them.'

'Will we get in?'

Jennifer lowered her voice, as if Elizabeth wouldn't hear, 'You mean will we be served? Of course. I know the guy behind the bar. Meet me in the pub garden, eightish.'

Richard looked to Anika, seeking confirmation she thought they'd be served but she said, 'Your choice. I'm not your mother. I'll be going if I'm not working in the B and G.' Anika looked to Elizabeth and shrugged. Elizabeth smiled back.

'Okay.' Richard turned back to Jennifer, 'And why don't you come with us to the cinema, on Tuesday.'

'Who's going?'

'Me and Anika.'

'Wotchya seeing?'

'The Omen. It's come back round. Only released a couple of months ago.'

'It's X rated isn't it?' Jennifer said quietly, conscious of Elizabeth.

'Tell you what, I'll get you into the film and you get me served in the pub.'

'Deal.'

'Coke only,' Elizabeth said, having heard the conversation, 'and if you get into the cinema don't get caught.' She added ambiguously and Richard thought it was more for Dudek's attention than theirs.

'Of course,' said Jennifer.

'Good to see them all getting along together.' Elizabeth shook Dudek's hand. 'Thanks so much for helping today, and for the offer of a room.' She thanked him again.

'I'm sorry we can't do more. Maisie has lost everything. I can't imagine how upsetting it is. God forbid we should ever have to know. And it makes it so true, we must make much of every day.' Dudek nodded seriously and asked, even more seriously, 'So will you come for dinner with me? One evening next week. We can take a taxi to Christchurch.'

While Dudek spoke Anika ushered Richard and Jennifer to the Mini, suggesting they should say goodbye to Maisie again.

A few minutes later Anika and Dudek sat on the patio, smoking. It was a beautiful summer evening and it was hard to believe the destruction and violence of the fire that destroyed Maisie's cottage was so few miles away and only a couple of hours ago. Bluey padded into the garden, exploring as usual and ignoring orders to go home. Richard ate a portion of Elizabeth's cake.

'So uncle. Did Elizabeth say yes to your invite?' Anika asked.

'Not quite, but she is thinking about it and I am hopeful. Can you drive me into Christchurch during the week to find a nice restaurant?'

'Of course. It was good of you to offer a room for Maisie.'

'It would be no sacrifice, poor woman. Should we try to find her brother? I can make some calls.'

'No. Maisie didn't want it and …. besides, neither would Elizabeth.'

'Why?'

'Elizabeth and Maisie's brother ran away together. It was a big story in the village. Elizabeth's mother wanted her to marry someone else but she loved Maisie's brother. Maisie's parents were ill and they needed her brother, but he went away, with Elizabeth.'

'Ah, I see. Love conquers all.'

'Hmmmm. Elizabeth was pregnant, he left her, so love doesn't conquer everything. And Elizabeth didn't come back for twenty years, with Jennifer as a baby.'

'How do you know so much?' asked Richard, impressed.

'Good, isn't she?' said Dudek. 'We could have done with you in my …. office, back …. whenever.'

'Elizabeth trusts me. So this will be our secret. Yes?' Richard and Dudek nodded.

'I don't know if Jennifer realises Maisie is her ….' Anika looked to Dudek for help.

'Great aunt?'

'So, Maisie's brother is Jennifer's grandfather,' Richard said to confirm his understanding.

'Yes. But she might not know. I think she doesn't.'

'What happened to Jennifer's mother?'

'I don't know. She died when Jennifer was a baby but I don't know how.'

'She will find out. It just takes a little time.' Dudek laughed.

Richard laughed along, even though he now had a secret he didn't like to keep. Perhaps not everyone did know everything about each other in the village.

'Anyway,' Anika interrupted his thoughts, 'Richard now has two dates with two ladies.' She stood and went to Bluey (he was sniffing at a border of dying flowers), bouncing her hip against Richard's shoulder as she passed. 'Hmmmm. Not to mention the girls he has back home. Should I be jealous?'

Richard hoped she was and wondered again how old was Jennifer.

From next door Young Samuel's plaintive saxophone was heard, lower in volume and slower than usual.

Richard couldn't remember who had first suggested seeing The Omen. The previous Thursday he had been practising on his Bontempi - not with any structure or with his grade books, but playing along to the cassette and 'improvising', as he was sure the greats (Wakeman, Emerson) must have - when he stumbled across the refrain for The Addams Family. Though he hadn't seen the programme on tv for years there was no doubting the quirky, catchy sequence. He was refining the timing when Anika walked past the door and he called her to guess the tune. She listened (not very carefully) and shook her head. 'I don't know.'

'It's The Addams Family. Isn't it?'

'Are you asking me or telling? I've never heard of them.'

'What about The Munsters?'

'I don't know what you're talking about. Sometimes I think English isn't your real language. Are you speaking Vietnam?'

Richard tried to describe the old tv programmes (not seen since he was many years younger) but such odd characters were hard to explain and references to Hammer House of Horror movies was little help. When Richard claimed Anika had never seen a proper horror film (he was adamant Jaws didn't count), she countered Czech horror films were far scarier than American or English. It was only a small argument from there to the challenge to go and see The Omen, being re-run in Christchurch, but Richard couldn't remember if it was he or Anika threw down the gauntlet.

Now Tuesday was here he had doubts; not so much for the film, but about getting in to an X-rated showing, and he had invited Jennifer. It would be embarrassing if he didn't fulfill the promise to get her in as well. True, he had got into the X-rated 'To The Devil A Daughter' a few months back, but he was with Malcolm who looked older than he did and was bigger and had bought the tickets. Of course Anika would get in, but Jennifer looked younger with her fresh face and pixie cut.

Anika rested in the sun lounger in the morning (wearing red gingham check rather than blue, Richard noticed - and a part of him wondered why he had invited Jennifer at all) while he finished painting the Hurricane. It was one of his best paint jobs and he took it to the shade of the apple trees to show Anika. She was complimentary and he said she could keep it; the pleasure for him was in the building and painting. She accepted gracefully.

She put on her baggy white t-shirt and they made an early lunch together, the showing was scheduled to start at 1:40 pm. Richard and Dudek cleared the table while Anika went to change. Dudek told Richard he should say how nice she looks when she comes down, and she did (in the dress she had worn when working in the pub the previous Friday), so he told her and she smiled demurely. Richard hoped he wasn't underdressed in his plain jeans and favourite Montreal Olympics t-shirt. They performed their usual routine of waiting outside the open car for a few minutes to let it cool and Dudek waved them off from the front door. It was a minute drive into the village and Jennifer was waiting outside the post office. The Citroen bounced to a halt and Jennifer struggled to get in the back elegantly in a knee length denim skirt and striped blouse. Richard had never seen her wear anything other than jeans before and, still following his uncle's advice, mentioned how nice she looked in a dress,

'Skirt,' she said.

Anika laughed. Richard shrugged his shoulders and waved at Elizabeth, watching from the post office window.

'Don't.'

'Don't what?'

'Wave.'

'Oh. Too late. Sorry.'

'Hi Jenny.' Anika looked over her shoulder as they pulled away.

'Jennifer. Or Jen. Never Jenny.'

'Okay Jenny.' Anika laughed before asking, 'How's Maisie?'

'Okay, when she's not crying.'

'Oh.'

'Not that I'm saying she shouldn't be crying, I mean, who wouldn't, I just mean, she's ....'

'.... crying a lot.' Richard finished the sentence.

'Yeah. A lot. But who wouldn't. We try to cheer her up. I made her a cake.'

'Did it help?' Richard asked.

Anika looked sideways at him. 'You're doing that funny thing with words again, aren't you?'

'No.'

'He is. When a house burns, cake doesn't put out fire.' She spoke over her shoulder to Jennifer and used the car park of Devil's Peat to turn round the car and head back through the Oakjack Ford and onto Christchurch.

'Is that an old Czech saying?' Richard asked.

'See?' Anika gestured back towards Jennifer. 'He's doing it again.'

Jennifer laughed, though Richard doubted she understood Anika's point; he didn't, but that was okay. 'Anyway,' he changed subject, 'you okay for the film?' He turned in the seat to see Jennifer. 'Won't be too scary for you?' It was asked sincerely.

'Just get me in and I'll be okay,' said Jennifer with forced bravado. She had to shout above the wind-roar from the air rushing in through the Citroen's open windows. The incoming air was warm and barely cooled the car's stifling interior.

'You look too young and pretty. But don't worry, we have a plan,' said Anika.

Christchurch's largest cinema looked closed. The foyer below its art deco façade was in deep shade and there were no customers queuing or loitering. There was less than ten minutes to curtains open.

'That's good,' Richard agreed as Anika linked her arm through his and steered him to the little box office. 'Hi. Two tickets for the one forty show please. Stalls. Are there seats left?' He spoke to the top of a middle-aged lady's head - she was counting receipts.

'Oh yes, lots, there's only seven or eight people in. An afternoon showing? I told them. They never listen.' She smiled as she looked up but the smile froze as she tried to reconcile the deep voice with the fresh young face looking at her through the glass. Richard didn't look away, despite the temptation. Anika tried to look bored and succeeded. The box-office lady looked from Richard to Anika and back.

'Are you eighteen?'

'Nineteen.' He answered without hesitation and calmly, belying his pounding pulse. Anika nodded.

'Really?' the lady asked.

'Of course.' Anika spoke and her accent was more noticeable and staccato than usual, lending it an assertiveness that was compelling. 'He is from Vietnam. They look younger over there. I'm from Czechoslovakia.'

'Oh.' The woman didn't know what to do with this information. Before she could ask anything else Anika spoke to Richard.

'See I told you the English do things properly.' She turned back to the box office. 'He is my half-brother, on my father's side, and has only been here a week and is looking forward to seeing this film.'

'He speaks good English.' The ticket lady spoke direct to Anika.

'Yes. He has had many lessons in Vietnam. Since a child. Like me. Though, of course, I learn in Czechoslovakia. And of course, your country would not give us a visa if we didn't speak English and were at least eighteen, would they?'

'I .... suppose not,' the woman said, not wanting to show any ignorance.

'How much?' Richard smiled at her and passed over two pound notes.

'Is it just about to start?' asked Anika. 'We don't want to miss the start.'

The lady hesitated but took the notes, punched out a couple of tickets and handed them over with change.

'Thank you.' They said simultaneously. Anika took the tickets and they walked through, not stopping at the refreshments kiosk, Richard enjoying the contact of her arm through his.

Though the presentation hadn't started the lights were dim and an usher lit their way with a torch, showing them the central aisle. When they were under the balcony overhang they took their seats, Richard sitting on the aisle. As the curtains parted, and the Pearl & Dean advert flew at them, Anika checked round the cinema. There were few other people there, as far as she could see in the dark. At the front, dwarfed by the screen, was another usher, wearing a tray crammed with Kia-Ora cartons and Wall's ice cream tubs; ambitious considering the tiny audience. They watched the trailers for coming films, Richard fidgeting nervously in contrast to Anika's calm, and as the censor's certificate filled the screen the usher left the theatre. Anika waited until the twentieth century fox search lights were gone and nudged Richard. He nodded, though Anika would not see in the dark, and left his seat, half-crouching as he went across the aisle and along the row of empty seats in the next block until he reached the aisle at the far edge. Still half-crouching he walked down towards the screen to the fire exit two-thirds along. He felt sick with nerves and jumped at the noise of the door when he managed to push the bar firmly enough at the second attempt. He opened it as narrowly as possible to squeeze through but still the light appeared to flood into the auditorium. He pulled it carefully behind him, leaving it unlatched and fretting over how much light was spilling through the crack. He blinked hard to adjust to the now bright light. He was in a short, bare corridor. At the end was another double door with another fire exit sign above. He pushed the bar hard first time and it opened onto the small alleyway between the cinema and a terrace of shops. Jennifer was a few yards away, trying to look inconspicuous but there was an attraction to her nervous energy Richard thought made her noticeable. Surely others would be looking at her but there was no-one else in the alley and Richard called. She stubbed out the cigarette and walked quickly to join him. He closed the door behind and went to her as she stood by the inner door at the end of the short corridor, stifling a giggle.

'Ready?' he whispered.

'Some say,' she whispered back. Richard took that to mean yes and pushed the door open as little as needed to let her squeeze through. He followed. Jennifer copied his half-crouch walk back up the edge aisle, through the empty block of seats and across the centre aisle. Anika was now two seats along, slouched in the chair and smoking. Richard sat next to her and Jennifer took the aisle seat. He tried to slow his breathing, and slouched as low as Anika. She didn't acknowledge his return except for patting his leg as if to say 'well done.' A sliver of light slipped in from the still open fire exit they had used but there was nothing to be done about it. Next to him, Jennifer rummaged through her small denim handbag for her pack of ten cigarettes and lighter. The fidgeting was a distraction and Richard looked to her as she lit a cigarette. The burst of flame showed her flushed cheeks and she smiled an apology with a shrug. She stretched her arm over the armrest between them and took his hand, squeezing it once. Richard returned the squeeze, with a flush of excitement that built on the thrill of slipping her into the cinema but a tightening gut in case Anika saw, despite the dark. Though Richard was looking at the screen he wasn't watching - Jennifer's hand was cool - but the film was only minutes in so he had time to catch up. He took a few slower breaths, determined to concentrate (though he didn't let go of Jennifer's hand) and find out if the film was as frightening as Malcolm's older brother claimed. On the screen there was terror in a priest's eyes and Richard sensed Jennifer tense in preparation for something but before he could focus on the film a torch light flicked from Jennifer's face to his and Anika's and back again and a voice, low in tone and volume, hissed, 'Out. Now!'

Jennifer started and dragged her hand from Richard's. He sat upright. His stomach lurched. Anika shrugged. The man with the torch at the end of the aisle shone it to hide his face. He hissed again, with a venom Richard had never heard in a hiss. Jennifer was quick to her feet and the man took a step back to let her out of the row. Richard followed, trying not to show fear. Anika nodded casually and tried a demure smile as she went past the man, but he kept his torch high and Richard couldn't see his face. They walked ahead of him towards the screen and out of the main entrance.

'Stay there!' The angry man hissed at them in reception. Jennifer's head was lowered but Richard made an effort to look him in the face. The woman in the box office looked smug.

But Anika didn't stay there. She took a step to be close to the suited man and said, 'Sorry,' with a natural sincerity. 'We are going. Sorry to be trouble.' With her accent a little softer and her blue eyes a little closer the apology was hard to ignore but it looked to Richard the man was going to try and he began to splutter threats. Anika apologised again, turned to Richard and Jennifer and said, 'Come.' She started walking to the sunshine of the open exit. The man grabbed her arm and Richard took an instinctive stride towards him but Anika raised her other hand to still him and said to the man, 'We are sorry and we are now going.'

'No you're bloody not.' The man hissed - still, even though they were no longer in the auditorium.

'We go. And we won't ask for our money back though we haven't seen the film.' Anika stepped even closer to him and placed her other hand over his. 'Sorry,' she gave his hand a couple of light rubs, 'And you shouldn't be …. touching me. We are sorry.' There was an emphasis on the 'touching'.

She rubbed his hand again and it dropped from Anika's arm. She thanked him and walked out; confident Richard and Jennifer were behind her. They crossed the road as the man shouted a belated threat. Anika waved nonchalantly without turning round and wiped her hand, the hand that had touched the man, on her jeans, complaining of 'his sweatiness' to no-one in particular. They walked ever more hurriedly back to the car park, not speaking until they reached the Citroen, and didn't wait for the car to cool before driving away, taking a route that avoided the cinema.

'Oh well, perhaps we will see the film another time,' said Anika as they reached the outskirts of town.

'Shame. It was looking good.' Richard tried to sound as relaxed as Anika. 'You okay?' He turned and asked Jennifer who was red in the face and close to crying.

'Yeah.' She looked away.

'Really?' Anika looked in the mirror. 'Don't worry. It doesn't matter.'

'Not to you. But Elizabeth ….?'

'Elizabeth won't worry. What harm done? Just say we didn't get in.'

'I …. I can't. She changed her mind about me going to an X film so I told her we were going to see Gumball Rally instead. I can't tell her we didn't get into that.'

'But what if Elizabeth asked us if we enjoyed Gumball and you hadn't told us we were meant to be seeing it?' Richard asked.

'What is Gumball?' asked Anika.

'American comedy. About a car race,' Richard explained.

'Okay. Not my thing but hey, okay. What do you want us to tell Elizabeth?'

'I don't know.' Jennifer swallowed hard to fight back a tear.

'No matter. Say we changed our minds and didn't go in.' Anika was pragmatic.

'No. She'll know. She always knows. We'll have to pretend we saw the film and say it was okay, but we can't go home yet.'

'We can't drive around all afternoon. Dudek doesn't have enough petrol.' Anika pointed at the fuel gauge.

Jennifer brightened as an idea came to her. 'I know. We'll hang out in my den.'

'Den? What's a den? And do what?' Anika asked.

'Just hang.'

'Just hang? What does that mean? Where?'

'My den. Safe place.'

'Why do you need a safe place?' asked Anika.

'Everyone needs a safe place. A den,' said Jennifer.

'Hmmm. I suppose. But I have things to do. And I'm working in the pub tonight.' Anika wasn't convinced. 'You two go.'

'I don't mind. Whatever suits you two.' Richard's spirits were high. Nervous fear had been replaced with triumphant relief and he was happy to go along with either or both of the girls. He turned on the radio and even though 'Don't Go Breaking My Heart' was playing (again - still number one) he didn't mind. It suited the sunshine and he increased the volume.

'Okay. For a short while,' Anika conceded. 'Where is this den?'

Jennifer leant forward from the back seat to fill the space between Richard and Anika and gave directions.

The den was on the edge of a field a half mile north east of Oakjack Ford (walkable from the post office as Jennifer told them). The field was surrounded by gorse and accessed via a single track lane off the main road into the village. The den itself was an abandoned storage shed, half-brick, half-timber, camouflaged by the gorse swarming around it. Anika pulled off the track when directed by Jennifer, who led them round to the shed's door. Jennifer closed the door behind them and because the roof was partly missing there was plenty of light. Empty fruit crates were stacked to provide two chairs and a table and an upturned box was a waste bin, holding four used coke cans and two empty crisp packets. A wasp buzzed round the bin which Jennifer put outside. She motioned to Anika and Richard to sit, while she dismantled the crates that made the table and re-arranged them into another chair.

'Clever eh? I should design furniture when I leave school,' she said proudly, taking cigarettes and lighter from her handbag. Anika did likewise and they settled uncomfortably on their boxes.

The girls were both overdressed for Jennifer's den. Richard watched them smoke.

'So, we won't be going back to that cinema anytime soon.' Jennifer spoke. The anxiety she'd expressed in the car fading.

Anika nodded.

'Maybe I'll catch the film when I get back home,' said Richard. He was aware he was only just calming since the cinema's adventure but that was okay. The afternoon hadn't gone as planned but there was no denying its excitement (highlight: Jennifer's hand-holding or Anika's arm-linking) and it was a shame he couldn't share it with Malcolm. It was a good story to tell when he was home and he daydreamed about embellishing the tale further when telling Julie and Carol. He wondered what they were doing. He wondered if they should tell Dudek what had happened and thought they should, he could imagine Anika underplaying the bit when they were thrown out and Dudek would understand when they asked him not to tell Elizabeth, for Jennifer's sake. Dudek was good at keeping secrets. Richard looked at Anika smoking and thought of Carol again. Perhaps he wouldn't tell her this part of the story, the part in a den with two pretty girls. Or perhaps he should. Or rather, tell Julie but not Carol. Or just maybe not - at all. He nodded to himself but his thoughts were jumbled as he relaxed further and they slipped back to the secret they would want Dudek to keep. Or did they? His thoughts were scattering but before he found focus Jennifer's voice distracted him. She called his name. He began asking her to repeat the question but the words were not there and neither was Jennifer. But of course, she was - he just couldn't see her. She shifted to her left and he saw half her pretty face. The half blouse he could see was confusing - the vertical stripes were uncomfortable colours blinking in and out of his sight. He looked back to her face where the other cheek jumped into view but disappeared immediately. She said something and forced a smile (half) and he felt sick with an immediacy that came from fear.

Migraine.

He moved his arm to tap Anika's shoulder, except his arm hadn't moved. He looked at it and made it a conscious decision it should lift and move to his right. It obeyed. But even though it was his decision, it didn't seem to be his arm. Of course it was his, but could have been someone else's, though why it should answer to his thoughts would be a mystery. It nudged Anika. She looked from Jennifer to him for a second or two or three or …. Jennifer was still talking, as far as he could tell. Anika's half mouth moved. He heard the word, said it again to himself and tried to decipher it to a meaning but couldn't. He made his arm nudge Anika again and concentrated hard as she said her word again, 'What?' and focused all his efforts into saying, '....head's .... gone ....' and touching his forehead.

'What?' she repeated, then understood. 'Oh. We have to go home Jennifer. We have to go home. Richard has one of his bad heads.'

'Bad heads? What does that mean?'

'I don't know. But I want to take him home.'

Richard tried to follow the conversation and Anika asked him, 'Have you tablets?'

He thought about the words and repeated them to himself slowly, giving each its discrete meaning until he worked out the question and could plan an answer, 'Mmmm .... no.'

'That doesn't help. Lights?' Anika asked.

'N .... not .... yet.'

'Lights?' Jennifer repeated the question.

Anika told Jennifer the little she knew of 'the lights'. Richard was already sweating more heavily than just the heat caused and wanted to leave; Jennifer's safe place was no longer safe for him.

Anika drove them to Dudek's, avoiding the post office as asked by Jennifer. Dudek was calm, as ever, and amused by Anika and Jennifer flanking Richard and helping him into the sitting room. Jennifer closed the curtains (instructed by Anika) and Anika went to Richard's room to find his tablets. Richard and Jennifer sat on the settee. By now 'the lights' were in his eyes and he sat with them closed tight though it made no difference, they didn't go away. Jennifer held his hand, but matronly, not like in the cinema, and though he knew he would be better off alone, he didn't want to ask Jennifer to leave. He heard the door open. Jennifer took her hand away.

'I found them,' said Anika, 'you haven't opened the packet yet.'

Richard opened his eyes to see what was happening. Anika tore at the paper bag and took out the small box of tablets and the dosage instructions. She read slowly and shook her head. 'I think it means you need to take a tablet in water when the bad head starts. But we should try one now maybe. My English to read is not so good. Jennifer, does it say that?'

She passed it to Jennifer who took her spectacles from a handbag to read and confirmed Anika's under-standing. Anika brought a damp flannel and glass of water from the kitchen and dropped in a tablet. It fizzed loudly (to Richard's ears) and he drank it in one to minimize the metallic taste. He ignored her question as to why he still hadn't read the dosage instructions and her suggestion if he kept a tablet with him maybe he could have taken it earlier. Anika sat beside him (he was now between the two girls on the settee) and pressed the cold, damp flannel to his forehead. Although it was comforting he preferred to be alone, especially when Anika and Jennifer started chatting and their voices were painful to him, even though they almost whispered. Anika was asking Jennifer why she used the shed as a hideaway but the answer was vague, rambling around needing space and Elizabeth not understanding her and needing more space, especially now Maisie was living with them. They fell into silence (welcomed by Richard) and over the twenty minutes his lights went away and his thoughts untangled and steadied. He had maybe another fifteen minutes before the pain would come.

Anika went to finish her chores, leaving Jennifer to re-arrange the flannel. She sat close to him, folded it again and placed it back on his forehead. He murmured thanks and tried to rest his head on the back of the settee but was too tall and stretching his neck backwards hurt. He moaned with the pain and Jennifer rested her hand on his. With no plan or forethought he turned his body and shuffled down the settee enough so his head rested on

Jennifer's shoulder. It wasn't comfortable for either of them and made him hotter and wouldn't help his coming headache but her scent was stronger than before and she didn't resist. To make it easier she slid further away on the settee and lowered his head into her lap; he pulled up his legs and was able to lie on the couch even though he couldn't stretch. His heart rate picked up, which wasn't a good thing as the steady throbbing in the side of his head was already a discomfort, but what else was he to do? The afternoon had a new highlight - in the middle of its lowest point. The room was still dark with curtains closed and the flannel was cooling but it took only a minute before he was uncomfortable and he sensed Jennifer's tension. Her left arm hung uselessly over the back of the sofa; she couldn't decide where it should rest. His head began to hurt more and laying this way didn't help. He was reluctantly grateful when Anika came back in and 'tutted' theatrically. She went round the back of the settee to take Jennifer's arm and rest it across Richard's chest, 'That's better Jenny, isn't it?'

Jennifer blushed but said, 'Jennifer, or Jen. Not Jenny.'

Anika nodded but took the hand away again, saying, 'Another time though. Richard, I think you should go to bed. Alone. Has that tablet worked?'

'Not that I can tell. And it does hurt a lot.'

'You should have a proper lay down.' Jennifer took back control, bending over her lap to whisper, 'And you can call me Jenny.'

She helped Richard to stand, though it was unnecessary. He turned at the door to remind them, 'Gig tomorrow, right?'

Both girls nodded and as Richard left them to go upstairs Anika led Jennifer out to the garden for the late afternoon sun, though Anika went back under the apple trees.

In his room Richard tried to settle on the bed but

the pain was building and there was no position that didn't make it worse. The room was too light and he went to the window to close the curtains and would have spent longer watching Anika and Jennifer if only the pain was bearable.

Chapter 10
One Unlucky Bunch

The weather forecasts carried a hint of rain. A few areas in the South-East had a tenth of an inch at most (never enough to threaten the drought) but The New Forest didn't even get the hint. 11th August was bone dry, again.

Anika, Richard and Dudek watched the early evening news and weather on tv (the repair man had turned up with new valves that morning) and tutted harmoniously, not that Richard cared much but it seemed appropriate, especially when the newscast reminded viewers of the drought orders. Anika and Richard went upstairs to change and Dudek limped to his study, saying he'd found another pile of papers he'd brought from London needing a sort and complaining about the television choices - three channels and nothing to watch.

At close to eight o'clock Anika knocked on the study's open door and entered without invitation. Richard was behind her.

'We're going now uncle,' Anika said – or, Richard assumed, something like that. She spoke Czech. Richard liked the staccato sounds and erratic melody of the language, but had to guess at the meaning. Dudek was sitting in the chair behind his untidy desk, head back and eyes closed. Anika repeated it in English - louder to be sure Dudek heard above the Radio Four broadcast. Dudek opened his eyes and leant forward to take the bottle of Johnnie Walker Black Label from the desk. There was a measure or two left in the bottle. He emptied it into the tumbler he was holding.

'Okay. See you later,' he said and took a sip. 'Oh, wait. Where are you going?'

'The pub. We told you.'

'I'll come with you.' He looked at the empty bottle and downed the contents of the tumbler in one.

'What, to see the band?' Anika asked.

'What band?'

'We're going to see a band at Devil's Peat. Remember?'

'Oh. I thought you were going to the B and G. What night is it?'

'Wednesday.'

'Of course. Skittles night.'

'Not for you.' Anika pointed to his strapped ankle.

'I can watch.'

'While you have a drink,' Anika said.

'Of course.' Dudek winked and raised his empty glass to Richard who stood in the doorway.

'But we're not going to the B and G,' Anika reminded him.

'Oh. But you can drop me on the way.' He put the tumbler on the desk and started to raise himself up using the chair's arms. Anika pressed him back down, saying,

'Wait there. You need jacket and shoes.'

Richard stood in the doorway, feeling an intruder for the first time as his uncle examined the tumbler for drops. The radio signalled eight o'clock. The anodyne news reader reported the headlines so clearly they were almost inconsequential with a lack of drama. Anika brought shoes and jacket and Dudek turned off the radio, bringing silence except for the faint melody drifting through the open window.

'Young Samuel is late today,' Dudek said. 'I am recognising the tunes now. Perhaps that's a good thing and the longer I keep hearing them the better. It means …. they still have each other, for now anyway. That's good, isn't it?' he asked vaguely.

'Yes uncle.' Anika helped him with the jacket.

'Nephew!' Dudek called to Richard, still standing at the door. 'We should find someone for Anika. She should have someone, everyone should.'

'Yes uncle. I'll keep an eye out for someone tonight.'

'At skittles practise? They're older than me.'

'No, we're going to see the band. Remember? We'll drop you off first.'

'Oh, yes, I forgot.'

Dusk was falling and the Citroen was parked in the long shadows thrown by the trees between Dudek and Samuel's front gardens. Samuel's saxophone was just audible from his back garden and Dudek took a couple of seconds to listen before sighing.

'You okay uncle?' Richard asked as he helped him into the car.

'Of course. If someone takes trouble to play, we should take time to hear their story, not just the tune. We forget.'

'I suppose so. Are you sure you want to go out tonight?'

'Of course.'

'What if Larry is there? You haven't been back to the pub since the argument.'

'Ah, tonight I'll sit with my back to the wall and he is no match anyway. He has no balls to argue again. Come princess, drive.'

Anika parked in the B and G car park. They walked him to the door, nagging him to be careful, before walking on through the village.

161

There was little traffic on the road through Oakjack Ford. Evening birdsong was exaggerated in the quiet and there was calm in the dusk not unsettled by the smell of burning. Now Richard thought of it, it wasn't until he thought of it he smelt the burning; surely a bad thing if familiarity brought such contempt. He sniffed harder but instead of burning gorse caught Anika's scent, not 'soapy' tonight, more something he couldn't describe – thoughts of the burning gorse and peat vanished. He and Anika were half-way between The Blue And The Gorse, at one end of the village, and Devil's Peat, at the other, strolling the short length of the village. They talked little, but that was okay. It was a beautiful summer evening, Anika smelt good and looked stunning, with just a little eye make-up this evening (he'd noticed when she had given a last check in the mirror in the hall). And if the now was good, the near-future could be great; a band, a pub and another girl - Jennifer. He soaked in as much detail as possible for the story he wanted to tell Malcolm.

Anika led him round the side of Devil's Peat to the garden, next to the rear car park. There were five sets of wooden tables and benches, scattered on a dying lawn, kicked to bare earth under the tables. The umbrellas were closed and the tables in deepening shade of the pub. The sun was nearly gone and the garden lighting sparse. Brighter light spilled from the pub's windows but had little effect on the shadows in the garden. Jennifer sat at the table providing the best view into the pub of the small riser in the far corner, the stage for that night's band - Rocknow Station. The window through which she looked was open to the warm evening and the constant chatter of anticipation added to Richard's excitement. Jennifer hadn't seen them enter the garden. She didn't react when he called her name until he sat opposite her, but with an equal view into the pub.

'Hi townie. How's the head?'

'Better, thanks.' Richard had spent much of the morning in bed and the afternoon in the shade. It would be a day or two before the feeling of not being tuned-in would pass. 'You okay?' he asked.

'Yep. Spent the day helping Bill in the newsagents. Not much fun but worth a couple of quid. Bring your tablets tonight?'

Richard felt Anika watching him; she'd cut a couple from the blister pack and insisted he put them in his back pocket. He'd forgotten. He tapped his jeans where they should have been and said, after hesitation, 'Of course.'

'Liar,' said Anika. She opened the small linen handbag hanging from a cord over her shoulder, pulled out the tablets she'd cut off earlier and dropped them on the table in front of him.

Richard hoped the shadows hid his blush. He slipped the tablets into his pocket and started to speak but Anika put a finger to his lips and shook her head. He shrugged.

'Nice dress,' Jennifer said to Anika.

'Yes. It is.' Richard was quick to agree.

'And mine?' Jennifer asked.

'Yes. Very nice.'

'Nicer than Anika's?'

'Er …. they're both …. lovely?'

'Of course,' Anika rescued him, 'what do you want to drink?' and offered Jennifer a cigarette. She shook her head,

'No thanks. There'll be people here who know me and Elizabeth. They'd love to tell.'

Anika nodded and lit her own cigarette.

'I'll get the drinks,' Richard offered.

'Anika will have to go in though,' said Jennifer. 'Turns out the new owner, Slim Tim or something, doesn't serve under eighteen. He doesn't even want them in the pub. It's why I'm sitting here. And if he sees Anika is buying beer for us he'll ban us all. He's a wanker.'

Anika shrugged as if to say 'whatever' but Richard said, 'I was gonna have a coke anyway.'

'Me too,' said Jennifer, 'but ask for ice and a slice of lemon. That's how they serve it in the best hotels now.'

Richard pulled a couple of screwed up pound notes from a pocket and gave them to Anika. 'But I'll pay.'

Anika took the money and was half way to the pub's back door when she turned to shout a question, 'Crisps? Straws?'

'No. No way.' Jennifer was adamant and to Richard, 'It's bad enough we can't go in, but a straw? Right?'

'Right. But we can see and hear okay.' Richard pointed to the window.

'Until the crowd gets excited and stands. Anyway, it's a nice night.'

'And it'll be hot and sweaty in there. We have exclusive seats.'

'Some say.'

'You say that a lot.'

'Some say.'

'Ha ha.'

'Anyway, this'll do. Perhaps it's just as well it won't be too loud out here, what with your bad head and all. Hope it wasn't the excitement of coming to my den caused it.'

Richard shook his head, 'No. It's a fine den.'

'Thank you. Heard of this band before? Being a townie and an MM reader and all?'

'Rocknow Station? No. But that reminds me, I owe you for that Melody Maker.' He fished in his pocket for change.

'No, s'okay. I …. I haven't paid for it yet.'

'What, you nicked it?'

'In a way,' Jennifer said with a hint of pride.

'Won't you be in trouble if whatsisname finds out?'

'Who? Big Bill?' Nah. I look after all the magazine racks. He won't know it's gone.'

'Even so, I should pay. Don't want you to get in trouble.'

'Nah, s'okay. Our secret. Let's see what happens when this week's comes in.'

Richard nodded uncomfortably. Anika came back carrying two bottles of coke and two glasses, 'Ice okay but no lemon. He says that costs extra. I don't believe him but ….'

Richard took the glasses and Jennifer the bottles. 'Where's yours?'

'Inside. I'll be out later, the band is on soon.' She gave Richard his change and turned to leave them in the growing darkness but had made only a yard or two before returning to ask Jennifer, 'Why did Elizabeth not want to go to dinner with Dudek? Dudek said she rang this morning to tell him she's changed her mind.'

'I don't know. I thought they were going out tomorrow.'

'Not any more. Do you know why?'

'Nope. But hey, they're old, it's not like there's a boy girl thing happening.'

Richard looked at her but in the darkness couldn't tell if she was being sarcastic or insensitive. There was often a mischief in her spoken thoughts which was entertaining, but without catching her eyes he couldn't tell.

'Hmmm. Dudek is …. young in the heart …. I think so is Elizabeth. They can be …. good friends. Dudek …. deserves that, after what he has done. You should help your grandmother,' Anika said and walked away before Jennifer could respond, so she spoke to Richard,

'Anika wasn't here last summer. Dudek and Elizabeth went out a few times. She didn't say much but your uncle might be a little …. too friendly sometimes, especially if he's had a drink …. and maybe Elizabeth thinks she's just too old to be getting …. too friendly. They're not young like us, are they?' She leant forward into the light from the pub's window and Richard saw her face this time. The unspoken tease was there and appealing and he wanted to ask something, the right thing, to draw it further. But he also wanted to echo Anika's words. He hadn't known Elizabeth was not going to dinner with Dudek - did it explain his uncle's behaviour earlier? He looked to Anika but she was already half-way to the pub's door and as he turned back an old Ford Fiesta pulled into the car park and next to a battered Transit van. Richard saw it was Erica and Larry. They walked to the pub and Larry stopped half-way when he recognised Richard sitting in the light from the pub's window. He was at least twenty yards away and though Larry's face was in the darkness, his stance was aggressive (or was Richard imagining?). Richard's stomach lurched; his chest tightened. Jennifer was talking to him but he didn't respond. He stared back at Larry, not with any bravado or defiance, but with frozen unease. Jennifer turned to follow his gaze. Erica had walked on but stopped when she realised Larry was no longer with her. She turned, saw Richard and there was a four-way hesitation. Larry took a step towards Richard but Erica called his name. There was another hesitation and Erica reminded Larry the pub were offering first drinks free for the brave volunteer fire-fighters; she said it loud enough to make sure Richard heard. Richard looked down and Larry followed Erica into the pub.

'Hmmm. Larry's not happy. Guess he's not over Friday. You okay?' Jennifer said.

'Yep. All under control.'

'You worried?'

'Nah, I'm sitting with my back to the wall, sort of, and no alcohol.'

'Which means?'

'That's lesson three. S'okay. We should ….' He stopped talking as the main lights in the pub were extinguished. The interior went dark, the chattering stopped and a small cheer went up as a single spotlight flashed to life. Four figures huddled on to the stage; one struggled to fit behind the drums without knocking over a cymbal while the others fussed with guitars and amps. Despite the spotlight the figures were mostly in darkness. They wore jeans, white t-shirts and long hair and it was hard to tell them apart. They fiddled for another thirty seconds or so while the crowd started ironic clapping but stopped with anticipation as the fiddling finished. Silence. The singer nodded to the figure to his left. The opening chords of 'Brown Sugar' exploded through the pub (Richard later swore the pub shook) and burst out into the night, swamping Jennifer and Richard with energy. The power carried in the driving rhythm was instant and overwhelming; the passion carried in the beat intoxicating. Though they were outside it thumped into Richard's chest and the volume was just short of painful; loud enough the sound was muddied, but that mattered not at all. It .... Was .... REAL! It .... Was .... LIVE! Rocknow Station was the first band Richard had seen live (albeit through a window) and he experienced it through a new sense, newly awakened. He looked to Jennifer and returned her wide smile. She nodded her head to the beat and banged the table. The three standing figures crammed on the stage front bounced rhythmically as one.

The silence when the first song finished was sudden but before applause could build the drummer called a count of four and the band kicked into 'All Right Now'. Jennifer shouted something Richard didn't hear; he nodded enthusiastic agreement. The crowd in the pub moved closer to the low stage as Rocknow Station gathered momentum and stormed into 'Jumpin' Jack Flash'. Jennifer sat on the table to see better over the heads of the crowd and Richard joined her, sharing both the space and moment. The sound was more than music. Richard wasn't hearing this - it was elemental, alive inside him. He took Jennifer's hand as the opening riff of 'The Boys Are Back In Town' engulfed them. The band was relentless and a succession of high energy covers surged inexorably through the night.

The first set ended. Richard and Jennifer yelled for more, along with the crowd inside, and were only placated when the singer said they'd be back in twenty minutes. The pub's lights went back on. With ears ringing, Jennifer and Richard sat back on the benches, opposite each other as before. Richard started to ask what Jennifer thought; it was clear she was as impressed as he. They were buzzing with excitement, matching each other's chattering high, and Richard didn't notice he was still holding her hand until he wanted his drink. They both slipped into silence as they realised and took swigs from their cokes and a relative calm eased them.

'Anyway,' Jennifer asked, 'do you think you'll ever be good enough to play keyboards in a band?'

'I didn't, until tonight, and I'm not saying I am good enough, but after that, I just have to do it, good enough or not, and I know that doesn't make sense but ....'

'Me too. I've been learning a bit of guitar and trying to sing. I wasn't sure, but now, definitely. I'm gonna do it. Blue Jean Jenny. That will be my stage-name.'

'I didn't know you were learning guitar. You didn't say. That's great.'

'I thought you'd laugh. No-one takes me seriously. But after that,' she nodded towards the pub, 'I don't care.'

'Good. Do it!' said a new voice.

They hadn't noticed the figure that walked from the pub and was now standing close to their table. In the light from the pub they saw a young guy, mid-teens maybe, shoulder length hair, big smile, black jeans, plain white t-shirt and sun-glasses. He sipped from a bottle of coke, sat next to Richard, took off the sun-glasses and reached over the table to tap Jennifer's arm and repeat, 'Go for it. Blue Jean Jenny is a great name for a rock star. Trust me. I know. And we're looking for a girl backing singer. Someone that looks good and can hold a tune. You look good, wanna audition?'

'Er, who are we?' asked Richard.

'Rocknow Station. You heard us? We're good right?'

'You're with the band?' Jennifer asked.

'I know. You're thinking, cliché. Guys will say anything to get with a chick. But yes, I'm with the band. Honest. Bass. Did you not see me?' He stood to look in the pub window, 'Oh, not a good view, spotlight's shit, but it was me, straight up, on the left. And Blue Jean Jenny is a great stage-name. Can I call you that? I'm Mike but everyone calls me JB.'

'JB?' repeated Jennifer.

'Yep, JB. It used to stand for junior bass 'cos when I turned up at the first rehearsal that's all I had, this short little bass guitar and tiny combo and I was just a kid but I got the gig and the nickname stuck. JB. Everyone calls me that. You can.'

'So why say your name's Mike if you want to be called JB?' Richard asked.

'Hmmmm. Good question. No-one's ever asked. I need to think about that. I know, if you think we'll be friends call me JB. If not, Mike. Is that okay?'

'But how do I know we'll be friends? We've only just met,' asked Jennifer.

'Hmmmm. Another good question. I need to think about that too .... meantime, assume we'll be friends, call me JB and if you start calling me Mike I'll know you don't want to be friends anymore. That works right?' JB addressed the question to Richard who nodded agreement. JB drew breath to take a drink from his bottle. Richard asked before JB could start talking again,

'And you're with the band. Really?'

'Really.'

'So why you out here?'

'Landlord's a prat. Fucking stupid. Says I can play with the band but can't stay in the pub. Some stupid rule about being eighteen. Said I had to wait outside. Prat. Hence this,' he held up the bottle of coke.

'So you're not eighteen yet.' Jennifer made the connection.

'No. Not long though. Like you guys I guess.' He clinked his bottle against their glasses. 'What's that smell?' He turned around as if expecting to see its cause.

'What smell?' asked Jennifer.

'I don't know. That smell. It's usually pot or fags when we're gigging, but what's that?'

'Oh, the heath. As fast as they beat them out they start again.'

'What do?'

'The fires.'

'Oh. We're safe here right?' JB asked.

'We're safe.' Richard was almost patronising.

'Good. We're playing another set in a few minutes. You heard the first set right? Was it okay?'

'You guys were great,' said Jennifer.

'Pretty good. Need keyboards though,' added Richard, pretending a reserve he hadn't felt earlier.

'I know. I've been telling them,' JB agreed readily and turned to Jennifer, 'and a girl backing singer. Blue Jean Jenny is a great name. We should audition you. Tonight.' He paused to take another sip of coke and Richard tried to speak but JB was talking again, 'You sure that fire's okay? Smells close. Don't want to be stuck here. Not that here's not nice, but it's a long way from home and we need to get back. We've a gig in London tomorrow night. Could be the break we need. You guys should come along. I'll get you in. Not like this place. Prat landlord. You should come.'

'London?'

'We're supporting a punk band. Not my thing but a gig's a gig right? Nashville Rooms. Do you know it?'

'Er, it's a bit far,' said Jennifer, 'he might know it.' She pointed at Richard.

'I live in Hounslow. I've heard of the Nashville.'

'I'm in Richmond. We're almost neighbours. Hello ….'

'…. Richard.'

'Richard? Not Rick or Ricky? You look like a Ricky to me. What do you think?' he asked Jennifer but before she could answer he continued, 'I'm JB.'

'I know. But if you're a London band why you here?'

'Another good question and the answer is not money. It barely covers the petrol.' He pointed to the old Ford Transit parked in the corner of the car park. 'Hope it gets us home. Used to have our name, Rocknow Station, painted on the side, but thieving gits worked out gear was inside and kept breaking in. Bastards. Can't get insured anymore. Only came here 'cos the singer knows the landlord. He used to be a record producer. Slim Jim or something. Bought the pub and moved here after a heart attack or something. Slim Jim. Must be ironic, he's a fat git. The gig's practically a favour, hoping he'll mention us to his old muckers in the business. Not that it isn't a good gig. Good crowd an' all. They like us. Even without a keyboard, eh?' JB nudged Richard as if sharing a secret. 'And I bet you play, don't you?'

Richard nodded.

'I knew it. I'm psycho. No, that's not right. I mean psychic.' He waited for a laugh, or at least a chuckle. None came. 'Never mind. You like prog rock right?'

'Yep.'

'See. I'm right again. But maybe you're a Rick rather than a Ricky then.' He looked to Jennifer for confirmation. She nodded. JB continued, 'You should have seen us last week if you like prog. We supported some old fuckers called Dogs Of Seville or something. You'd have loved them. Not my thing but a gig's a gig right Blue Jean?' he asked Jennifer.

She nodded and tried to speak but JB was flowing, 'And you do sing right? We need a girl backing singer. I've been telling them and ....'

'.... Blue Jean Jenny would front her own band, wouldn't she?' Richard interrupted the flow.

'You're right. What was I thinking? Looking that good, with such a great name. You'll have your own band. We'll support you. Ha ha,' JB agreed. Richard was disappointed. At last, there was a moment's silence. Jennifer watched JB, as if waiting for him to fill it. He did,

'I know what you're thinking. I look like Peter Frampton, right?'

He did, but Jennifer didn't want to agree too readily. 'More a spaniel. Nice ears, I mean hair.'

It was true. In the poor light JB's long curly hair hung either side of his face like a dog's ears. Richard laughed. JB laughed, 'Ouch, that's gonna hurt all the way home, which is a long way. Wish I had a beer instead of this.'

'So how old are you?' Jennifer asked.

'Sixteen.'

'Sixteen?' she repeated.

'Yep, and never been kissed. Ha.' JB laughed.

'Does your mum know you're here?' She ignored his remark to ask her question.

'Of course. She always knows where I am. She's watching. I'm sure.'

'Watching? She's here?'

'Sort of.' JB pointed to the sky. 'She's not here, as such, but watching, I'm sure.'

'Oh, I'm sorry. I didn't know she was .... you know.'

'That's okay. Long time ago. But she keeps an eye on me. I'm sure.' He looked up at the clear, dark sky. 'Sorry for the swearing mum. Don't tell dad.'

'What? Your dad's there as well?'

'No.' JB smiled. 'That would be really sad. But he says mum talks to him sometimes, which is cool. Perhaps she'll talk to me sometime. That would take a miracle right? But they happen …. right?' JB's voice tailed away. The silence was uncomfortable.

'My mum's dead too,' Jennifer said.

'Oh, Blue Jean. I'm sorry,' JB offered sincerely but the silence that followed again was uncomfortable, again.

'My dad's dead,' said Richard, as if it had just occurred to him.

'Really?' JB asked.

'Of course. I wouldn't lie about that.'

'I guess not. Wow. We are one unlucky bunch. You couldn't make it up. There's a song in there somewhere. Maybe a bit country, 'bout three young kids with dead parents. I'll play around with it on the way home and if it makes the top ten I'll cut you guys in on the credit. Wow, we are one unlucky bunch.'

'Some say,' muttered Jennifer.

Silence, again, until Anika came from the pub, carrying two bottles of coke. 'Quiet. What's wrong?'

Three young faces looked up at her. JB said, 'We are one unlucky bunch and in the words of the great Bob Dylan, just knockin' on heaven's door, sort of. I gotta go.' He pointed to the figure in jeans and white t-shirt waving at him from the pub doorway. 'The show must go on. Will you guys be around after? I want to hear Blue Jean Jenny sing.' But he didn't wait for an answer.

Anika gave the bottles to Jennifer and Richard, 'Was that one of the band?'

'Yep.'

'Nice hair.'

'I thought you didn't like long hair. You wanted to cut mine,' said Richard.

'Hmmmm. Maybe it should be longer then. What do I know? Who's Blue Jean Jenny?'

'I am,' said Jennifer proudly.

'Good name. What's his name?'

Jennifer said, 'JB.'

'Mike,' said Richard.

'Boy with two names. I like that. Who is the unlucky bunch knocking on heaven?'

'I think he was saying we're sad 'cos his mum is dead, Jennifer's mum's dead and my dad's dead. What are the odds of three like us meeting up? Wait. Your dad's dead.' Richard almost shouted the last realisation but Anika waved a hand carelessly at him,

'No. I didn't say he was dead. I just didn't know him. Big difference. Especially for my father. Last I heard he was working on a ferry on the Danube, but he never learnt to swim and the ferry wasn't so …. big, so who knows ….'

'Still, we were all brought up by just one parent.' Richard sought empathy.

'Not me. I was brought up by my nan. Remember? I didn't know my father either. No-one knows who my father was.' Jennifer said the last part with an exaggerated east European accent.

Anika looked at Richard before speaking to Jennifer, 'Elizabeth loves you very much. Do you want to know your father?' She lit a cigarette and offered one to Jennifer. She took, but didn't light it.

'I don't know. I didn't care, but a couple of days ago my nan and Maisie were in the kitchen, talking. Maisie said something about my mum's dad; she seemed to know him but Elizabeth didn't want to talk about it. I don't even know if my mum knew her dad, and now I don't know mine. Pretty shit eh?'

'But do you really want to know? What if he was a bad man?' Anika asked. 'Not all fathers are heroes like Richard's.' She tried to joke.

No-one laughed. Jennifer looked at her. 'And I don't know why Elizabeth won't talk about it. Any of it.

My mum died in a car crash when I was a few months old. I don't even know if my dad ever saw me. I don't know if my mum ever knew her father. I'd like to know. I don't know why.'

Anika placed an arm around her, 'I don't know if your father ever saw you, but your grandfather did know your mum.'

'How do you know?'

'I know a little. From Elizabeth. Sometimes …. sometimes people need to tell things.'

'What do you mean?' Jennifer asked, almost angry.

Anika looked to Richard, possibly for permission to continue but Richard didn't think it his to give. Jennifer tried to hold back tears and the turnaround since the excitement of the gig and meeting JB was unnerving. Jennifer watched Anika's face. Anika dragged from her cigarette and said, 'Elizabeth told me your mum's father was Maisie's brother.' Anika waited for a reaction. It was unexpected,

'Is that it?'

Anika thought for a moment. 'And Elizabeth ran away with him when she was …. pregnant …. with your mum. There was shame, bad days. Maisie's brother stayed with Elizabeth for the first few years but left them, Elizabeth and your mum. Not seen since.'

'So Maisie is my …. great aunt. Is that it? Nothing about my own father?'

Anika shook her head. 'He left when you were born. I don't know if he ever saw you. When your mum died, you were a baby, Elizabeth brought you to Oakjack.'

'That's it?'

'Sorry.'

'Sorry that's it?'

'No. Sorry I don't know more. Are you going to smoke that?' Anika pointed to the cigarette held by Jennifer, who shook her head. Anika took it back.

'And I thought everyone knew everything about everyone here.' It was Richard's turn to try a joke.

'Nothing about my father?' asked Jennifer, stressing 'my'.

'Er, no.'

'Big fucking deal. How long have you known? About Maisie?'

Anika shrugged.

'So much for friends right?'

'And you?' she asked Richard. She was no longer crying; her anger was enough to stop tears but not so much as to bring more. 'Thanks a fucking bunch. And when we sat in your uncle's house with Maisie, did you know?'

'No, not then. Honest. I'm sorry,' Richard apologised, head lowered. Jennifer shrugged off Anika's arm. Anika dragged on her cigarette. They sat in morose silence, saved by the pub lights dimming, the spotlight illuminating the stage again and JB's voice calling loud over the PA system,

'We're back! And this one is for Blue Jean Jenny. Remember that name. Blue Jean Jenny. This is for you.'

The band launched into 'I Can't Get Enough'. Anika stood without speaking and went back inside.

Rocknow Station's second set carried even more energy than the first but though Richard recognised most of the songs he didn't feel them in the same way. Richard and Jennifer couldn't see well but stayed on their benches, opposite each other. Richard took occasional glimpses to check if Jennifer was smiling, but her face was in darkness. He hadn't noticed in the first set but JB (Mike) did most of the talking between songs and Richard felt young in comparison to JB's sixteen. And he worried at how easily Jennifer had spoken to JB; for his sake, not hers, which he knew was selfish. Blue Jean Jenny. It was a good name. Why hadn't she mentioned it before? He thought they were closer since she looked after him the previous day and said he could call her Jenny - but not Blue Jean Jenny.

The band played 'Won't Get Fooled Again' for their second encore and the audience finally gave up calling for more when the meagre spotlight went out, the wall lights came on and JB unplugged his bass. The barman rang the little bell behind the bar and shouted for last orders. Richard looked at his glass, long empty and it was too late for Anika to bring another. He wondered if his uncle was okay.

'Good, weren't they?' Jennifer said, for something to say.

'Yep. Hot. When I'm back home I'm gonna look out for them. The guys would love to hear them.'

'He does look like Peter Frampton, doesn't he?'

'Who is Peter Frampton?' Anika asked, joining them from the pub.

'You know. Peter Frampton,' Jennifer repeated the name slowly, as if it would help.

'No. My ears hurt. Good but time to go. We have to get Dudek.'

Richard stood.

The pub's customers filed out into the still warm darkness, talking loud with ringing ears, sated with drink and music. Erica and Larry were amongst them.

'Er, did you see Erica inside?' Richard asked Anika.

'I did. It was too loud to talk.'

'Well I think she wants to talk now.' Richard nodded over Anika's shoulder. She turned to see Erica and her brother approaching. Erica led.

'Cow. I thought we were friends.' There was more hurt than anger in Erica's voice.

'Erica, we are. I'm sorry.' Anika looked over her shoulder to Larry and apologised again, 'I'm sorry.'

'Fuck off,' Larry mouthed.

Richard moved round to Anika's side of the table. Jennifer turned on the bench to watch.

'What's your problem?' Erica demanded. 'Your fucking uncle hurt him last week. He was out of order.'

'It's just that …. Larry, come on, you were drunk and angry, I don't know why, but it wasn't the right place for an argument was it?' Anika tried to appeal to Larry.

'Fuck off,' he mouthed again.

Anika turned back to Erica. 'Dudek is sorry, I know he is. It was a silly fight started by money. Not worth arguing over, not like women, as Dudek says.' She tried to lighten the situation, but failed.

Larry stepped out from behind his sister, 'Money? You think it was over money? That fat old man …. you think I'm to blame? Get fucking real.'

Richard tried to remember the lessons, there was one about recognising anger, but that was easy to do here; Larry was angry, very angry. 'I'm gonna fucking 'ave him. And you, little fucker.' He pointed at Richard and took a half step. Fear shuddered through Richard; Dudek's lesson said to kick him the balls and run, but that meant leaving Anika. Fear of the shame afterwards outweighed fear of the moment.

'Okay Larry. I …. I understand how you feel ….' Richard thought it was what his father might have said, though he had no way of knowing.

'No you fucking don't. Do you know how your uncle treated me? Have you any fucking idea?'

'It was just a disagreement over money. Not worth fighting over, not like women eh?' He tried the joke again but rage blazed in Larry's eyes and he took another half-step forward. Erica didn't try to stop him and Richard tensed. He didn't see from where the short man came, but then he was between him and Larry, dressed all in black and shaking his head. Larry looked down at him. A voice called from behind Erica,

'Hi all. This is Sunny Steve. We call him that 'cos he's always smiling, though you can't tell at the moment. Actually, that's not true. I've never seen him smile, but he comes everywhere with us. I won't do a gig unless I know he'll be with us. Steve, say hello to Blue Jean Jenny and her friends.' JB's tone was cheerful but his voice hoarse.

'Hello Blue Jean Jenny,' the short man said without taking his eyes off Larry and with a hint of accent Richard didn't recognise.

'Did you enjoy the second set? My voice was going toward the end. I should stop talking as we've a gig tomorrow as well.' JB edged between Richard and the short man and took both Richard and Anika's arms and ushered them to one side, adding loud enough for Erica and Larry to hear, 'We don't want to be too close in case we get blood on our clothes.'

Larry took a step to one-side to be closer to Richard and Anika but the short man in black moved in tandem with him. Erica looked at the short man. He ignored her to stare at Larry. Erica whispered something to Larry and pulled him away. He walked backwards, alternating a hateful stare between Richard and the short man and nearly stumbling into the small Ford Fiesta while Erica unlocked the doors. They sat in the car for only a few seconds before driving away, Erica revving the engine unnecessarily hard.

'Thanks Steve.' JB patted Sunny Steve on the back, 'We better help the others pack up.'

Sunny Steve went over to the old Ford Transit van and backed it up to the pub doorway as the band's equipment was brought out.

Richard nodded a thank you to JB. Jennifer offered to help the band pack their equipment. Anika told JB his band were 'very good' and reminded Richard they needed to meet Dudek. Richard, silent in his relief at a fight avoided, gave a simple goodbye wave to Jennifer and followed Anika. After a few yards he heard JB call, 'Don't forget. If you're near the Nashville tomorrow, come and find me.' And it sounded sincere.

Anika and Richard walked in silence until back at the B and G, when Anika said, 'Don't tell your uncle about Larry.'

'Okay. But why did Larry say it wasn't over money?' Richard asked. Anika stopped walking and was thoughtful before replying,

'I don't know all, but Dudek tried to .... help Larry. And Larry was too .... friendly and your uncle didn't .... help ....'

'And?'

'Does that help?' Anika made it a question.

'Not really.'

'Okay,' Anika said, as if satisfied she had answered and walked on before further questioning.

The regulars at The Blue And The Gorse were enjoying a lock-in and Anika had to knock hard to gain anyone's attention. Dudek insisted she and Richard stay for a drink and though Richard wanted to go home and think through the evening (so much had happened, so much had been said and not said; he worried if Jennifer sang for JB) he didn't know how to say no to his uncle, but did talk the drink down to a weak shandy.

Chapter 11
Choices

Despite not sleeping until well past midnight (too excited after watching the band), Richard was down for breakfast early. Dudek was still in bed, unusually for him, but Anika was up as normal and, fuelled by coffee and tobacco, already into her Thursday cleaning routine. Richard picked at a bowl of cereal and tried to catch Anika's attention but she moved in, out and around the rooms with a ferocious dedication to the yellow duster and spray polish. His thoughts jumped from Rocknow Station to Jennifer to JB to his Bontempi to the short man in black to Anika to Larry and back to Rocknow Station, where he tried to focus them and rekindle the natural enthusiasm generated by the gig. He wanted to experience that moment of awakening again, and to share it again, but there were too many distractions: Jennifer and JB and Larry and Anika and the short man in black. Frustrated, he went to the Bontempi to practise, hoping Rocknow's inspiration would bring focus. He was trying the introduction to 'Dreamer' (though he doubted JB would approve) for the sixth time when the clanging bell cut through percussively, a painfully loud assault. Richard's thought jumped to the fire engine he'd seen on the way down (less than two weeks ago) and there was a rush of fear the heath fires were close to Oakjack Ford and Dudek's house. He went to the hall. Anika was already at the front door and as she opened it Dudek was edging his way down the stairs, leaning heavily on the bannister. Richard helped Dudek the last few steps and out to the front porch. Anika was already at the end of the drive. She waved Richard and Dudek to join her and led them next door into Young Samuel's front garden. There was an ambulance as close to the front of the house as it could be. The door was open and Anika stood in the doorway calling through to ask it if was okay to go in. Richard was relieved the alarm hadn't been a fire engine but then guilty - this was an ambulance; his relief was someone else's pain. Anika called him to help Dudek, she was going inside.

Dudek and Richard caught up to Anika in Young Samuel's hallway. The house was dark after the sunshine and the kitchen curtains still closed. Samuel was next to Anika. He was pale and drawn with red eyes. Dudek limped down the hall to his friend and Anika took a step away, leaving Dudek room to hug Samuel, muttering something in Czech Richard didn't understand. Anika nodded. Young Samuel eased away from the hug, saying, 'Megan is .... is ....'

'.... being looked after by the ambulance men. In there.' Anika pointed to the sitting room. Richard saw a man in a dark blue uniform bending over the settee. Another man was holding a small bottle of tablets, reading the label and writing something in a notebook.

'She's not ....' Dudek hesitated.

'.... dead?' Anika both completed and answered the question, 'No.'

'Thank God,' said Dudek.

'My fault ....' said Samuel, trying not to cry, 'I .... I thought there was enough oxygen in her tank for another day but .... but .... fucking idiot .... it ran out this morning. Poor Megan, she was gasping and gasping and gasping. It was terrifying, she thought she was going, she couldn't breathe, there was nothing I could do, such a fucking idiot. I'm supposed to be looking after her. She was so scared. She thought .... I thought, she was .... you know …. such a fucking idiot.' Young Samuel let his tears flow and Dudek hugged him again. Richard had never seen a grown man sob in such a way; terrified and angry, beyond control. Richard moved closer to the sitting room door. The ambulance man near the settee was kneeling and Richard watched him fiddle with the tap on top of a small gas bottle, from which a tube draped to Megan, lying on the couch. The other ambulance man adjusted the position of a mask on her face but it didn't hide her white cheeks and wide eyes. Her chest rose up and down arrhythmically. Richard was relieved she wasn't gasping painfully. She wore a pale white night dress and matching dressing gown, despite the day's heat, but their blanching was nothing to Megan; she wasn't just white or pale, she had no colour; she was drained of any hue, almost translucent. Her eyes searched the room. Richard took a half-step back rather than be seen. The ambulance man with the notebook stepped away from Megan and came to the hall, speaking to Samuel.

'We need to take her into hospital. We don't have everything we need here and she …. needs to be …. somewhere she can be helped …. to …. to be where she can be looked after. To be comfortable.'

Samuel wiped his face, looked into the room and forced a smile at Megan. She saw him and shook her head, fear showing.

Dudek eased Samuel into the sitting room to be with Megan and rested a hand on the ambulance man's arm. Anika did likewise on the other arm as Dudek said, 'My friend Samuel is a good man, a devoted man. He is looking after Megan better than anyone. Isn't he?' He looked to Anika who confirmed,

'He loves her very much. See, she is calming now he is with her.'

'Better they stay together. Don't you think?'

The ambulance man lowered his voice to a whisper, 'You know she won't .... live .... much longer, right? Better she should be in hospital, isn't it?'

'We understand there is nothing they can do. Better she should be with Samuel. He loves her so much. She loves him. Wouldn't you want that?' Dudek's voice was both calm and calming.

'But he let the tank run out of oxygen.' The ambulance man pointed to the tall thin gas bottle in the kitchen. 'And she needs drugs.'

'They have all the drugs they need. And the oxygen? You can leave a tank or two, surely?'

'Only that small one. I doubt it will last more than a couple of days.'

'Samuel will go to the doctor later today and they will order another. It will be here tomorrow morning. If, in meantime, there is an emergency we will take her to hospital.'

Dudek didn't wait for an answer but looked at Samuel and Megan, holding hands, and subtly turned the ambulance man so he would see. Megan smiled; she watched Samuel's face as though searching his thoughts to know him better and for his sake, not hers.

'I should have such a love,' Dudek said, with unaffected honesty.

'See, she has calmed,' whispered Anika. 'If you take her to hospital, we fear for Samuel. They are everything to each other.'

'He can visit.'

'His heart would break. He cannot leave her side.' Anika's appeal was sincere and irresistible.

'I should have such a love,' Dudek repeated, to no-one in particular.

The walk into the village was a slow one. Richard dawdled without (he hoped) drawing attention to himself but it was still only a short walk. He loitered outside the newsagent, reading the handwritten adverts on postcards in the window - an eclectic mix with an unusually high (Richard thought) number of secondhand dressers for sale. He waited until a couple of customers had come out and none went in, before entering and browsing the magazine rack in an overly casual manner. Big Bill saw him and called through the door to the back of the shop, 'Jen. Your .... townie is here.'

There was no response and he called a couple of times before Jennifer came from out back. Richard thought her smile genuine enough. She nodded a welcome, 'Wotchya looking for?'

'Wondered if Melody Maker was in yet. Seeing the band last night reminded me it was due. Good weren't they? Did you enjoy it?' But he really wanted to ask if she sang for JB after he'd left.

'Ace. It was a good night, on balance, as some say, wasn't it .... Ricky? And yes, the MM did come in. We were gonna deliver it tomorrow morning. Wait there.'

Jennifer went out to the store room and came back with a few copies of the paper, handing one to Richard and placing the others on the rack.

'Shall I pay now?' Richard offered.

Jennifer made a show of looking to see if Bill was in the shop before whispering, 'Nah, just take it. Our secret.' Her mouth was close to his face and he felt her breath on his cheek.

Richard didn't back away but looked at the paper suspiciously. 'No, I shouldn't. I don't wanna get you in trouble.'

'You wish. Ha ha,' she whispered again and pretended the laugh.

'No. I'd rather not.' Richard missed her innuendo.

'Such a .... townie. Don't worry, take it.' She stepped away from him.

'But that'll be the second one. I can't ....'

'Don't be such a wuss. You telling me you haven't nicked anything before? A stick of gum or a pack of fags or a coke or something? Come on. Be brave. Like last night when Larry had the hump and you stood next to Anika. Her hero,' Jennifer said, but with no obvious sarcasm.

Richard hadn't felt brave the previous night. He was too ashamed to admit he was grateful for JB's intervention. 'Right. Lucky for Larry JB's roadie came along. Who knows what I might have done to him.'

'Would you be that brave for me?'

'Of course. I let you in the cinema didn't I?'

'True. That was a buzz wasn't it?'

'I guess.'

'You got the buzz right?'

'I guess,' Richard repeated. It was true, the excitement had overridden the fear.

'Of course. Here take the MM.'

'No. You'll get in trouble.'

'That again? Come on, show me you can be brave for me as well as Anika.'

Bill came back into the shop from out back and stood behind the counter. He leafed through a copy of The Sun, taking no notice of Richard and Jennifer, but Richard placed the magazine in the rack theatrically, saying quietly, 'Okay, but not now.'

'I know. Come on.' She took Richard's hand and led him out the shop, shouting over her shoulder, 'Back in a minute Bill.'

Bill nodded.

They walked to the post office, Jennifer explaining, 'Go on, nick me a present from here. If Elizabeth finds out I'll tell her I said it's okay. She'll be fine. Come on.'

Jennifer pulled Richard into the post office and called out a hello to both her grandmother and Maisie, who was standing next to Elizabeth behind the counter.

'She's always here now,' Jennifer whispered, 'I haven't asked her about …. about what Anika told me last night. But I will. Later. I'm pissed off with their secrets. Whenever I walk in they stop talking. Like just now. Did you see?'

'Er, I suppose.' Richard hadn't noticed.

'Well go on. I'll distract them. We'll be Bonnie and Clyde, right?'

'That didn't end well for Clyde, did it?'

'Or Bonnie,' Jennifer said over her shoulder as she walked to the counter. He stood awkwardly for a few seconds, unsure how he was in this position but understanding what was expected of him and though his heart beat heavier in his chest, he wasn't afraid. He browsed the shelves with false interest and when he heard Jennifer asking Elizabeth about dinner he went down the aisle most hidden from both the post office and pharmacy counters. He had no idea of what he should take and, later, claimed it must have been the adrenaline fogging his thoughts; the sun-faded, dust covered Airfix box with a grey war ship pictured on the front was irresistible. It was too big for a pocket but not so big he couldn't slip it under his t-shirt and, as long as he didn't turn around, it wouldn't be seen, except by someone coming in as he went out - but too late for that thought; he was already at the door. The bell rang louder than it ever had as he wrenched the door open but there was no shout to stop him and no other customers rushing to grab or accuse. He walked self-consciously towards the bus stop. No-one waited there so he sat and took the model kit from his t-shirt, brushed off the dust and inspected it, trying to ignore the guilt.

He placed the model on the bench next to him and watched for Jennifer to come from the shop. From the bus stop he could see the bakery; Larry walked through the door, turned to call a goodbye to Erica but stopped on seeing Richard at the bus stop. He stood in the doorway to the bakery, looking at him. Richard looked away, not wanting to provoke a reaction and unsure how the previous night's confrontation had left matters - uncomfortable, to say the least. He glanced sideways and was glad to see Larry gone and Jennifer running toward him. She stood over him, laughing, 'Well. What did you get me?'

Richard passed the model to her, suddenly aware it was inappropriate. She turned the box over a couple of times, checking to make sure she wasn't missing something, and said, 'A toy? A toy boat? You are soooo sweet,' heavy with sarcasm.

'It's not a toy. It's a model.'

'Some might say. Still, thanks.' She pecked him on the cheek and sat next to him. 'You were very brave. Clyde.'

'Thank you, Bonnie.'

They went silent as Jennifer opened the box. 'I really do have to put it together?'

'I'll do that for you. I haven't the right paints though.'

'Oh. We should go back and nick them too.'

'Does your nan have them?'

'I'm joking.'

'Sorry.'

'No, It's …. different. I wasn't expecting a toy …. I mean, model. And you can put it together for me. Though I probably won't put it on my dressing table, if that's okay?'

'Of course. Sorry.'

'No, it's …. lovely.'

'No it isn't.'

'Okay, not lovely. Thoughtful?'

'No it isn't,' Richard admitted.

'Okay. It's …. you. Thank you.' She pecked him again, harder.

It was nearly mid-day and the bus-stop offered shade so they stayed there for a few minutes but there was no breeze. Richard fidgeted and sweated and stood, said, 'Stay here,' and walked off before Jennifer could reply.

By the time he returned to the bus stop sweat was showing on his t-shirt and he had to clean a drip from his spectacles.

'Well, what is it?' asked Jennifer. She had watched him go back into the post office/pharmacy. 'You look …. hot, and even a bit red. As much as I can tell.'

'No I don't. Come on, let's go to your den. Find proper shade.'

'Why did you go back to the post office?'

'I'll tell you when we reach your …. safe place.'

'I should go back to the newsagent.'

'Oh. What time do you finish?'

'I'll tell him I can't work this afternoon. Truth is, there's not much to do anyway. He just likes me hanging around sometimes. Should that worry me?' She laughed. 'Wait here.'

'Hang on.' Richard dug in a pocket for coins and gave them to Jennifer. 'Buy a couple of cokes. Cold ones.'

It was a ten minute walk north out of the village and through the heath to Jennifer's den and they were half way there before realising they'd left the Airfix model on the bench at the bus stop. Richard pretended to be offended Jennifer hadn't picked it up; she pretended to be upset at losing it. Both pretended not to know the other pretended.

As they neared the den Richard grew uneasy. It was here he'd suffered the last migraine and the association meant this was not the 'safe place' Jennifer claimed. Of course there was no reason to assume the den itself had caused the migraine, but even so, he felt a mild panic and hesitated before following Jennifer through the door. She was already sitting on one of her box chairs and handed him a can as he sat next to her, 'Not so cold anymore, sorry,' but it was still refreshing after the sun and difficult to resist gulping. Jennifer put her can on the floor and reached under her box to pull out a pack of ten Players number six, a matchbook advertising a Berni Inn and a small, bright red transistor radio.

'The battery's dying,' she said, extending the aerial and fiddling with the tuning dial. The hiss was almost drowned out by Radio One playing 'You Should Be Dancing'. 'I don't think JB would approve,' she said, balancing the radio on one of the other boxes. It was similar to the little radio Julie listened to through an ear-piece and Richard nearly said so, but didn't want to talk about Julie.

'That's better,' said Jennifer as the song faded to be replaced by 'The Boston Tea Party'. 'Like this?'

'S'okay.'

'You do know it right?'

'Of course.'

'Good. Anyway, where is it?'

'What?'

'My present. Come on Clyde. You went back in to the post office and came out red faced. You nicked something else for me, didn't you?'

'Maybe,' he tried to sound relaxed and not blush.

'Ha. Bad liar. Come on. Show.' Jennifer lit a cigarette.

Now that he was blushing fully, visible even with his colour, there was no point pretending. From a back pocket he took a small blue aerosol spray can with gold writing on the side. 'I got it from the pharmacy. Perfume.' He turned it on its side and showed it to her.

'Blasé?'

'Do you use it?'

'No. But I will from now on.' Jennifer took the aerosol and raised her head to spray a mist onto her neck. She looked at the small can, 'You know this is a tester, right?'

'A tester?'

'Yep. It wasn't in a box was it?'

'Er, no. But it was on the counter. There was no-one behind the pharmacy and Elizabeth and Maisie were talking, and I thought …. I mean it looked like a proper perfume. Sorry.'

'It is a proper perfume. Smell.' She leant towards him and offered her neck.

He didn't know what a proper perfume should smell like, but was sure the flowery scent at such close quarters qualified - it might even be the same perfume Carol had worn.

'Like it?' she asked.

'Yeah. Nice.'

She wore jeans and a white blouse with the top three buttons undone, he couldn't help but notice, and couldn't help but notice that by tilting his head, still at her neck, he could see her small breasts, nestling in a plain white cotton bra. He stole another glance and sat back on his box.

'And it will look better on my dressing table than a model ship. Thank you. My hero.'

He knew there was nothing heroic about theft but easily ignored the guilt while she smiled so brightly at him.

'My pleasure Jenny. I can call you Jenny, right? And it does smell nice. Can I?' He moved towards her again. She leant into him and his nose grazed her neck. He thought she breathed in sharply. He nuzzled and kissed her neck.

'Wait,' she said and moved away. She dropped her cigarette on the hard, dry earth and stamped it out before moving her box closer to his and taking his arm to put it around her shoulder. He pulled her close and kissed her on the lips, hoping it was the right thing to do and unable to stop. She pressed her lips hard against his and he slid his free hand to her waist. She put a hand on his thigh. It was hot in the den and he was sweating and he heard the buzzing of insects on the gorse outside and felt the rise and fall of Jennifer's breasts against his chest as she breathed. She pulled her mouth away from his just enough to flick out her tongue and lick his lips and he copied her and dared to move his hand to cup her breast and she didn't withdraw and the radio played 'Show Me The Way' and though he was no Peter Frampton fan, he knew that track would now forever be a favourite. She slid her tongue into his mouth and moaned as he held her breast tighter (not in pain, he hoped - but released slightly just in case) and rubbed the back of her neck with his other hand. She took her hand from his thigh. There was a flush of further anticipation and he was only mildly disappointed when she placed it behind his head, but instead of caressing she pulled him closer and their faces pressed almost painfully. He had no conscious thought or expectation of where this might lead; the moment was all. Jenny bit his lip, not gently, not hard - just perfectly.

'Hi Jenny, Richard,' Anika said loudly.

Richard and Jennifer pushed away from each other, Richard speechless, Jennifer with an exclamation which was not a word, just a noise of surprise. Richard was too shocked to be embarrassed; how long had Anika been there? Jennifer regained composure first. 'It's polite to knock,' she said, adjusting her blouse. Richard didn't recall 'unadjusting' it.

'I did. A couple of times and called. You were .... busy. Beautiful day, isn't it?' Anika sat on the spare box, and picked up the can of coke at Richard's feet to take a sip.

'Again,' said Richard.

'You were busy .... again?' Anika asked.

'No. I mean a beautiful day, again.'

'Of course. Isn't it Jenny?'

'Jennifer.'

'Yes, Jennifer. Can I have one of your cigarettes? I left mine at home. I didn't think I'd be out long.'

Jennifer passed them over. As Anika lit up Jennifer asked, 'So what brings you to my den?'

'I needed …. things from the chemist,' she answered after taking a drag.

'I'd have done that for you,' said Richard.

'No, I needed …. things you wouldn't understand. Lady things.' She looked to Jennifer and mouthed, 'Tampons.'

Jennifer nodded to show she understood and smiled, happy to be sharing.

Anika continued, talking to Jennifer, 'And when I saw Elizabeth she said if I saw you, to say she had a phone call from your friend with the puppies. She said if you want to go and see them, Friday, Saturday or Sunday will be okay. And when I couldn't find you, or Richard, in the village, I thought I'd try here.'

'I can go and see the puppies?'

'Elizabeth says.'

'Would you take me? You can see them too. You'll love them. Their farm is only a short drive.' Jennifer's enthusiasm was an age of innocence away from her passion just minutes earlier.

'Okay. Tomorrow afternoon?' Anika asked.

'I'll ring my friend and find out what time and let you know.' Jennifer turned off the radio and stood.

'Okay. I need to get back and see if Samuel and Megan are all right,' said Anika.

Richard had forgotten Samuel and Megan's crisis that morning. 'Was she okay when you left?'

'Too late for her to be okay, but better. I should go back. Dudek was to look after Megan while Samuel went for more oxygen.' She stood alongside Jennifer but only for a second or two before sitting back on the box. 'Or do you need to stay seated for a while?' she asked Richard. And it was made worse that she asked sincerely, not in a tease.

Richard's embarrassment reached a new level.

Although it was only mid-afternoon, Anika and Richard heard Young Samuel's saxophone as they neared home. They had split from Jennifer soon after leaving her den and strolled home, saying little, which was okay with Richard - the encounter with Jennifer filled his thoughts. They went straight round the back to the garden and found Dudek asleep under the umbrella on the patio. Anika smiled at Dudek's snoring and whispered to Richard, 'It was a late night for him, he drank too much I think, and a busy morning looking after Megan. We should leave him. Come.'

She took her favourite spot on the lounger under the apple tree. Richard sat on the hard earth beside her. As she half-lay on the lounger she said, 'Oh, I forgot. I have a present for you. From chemist.' She sorted through her handbag to find a small plastic tub with a label printed on it saying 'PILLS'. It would hold three or four of Richard's tablets.

'You should put two tablets in and take it with you. They have to be taken at …. onset. Is that the right word? Have you read the paper that came with the tablets yet?'

Richard grunted vaguely.

'Why not?'

'I will.'

'Hmmmm. Does it worry you? This …. what did you say …. problem with reading …. does it stop you reading?'

'No. It's just …. difficult sometimes. With words I don't recognise. I will read about the tablets. Promise.'

'I'll read it with you. We'll read it together. My English read is not so good. We can help each other.'

'Maybe ….'

'Okay. Your …. choice. But if that school needs to help you more, perhaps Dudek could talk to them.'

Richard looked at her, the question about Dudek's cheques to the school on his lips but before it was formed Anika said, 'But before you go home, I can help. If you want. Your choice.' She laid her head onto the pillow on the lounger and closed her eyes. Richard watched her for a couple of seconds. Her skin was still pale (more so compared to Jennifer's) and clear; her lips were full, though she wore no lipstick, and her eyebrows were finer than Jennifer's (she plucked them, he supposed). He started when she opened her eyes and turned her head to catch him staring. Her head was level with his. Her blue eyes were clear and bright, but not with their colour; they were bright with a captivating energy and intelligence.

'I have noticed when Jennifer speaks to you, she sounds like a …. what is her word? …. townie. When you're not around she sounds more …. village. Do you know what I mean? Of course not, you're not around to hear her when you're not around. But you know what I mean. Yes?'

He didn't but nodded anyway. She leant up to rest on an elbow and reached over to take off his spectacles. 'Long eye lashes. Jennifer said. She was right. From your mother, right?'

'I suppose.'

'And dark eyes. Always watching. From your father?'

'I don't know.'

'Are you a watcher?'

'I don't know.'

'You are young. Time will tell. But already a hero, like your father.'

'Er, no. That wasn't heroic.' Richard's hasty assumption was somehow Anika knew he had stolen the perfume, which Jennifer thought made him a hero.

'I think so. Twice already you have wanted to help me when Larry wants to …. fight. So you are my hero.'

'Oh. No, not really. I was scared ….'

'…. even braver.'

'Er, no, I was scared of looking a prat if I didn't do something. Scared you'd think I was a coward. Not the same thing.'

'You think too much. A watcher and a thinker. You need to be careful, you may watch and think your life to a …. statue.'

The silence was broken by Young Samuel's saxophone from the garden next door. Anika was still holding Richard's spectacles and sat up fully so she could replace them, but stroked his cheek gently as she did so. 'What would have happened in Jennifer's den if I hadn't …. found you?'

'I don't know.' Which was true.

'Would you …. you know?' She took his hand and held it close to her cheek, barely touching.

'I …. I …. don't know. I …. I guess,' Richard stammered.

Anika let go his hand and lay back on the lounger. 'Okay. But don't forget. I am here.' She closed her eyes.

Richard watched her, trying to decipher her words and understand what she meant and if she teased or was sincere. The afternoon was hotter than ever and frozen still. Young Samuel's saxophone was rich in tone. Anika's chest rose and fell with slow, hypnotic rhythm.

Chapter 12
Friday 13th

'Oh, by the way, Melody Maker was delivered this morning, with uncle's Telegraph.' Richard turned in the Citroen's front passenger seat to look at Jennifer behind.

'I know. I mark up the papers for Big Bill, remember?'

'Yeah. And it's on uncle's account right?'

'Yep.'

'So, I needn't have worried about you paying for last week's. And what was all that nonsense about me stealing one yesterday?'

'I know. Nonsense right? But, more importantly, what sixteen year old boy says nonsense?' Jennifer asked the question to Anika who looked at her in the rear view mirror and laughed.

'Non-sense. A good word. I like that. I will try to use it later,' said Anika and looked back to the single track road ahead as the deer jumped through a gap in the low hedgerow. She stamped on the Citroen's brakes but had already hit the terrified animal with the near-side front wing before they took any effect. She steered away from impact but it had already happened and the animal was behind them. Richard called out something and Jennifer screamed as the brakes grabbed and the front wheels locked. Anika wrenched at the wheel to bring the car back into the centre of the lane but kept her foot hard on the brake pedal until the big Citroen slewed to a halt and stalled. Richard put out a hand to the dashboard and Jennifer slumped back into her seat. Anika held the steering wheel with white knuckles; her face more pale than ever. She held her breath until Richard said quietly, 'Okay? You okay?'

She breathed out and he turned to ask Jennifer the same question. She nodded and looked behind her, shocked into silence.

'We should go see,' said Anika, though her voice lacked conviction. 'Stupid animal.' She started the engine and reversed fifty or sixty yards to the deer, lying on the lane's verge. 'Stupid, stupid animal.'

The Citroen stopped five yards short of the wounded deer. Anika switched off the engine and got out slowly, nearly as slowly as Richard, who motioned to Jennifer to stay. He looked at the front of the car. The near-side headlight was smashed, the bumper was dented but still attached and the wing was damaged, but it didn't look too severe. Richard thought there a chance the deer might still be alive. He stood away from the car and heard Anika's quiet cry, 'Oh my God. You stupid, stupid animal.' She had her back to Richard, hands to her face, looking at the broken deer. Her shoulders shook but he couldn't tell if with fear, anger or shock. He went to her. The deer was still alive. It lay on the verge, half in a ditch, panting shallow with wide, terrified eyes. The front half looked okay but the back half was a grotesque malformation, its hips and back legs twisted into a sickening contortion. There was little blood and no gaping wounds.

'Stupid, stupid animal. Stupid, stupid animal,' Anika muttered repeatedly, now rocking back and forth. Richard tried to make her turn away but she was rigid, transfixed by the abhorrent sight.

'Oh my God.' Jennifer was behind Richard. He jumped when she spoke but composed himself to put an arm round her and lead her back to the car. When he went back to Anika she was breathing deeply and slowly.

'It needs to be out of pain,' she said, in a voice now so calm as to unnerve Richard. He nodded. She looked at him. 'How?'

'Ossie, our dog, once brought in a bird with a broken wing. My step-dad throttled it,' Richard said, to his own surprise.

'Throttled?' At last Anika looked away from the deer.

'Strangled,' Richard explained.

'You think you strangle that?' She pointed to the deer.

Richard didn't bother answering. Even if his hands stretched round its neck (doubtful) did he have the strength? (very doubtful) But more importantly, did he have the stomach? (absolutely not).

'I know. I'll be back in ten minutes. You stay here.' Anika started back to the car.

'Er, why?'

'Make sure it doesn't go anywhere.'

'Yeah, like that's gonna happen.' He looked back but the misshapen hind quarters were ever more sickening. 'Where are you going?'

'Ten minutes. I'll take Jennifer.'

Richard watched her turn the Citroen in the narrow lane with much to-ing and fro-ing and as she drove back the way they had come he crossed to be on the opposite side of the road from the deer. He hoped no-one would drive this way and stop. He had no answer to the obvious questions. For the first time since leaving the car he smelt a heath fire somewhere close. There was smoke over the gorse behind the field from where the deer had come, perhaps a quarter mile away.

Anika was back in fifteen minutes but it felt an hour to Richard, sitting on the hard, dry earth verge in the sun, occasionally hearing the deer gasping a deeper breath. She parked just past the deer. Jennifer was still in the back, but looking out at Richard, rather than back to the damaged animal. She stayed there while Anika climbed out of the car and waved Richard to join her.

'This will do it quick and no pain.' She showed him the pistol. 'Browning. Dudek's favourite.'

'What …. the …. fuck? Is it real?' Richard asked.

'Of course. You think a toy one would kill a deer? See, you do speak funny. Doesn't it look real?'

'How would I know? Apart from tv and film I've never seen one before.'

'It's real. Nine millimetre.' Anika shook the small box she held in her other hand.

'Of course.'

'The magazine can take thirteen but I've only brought three.' Her casual references were unsettling.

'Of course. It's not like you're gonna miss. Is it yours?'

'No. Why would I have a pistol?'

'I don't know. Whose is it?'

'I told you. It's your uncle's favourite. He told me he'd taken this one round the world with him, wherever he was …. working.'

'And he just gave it to you?'

'No, he's not at home. Now he's walking better he's gone into the village. I think he will be finding a reason to visit the post office and see Elizabeth. But I know the safe combination.'

'Oh, good.' Richard's sarcasm was too subtle for Anika. He asked, 'And you know how to use it?'

'Of course. Back home we hunt and your uncle made sure I knew of his pistol when I came to visit. But it is too hard a …. trigger pull for me. It is not a girl pistol. I may need two hands. So now, the deer. I need to …. help it pass. You must wait in the car. Guns are …. dangerous. Sit with Jennifer. But if the trigger is too …. hard, I may need you. I'll call.'

Richard wiped sweat from his forehead and sat next to Jennifer. She said nothing but took his hand. Her small face looked so young and her eyes were red with tears. Anika placed the box of ammunition on the Citroen's bonnet while she struggled to remove the magazine. 'See, it is …. hard for a girl,' she shouted into the car. Richard couldn't see what she was doing and was grateful when she managed to remove the magazine without asking for help. She loaded the three rounds, struggled to replace the magazine and went to the deer. Richard watched her face. There was no doubt. His heart was racing and he squeezed Jennifer's hand. She looked out of the window, to the other side of the lane. Richard could see only Anika's top half as she pointed the pistol into the verge with stretched arm and looked down its barrel. He saw the strain on Anika's face as she struggled to pull the trigger and joined both hands around the pistol's handle to use two fingers. Still she struggled and Richard tensed in expectation but still jumped as finally the pistol discharged and the explosion crashed in his ears, louder than expected. Jennifer jumped even more and shrieked. Anika lowered the pistol and watched the deer for at least a minute before looking to Richard and drawing a hand across her own throat to signal success. He started to leave the car but she indicated he should stay and struggled again with the pistol to release the magazine and remove the remaining two rounds. She waved him out. Forcing a brave face, he joined her to look on the deer. There was a black (not red, he later recalled and wondered at) hole in the side of its head and it was still. He spent another minute watching to make sure its chest did not show signs of breathing and there was no twitching or body movement. He looked to Anika. She was crying silent tears. He took the ammunition and pistol (careful to avoid even the slightest contact with the trigger) and lay them on the Citroen's roof to hug her. 'You have done the right thing and it was not your fault, you could never have missed it. There was nothing you could have done. There's no pain for it anymore.'

She kept her hands to her sides but pressed her head into his neck for a few seconds before mumbling, 'Sorry,' and pulling away from Richard with a deep breath.

'We should take the gun home. It's only ten minutes back,' he said.

'It's okay. It's safe without ammunition. We should go on to see the puppies. Jennifer wants to. I want to. Do you think it was running from that?' Anika motioned over to the horizon with smoke hanging as she took the pistol and ammunition from the car's roof.

'Maybe.'

'Stupid animal. Come.' She wiped her face with her t-shirt and went round to the driver's door, asking Jennifer if she was okay as she climbed behind the wheel and dropped the pistol into the door pocket beside her. She took the two rounds from the box and slipped them into her back pocket. Richard didn't hear Jennifer's answer; he was taking a last look to make sure the deer had not moved. Satisfied it was dead he sat in the front, next to Anika.

'Well, it is Friday the thirteenth,' she said, starting the car, 'and Dudek will be upset his car is damaged. He loves this car. You can tell him.' She looked at Richard who pretended not to see her new tears and thought about this new story he had to tell Malcolm when he went home.

The farm was a couple of miles further. Anika drove cautiously and they were silent save for Jennifer giving directions. Radio One played 'Here Comes The Sun', but it was never going to lift their mood.

Jennifer's friend lived on her family's farm a few miles outside of Oakjack Ford, on the boundary of the New Forest. They turned off the lane and onto a small track, the Citroen bouncing on the hard, rutted earth until Anika had to slow to a crawl. A couple of hundred yards up, a wooden five bar gate blocked the way. Jennifer left the car to open it and walked the rest of the way to the farmhouse, the Citroen following. The house was at the end of a collection of farm buildings and barns. Before they reached it two large black and white dogs appeared from a stable to bark at the visitors. Anika stopped the car. A girl (Jennifer's age, Richard assumed, though he was still to find out what that was) in jeans and wellingtons, despite the heat, came from the farmhouse and welcomed Jennifer. They chattered excitedly. Anika and Richard left the Citroen and Jennifer introduced them to Linda; red-face, red-hair and wide smile. She chatted quickly and incessantly and Richard liked her accent, which Jennifer adopted. Linda showed them the way to the barn where the puppies were kept, and introduced them to a menagerie on the way: dogs, chickens, ducks, one lazy cat and two horses. Richard hoped she wouldn't test them on the names - especially the chickens and ducks. Linda's mother came out of a small shed, leading yet another dog, and said hello with enthusiasm to equal her daughter's. She offered squash and shouted over to a thin man in blue coveralls who was cleaning a rusty tractor in the corner of the yard. The man looked up from the engine - Larry. He froze on seeing Richard and Anika and didn't answer the first offer of a cold drink but Linda's mother shouted again and he nodded. Anika nudged Richard (who nodded to indicate he had seen) while keeping the conversation with Linda's mum flowing. Larry stared at them and Richard stared back, hoping it appeared confident, not arrogant. Linda's mum left them to make drinks and Jennifer said to her friend, 'I didn't know Larry was here.'

'Larry? He does a couple days a week here now. Labouring and cleaning. Cash in hand I 'spect.'

'Where else would it go?' asked Anika.

Linda looked at her, said, 'Come on,' and led them into the main barn. The smell of animals and urine and manure and damp was strong but not unpleasant and the shade was welcome. Close to the barn's double door entrance was a pen where a litter of puppies tottered and climbed over and around a tired looking bitch. The puppies were mostly grey and white and as cute as expected. Jennifer and Anika 'aaaahed', Richard resisted. Linda was very proud. 'She's such a good mum. Six puppies. All doing well. Another seven or eight weeks and they can go. What d'ya think?'

'Adorable,' said Jennifer, 'can I go in?'

'Yes. They fed fifteen minutes ago, so they'll be awake for a little while and nap. It's a hard life.' Linda opened the pen's gate and they all entered. Jennifer knelt and three puppies came to explore. She picked one up; it was not much bigger than her hand and licked as she put her nose to its face. Richard missed Ossie, his dog. Anika picked up two puppies and gave one to Richard. The puppies were excited and their visitors besotted, so much that for a few minutes Richard ignored Larry and the collision with the deer was forgotten. Anika was smiling again. In less than five minutes Jennifer had chosen one and changed her mind at least three times and Richard hinted strongly a puppy would make a good companion for Dudek; Anika whispered Elizabeth would make a better one. Linda's mother brought squash and they stood outside the pen (apart from Jennifer) agreeing how sweet they all were and Jennifer offered to take two, one of which would be for Richard but she would look after it for him as it was too far to take back home. Larry stood by the tractor. The puppies slowed and huddled on and around the bitch, causing even more 'ooohing' and 'aaaahing', even from Linda's mum and they started whispering.

'Will your nan let you have one?' Linda asked Jennifer.

'I think so. I'll ask her for sure tonight. After dinner, if she's in a good mood.'

'What about you Richard? Would you really like one?' Linda's mother asked him.

'I'd love one, but I already have a dog at home, Ossie. I don't think my mum'd be happy.'

'You'll have to visit regularly to see Jennifer's,' she said kindly, and collected their now empty beakers. They strolled from the barn and squinted into the bright sunshine, discussing names for Jennifer's puppy (the second smallest one with the white flash under its chin) - Geddy was still first choice but Jaybee a close second. Linda's mother said goodbye and left them at the Citroen. As she took the beakers into the house Larry came over. Richard's chest tightened and he forced himself to stand tall. Larry loitered just out of range while Linda said her goodbyes but when she went to open the gate he approached.

'What is it with you? Wherever I go you fucking turn up. Old Dudek told you to keep an eye on me has he? Wants to know what I'm doing? Where I am?'

Anika moved close enough to Larry to whisper, 'Fuck off. Leave Dudek alone.'

Larry flinched at the venom in Anika's words but didn't move. 'That old fucker wanted me to believe him. He's a lying shit and I'll fucking do him one day. I'll fucking have 'im.' Larry spoke quietly so not to draw attention from Linda. He turned to Richard, 'Fuck Queen Dudek. And fuck you.'

In fear, rather than anger, Richard clenched a fist. He wanted this to be over, for Larry to be gone, but he couldn't walk first, just couldn't. Jennifer was speechless.

Larry pushed Richard in the chest, not enough to unbalance or hurt him, but enough to provoke. Before there was any reaction Anika shouldered him aside. 'Enough. You …. shit. I've had enough.' Before Larry came back at her she reached into the Citroen and took the pistol from the door pocket. She pointed it at him, who did a double-take at the black metal and tried to change the shock in his face to a smile; it stayed a grimace. Anika spoke as calmly as when shooting the deer earlier.

'Get in the car. I'm going to take you to a quiet place in the forest, where you won't be found.' The last few words were slow and deliberate.

Larry was scared and speechless. Richard remembered to breathe and took a couple of steps to move beyond Anika, saying to Larry, 'It's true. She will. She's Czech and can be on a plane home by tomorrow morning. They won't find your body for a few days and she'll be long gone. You better get in the car or she'll do it here anyway.'

Anika ushered Richard out of the way as Linda turned from opening the gate and screamed to see the pistol. Larry dropped to his knees. Anika bent over him to whisper again, 'Don't ever talk to me, my friends or family again or I will fucking kill you.'

She climbed into the Citroen and drove to the gate where she stopped and apologised to Linda while waiting for Richard and Jennifer to join her. Larry still knelt. Linda's mother had heard the scream and was running to the car. Richard heard Anika tell Linda, 'I'm sorry. There's been a mis-understanding between my uncle and Larry but it's okay. It's just a toy.' She showed the gun to Linda and tossed it on the back seat as Jennifer climbed in.

No-one in the Citroen spoke until they reached the lane, and Anika laughed quietly to herself, pleased with her game. She patted Richard's leg. 'You did well. He believed it. He is a …. what you say…. prat?'

'Yep, he's a prat. That won't be the end though, will it? He'll tell Erica.'

'I will go and speak to her first. Explain.'

'Good luck with that,' Jennifer said.

'She is my friend.'

'Was your friend. You're mad.' Jennifer passed the pistol to Richard.

'If only he knew it wasn't loaded,' said Richard.

'Wasn't it?' Anika asked innocently.

'You took the rounds out.'

'Oh, I forgot.' She laughed again and Richard didn't know if she meant it. Richard saw they were driving home a different way and wouldn't pass the dead deer.

'Anyway. What is Larry's problem? So he and Dudek argued over money or something. Gotta let it go,' said Jennifer.

'It is a long story. Dudek has tried to be kind to him. He didn't understand.' Anika shrugged.

'Who didn't understand? Larry or my uncle?'

'Perhaps both.' Anika shrugged her shoulders again and turned on the radio. 'Oh, I like this very much.' She turned up the volume for 'Dancing Queen'.

Chapter 13
Lesson Four, Part Two

Alan Freeman's Saturday radio show had finished over an hour ago and Richard was tinkering on the Bontempi, hoping to reproduce something resembling anything he'd heard, anything at all. It wasn't practise but Duded popped into the back room now and again to offer encouragement and praise and to remind him it was how to make his mum proud. Not that she wasn't proud anyway, of course, and, regardless of his soon to be received CSE and O Level results, Dudek was sure there would be a place in sixth form for him. Richard guessed there must have been a phone call from mum to his uncle in the last day or so.

'How can you know uncle? What if I fail them all?' Richard looked up from the keyboard.

'You won't. And even if you do, it'll be okay with the school. Trust me, I know about these things and I've spoken with your mother. She is excited to be seeing the results soon.'

Richard fiddled tunelessly while trying to find the words to start the conversation he wanted. 'But if I fail them why would anyone pay the school fees for sixth form? Was my father that much of a hero?'

Dudek moved to the other side of the table so his back was to the garden. 'Of course he was that much a hero. And more. Don't worry for the money. They will want you in their school. If you want to go.' He went out into the garden before further questioning. Richard pushed his chair away from the Bontempi. His uncle had side-stepped again and worse, raised the spectre of September. The last two weeks had been so full as to smother any thought of a future beyond a day or two. He didn't know what he wanted to do when summer ended and, despite his uncle's confidence, surely his results (lack of) must play a part. He went out to the patio. Dudek sat in shade, sipping from a glass, a half empty bottle of Black Label on the table. Richard must have shown unconscious disapproval. Dudek said, 'I know, it is early for a drink, but nearly five and the most beautiful evening.'

It was. Even the occasional bark from Bluey, gardens along, was gentle and well-placed - an addition to the peace, not a disruption. Richard sat opposite Dudek, 'Uncle, do you ....'

'I know, I understand. You want to ask, I understand. Anika told me what happened yesterday. The deer and Larry at the farm. Stupid, stupid animal, and so was the deer.' He tried to make a joke but Richard didn't understand. Dudek continued, 'It was right to kill the deer, don't you think? But .... bad .... to threaten Larry as she did, and I hear you played your part well and it was funny, was it not?' He laughed and Richard enjoyed the praise. 'But you want to know why Larry .... feels .... an anger.'

Richard nodded, though this wasn't the reason he had followed his uncle out to the garden.

'It is .... complicated. It is true I asked Larry to fix the fence, but more because he is a young man who needed .... needs, help, and perhaps a start. I thought I could help and perhaps offered the wrong way and he is .... emotional and I didn't handle it well, so we should think more kindly of him.'

Richard carried on nodding but was none the wiser. Before he could ask Dudek pushed himself to his feet. 'And now I must go. My ankle is much better and I am going to drive Anika to the pub. She is working this evening and is helping to set up. Anika!' He called unnecessarily as she stood in the door. She wore her favourite flared jeans and tie-dye t-shirt, tied in a knot to show her flat stomach. 'You need to change, surely,' said Dudek, 'we don't want to spend all day tomorrow turning young men away from the door. Do we Richard?'

'Er …. no, I suppose not.'

'It's okay. This is for cleaning. I have a dress to change into. The red one. Is that okay?'

'It's a bit …. low cut,' Richard said.

'You don't need to be jealous. Don't you know that yet?' she said and went back inside. Dudek followed, limping less and complaining of the damage to the Citroen. Richard heard Anika blaming the stupid, stupid animal.

The house was quiet, the garden serene and Richard bored. He checked the clocks in the kitchen (it was five-thirty and Dudek was not back, perhaps he was visiting Elizabeth) and noticed Kon Tum was running a little fast and Istanbul a little slow. He adjusted them using London as the baseline. He heard Bluey barking again and went to the bottom of the garden, but Bluey wasn't there and the barking stopped. He kicked a stone out of the dried earth surrounding the pond (had it shrunk a little more?) and tried to make it skip to the other side but it was precisely the wrong shape. He found a place on the sparse grass to lay and stare at the cloudless blue above. Shadows were encroaching but it was still hot and he wiped sweat from his forehead, from under his heavy fringe, and wished he'd had a haircut and thought he would ask Anika to do it in the morning. There was a rustle from his right and he turned. Jennifer pushed her way through the brown reeds.

'Shame. I was hoping to surprise you, make you jump. You look so relaxed.'

'You did. But I'm an expert at hiding reactions.'

'And emotions? Not surprised. Living here.' She half-smiled.

'Here?'

'Oakjack.'

'Oh. Why'd you come that way?' Richard sat up and pointed back towards the reeds.

'For a change.' She sat next to him. Richard lay back down. She copied him.

'See any fires?'

'Nah. But heard the fire engine go through the village earlier. Elizabeth won't let me go help the beaters.'

'Good.'

After a minute or two Jennifer said, 'We could've called the vet yesterday.'

'The vet?'

'To the deer. They might've done something.'

'No. You saw it. Too much …. damage. Horrible. It was never gonna live. Anika was right ….'

'Anika …. Where is she?'

'Working in the pub tonight. Lucky she knew about Dudek's pistol. Would've taken all three of us to throttle the poor thing.'

'I suppose.'

They fell silent again until Richard said, 'Not a cloud to work with.'

'Eh?'

He pointed vaguely to the sky. 'Not a single cloud to try and make into a shape. Not a car, a guitar, monkey, elephant, boat ….'

'…. deer, gun. Nope, not a single cloud.'

'Do you think that model ship I …. took, is still on the bench at the bus stop?'

'Model ship? You mean toy. Nah, someone's probably stolen it. Bloody cheek. We could check if you like.'

'Too far. Can't be arsed. It is bad about the deer though. You okay?'

'Not really.'

'Nice puppies though.'

'Yeah.'

'I miss Ossie.'

'Ossie? Oh yeah, Ossie. Honest, I could ask Elizabeth if we can have two puppies and you can have one and I'll take care of it and you can visit.'

'Nice thought. But it's a long way and I doubt your nan wants two dogs. Have you asked about yours yet?'

'Almost. We're not talking much at the moment. I asked her when she was gonna tell me about Maisie being my great aunt. Maisie was there as well. I wanted an argument but the two of them just sat there, calm, talking quiet. They'd been waiting for me to ask. Anika told Elizabeth.'

'Told her what?'

'I knew about Maisie, from Anika. She should have told me.'

'Who? Elizabeth?'

'No, Anika. She should have told me she'd tell Elizabeth and yes, Elizabeth should have told me, before.'

There was a brief silence. Richard looked at her, 'That's very complicated. I'm not sure I follow.'

'Is that 'cos you're …. dys …. dysil …. wass the word?'

'Dyslexic? No. How do you know?'

'Your mum must have told Dudek who told Anika who told Elizabeth who told me. Easy.'

'When?'

'I don't know.'

'Seems you can't trust anyone down here.'

'Does it matter?' Jennifer asked.

'What? The trust or being dyslexic?'

'Both.'

'Nah, not really,' Richard laughed weakly.

'Which?'

'Both. Ha ha.'

'Hang on. Wass that?' Jennifer pointed to a wisp of white in the sky.

'A shit attempt at a cloud. Not even a ball of cotton wool, which is the least a cloud can be. So you're not speaking to your nan?'

'Or my great aunt, which is funny as I didn't even have one a few days ago and now I'm already not talking to her. I miss my mum and dad. Can you miss what you never had? They …. they say not.'

'They know fuck-all.'

Richard slid his hand across the grass and took hers.

A long, slow, rich note from Young Samuel's saxophone floated to the pond, washing into Richard thoughts as he contemplated how hard (if at all) to squeeze Jennifer's tiny hand. 'Samuel's early this evening.' He sat up but still held Jennifer's hand though it was awkward for both of them.

'Doesn't it drive you crazy, every day?'

Richard shrugged. 'I don't suppose it will be for much longer. Either the summer will finish or Megan will ….'

'Come on.' Jennifer let go of his hand to stand but took it again as they sneaked past the pond's edge, into Samuel's garden and up to the bunker. 'Not as comfy as my den, is it?' she whispered as they crawled in.

'And colder.'

They edged to the letter-box window. Samuel was in his usual deck-chair, saxophone to his mouth, bottle of wine on the floor beside him. The oxygen bottle stood by one of the trees with the tube leading to the hammock. It was a familiar scene and some of Samuel's playing was familiar, but slower and with longer gaps between songs. He played a lingering version of 'The Last Waltz' (one of the few tunes Richard recognised), swapped the saxophone for the bottle of wine and swigged long. Samuel's eyes were rimmed red, his hands shook and, for a second it seemed he stared straight through the long grasses and into the bunker. Jennifer dropped to the hard earth and sat with her back against the bunker wall, pulling Richard down next to her. He waited a few seconds before easing up to peek. Samuel was still drinking and staring and Richard could see his teary stare saw nothing. Jennifer pulled him back down. The last time they had been this close Anika interrupted before …. before what? He hadn't known where that would lead; or this. She smelt of the perfume he had stolen. He put his arms around her and cuddled before pulling away to give enough room to kiss. She reacted and pressed against him. Lacking any finesse (which he thought a good thing) and with honest, naïve passion, they kissed and pressed and touched. Until the loud sob. And another. And another. Richard ignored it but there was another and another and Jennifer eased away from him, re-fastening the button on her blouse. Though Richard had little experience of 'the moment', it was clear 'it' had passed. They listened for the next sob. It didn't come but the sobs had been raw and the silence was heavy. They knelt to see. Samuel's top half was mostly hidden behind low branches as he hunched over one end of the hammock. He murmured rhythmically but the words were indistinct. Richard thought Samuel was repeating 'sorry, sorry, sorry,' but couldn't be sure. The tube from the oxygen bottle lay at his feet and the tiny bulge that was Megan's frail outline trembled, wrapped in the hanging bed, almost a shroud. Samuel went quiet and stood, dropping a pillow to the floor. He stepped away, picked up the pillow again and hunched again over the hammock for maybe half a minute. It swung as he bent away from it to drink again from the bottle. He finished the contents, dropped the bottle and picked Megan gently from the hammock; the pillow fell to the earth. He cradled her as the most precious cargo and carried her back into the house.

'Fuckin' hell,' said Jennifer.
'Fuckin' hell,' echoed Richard.
'Some might say.'

Jennifer lit a cigarette and Richard stifled a laugh. 'Aren't you meant to smoke after …. you know? Not after …. that.' He gestured to the letter box window.

Jennifer laughed nervously and offered a cigarette which he refused, though if ever there was a time to start, he thought this was it.

Jennifer had smoked half the cigarette before asking, 'So, did he really …. you know?'

'I think so. Don't you?'

'Nah. No way. People don't just …. you know, do they?'

'Nah. Even so, shouldn't we tell …. someone? Just in case.'

'I suppose.'

Dudek smiled as Richard and Jennifer found him in the kitchen, chopping at a raw steak. 'Ah, there you are. Tonight we will have a goulash. Jennifer, there is enough for you to join us, but I have just come from your grandmother's and she expects you home for dinner. You could ring her though.'

'Er, thanks, no. I better go home.'

'Okay. But welcome anytime. Are you hungry Richard?'

'Yeah, although, before you …. we …. I wanted to …. we …. needed to …. tell you …. about Samuel ….'

Dudek continued hacking at the meat but asked, 'Samuel? I heard him earlier. He is quiet now. Probably a good thing. I think his playing has …. peaked.'

'Yeah. Much quieter now. But, earlier, a little while ago, we think he …. might have ….' Richard looked at Jennifer, hoping she had a better word, but she shrugged so he said, '…. suffocated …. her. Megan.'

'What do you mean?'

'We saw him and Megan, and he …. it looked like he ….'

216

'…. suffocated her?

'Yes.'

'As in ….' Dudek put down the knife and mimed closing his hands and squeezing.

'No, with a pillow, we think. Don't we?' Richard asked Jennifer for support. She nodded. Dudek sat at the kitchen table and motioned to Richard and Jennifer to join him and tell their story. It didn't take long and though Richard was worried Dudek would want to know why they were in the bunker in the first place, he didn't question them. Instead he asked them to repeat exactly what they had seen. He listened carefully and repeated it back to them and, the way he told it, probably the oxygen bottle had run out (again - stupid Samuel) and the pillow behind her head simply couldn't be made comfortable, so he took her inside. And of course Samuel looked and sounded upset, the woman he loves is dying, isn't she? So, nothing to worry about, no need for them to fret and until they know more, they shouldn't assume anything and could Jennifer say thank you to her nan for the tea and scone, just an hour earlier.

Richard walked Jennifer to the front door and she said goodbye with a kiss (not a peck) on his cheek. Back in the kitchen Dudek was back to preparing his 'renowned' goulash, and casually asked Richard to tell again, what he had seen and what, if anything, he might have imagined.

The goulash was as delicious as Dudek promised and they ate from trays on their laps in the living room, watching Seaside Special; even after so many years living among them, Dudek was amused at how easily amused were the English. After washing up, Dudek insisted they play chess and predicted Richard would win if he kept filling up his uncle's glass with Scotch. As Dudek won the third game in a row, Anika came home from her shift in the pub, remarking there was an ambulance outside Samuel's and asking if they'd heard anything and wondering if they should go next door to see if help was needed. Dudek suggested not and indicated to Richard he should tell Anika. When Richard finished they went to the front sitting room (in darkness) and looked out the window for the ambulance, but in the darkness couldn't see through the bushes into Samuel's drive.

Richard went to bed, leaving Dudek and Anika to speculate. At first, visions of Samuel and Megan were intrusions but he worked through Dudek's interpretation and moved his thoughts to re-live the encounter with Jennifer in the bunker; the memory progressed further into fantasy and he slept well.

Although he was on the top floor Richard heard the doorbell chime. He put down the magazine and stood at his bedroom door. It was just past nine and he had been awake nearly an hour, flicking through the Melody Maker's pictures and listening for signs Dudek and Anika were up. From the landing outside his bedroom door he leant over to see the stairs down to the hallway. The doorbell chimed again and he heard Anika's bedroom door open. She came out, pulling on a light dressing gown and tying it at the waist as she descended. She looked up and smiled at him - that familiar, slightly crooked smile that teased and welcomed in equal measure. He heard her call for Dudek as she showed Samuel into the front sitting room. Richard's breathing shortened and his pulse quickened. He assumed Samuel was there to confront him over the ridiculous claim he, Samuel, could possible contemplate murdering his beloved Megan and how dare he spy on them in his own garden. And even though Richard doubted Samuel had seen him and Jennifer, a fear took hold and grew and it seemed yesterday's events must have been an imagining; it was too horrible to believe it had been real. He was embarrassed at his claims and wanted to go to Jennifer to ask what she now believed. He shrank back from the bannisters as Dudek left his room and hobbled down the stairs. The three of them stayed in the sitting room; Richard heard nothing of their conversation, but it was only a few minutes until Anika came out and upstairs. She saw Richard at the very top of the stairs and said, 'Samuel has asked if I will go with him to church this morning. There is a Sunday Mass at Holy Redeemer, Christchurch. He is not much of a believer but Megan ....was .... and he thinks today is a good day to start, perhaps. And I have persuaded your uncle to come with us. Will you?'

'So Megan is ....' Richard nearly smiled with relief he hadn't misinterpreted so badly.

'....gone. Yes. Are you coming?'

'No. Thanks, but no.'

'Of course. Though you are not so young as you might think now,' she said and went into the bathroom leaving him to wonder at her cryptic comment. He was anxious to know what would happen to Samuel now Megan was .... gone, and what it might mean for him, but Anika's attitude was calming and Dudek smiled at him as he came back upstairs, leaving Samuel downstairs.

Richard waited until Anika had finished in the bathroom before washing and cleaning his teeth. As he came out, Anika was leaving her bedroom, dressed for church in a simple dark blue dress, with little shape and a high neck. She wore black shoes with a small heel and barely a touch of eyeliner - but if she was hoping to appear formal and, perhaps, severe, she failed in Richard's eyes when she smiled and said she'd see him later. Dudek shouted a goodbye and when he heard the front door close behind them and the Citroen drive away he went to the kitchen for breakfast. Time passed slowly (watching all five clocks in the kitchen didn't help).

Just before mid-day (London time - seven pm in Kon Tum already) the doorbell rang again. It was Jennifer and Elizabeth. Jennifer smiled at him but Elizabeth was serious and asked for Dudek.

'He's at church, with Anika and …. Samuel.'

'Church? Dudek? Can we wait?' she asked, though her manner made Richard's permission redundant. Richard showed them through to the patio and offered them tea or coffee, which they refused. The guests sat opposite each other at the patio table and Richard didn't know whether to sit close to Jennifer, or even on the same side of the table, so settled for the low brick wall marking the patio's edge. He worried if Elizabeth was so serious because Jennifer had told of their intimacy or Samuel's actions and was then ashamed to put the two things on a par. Elizabeth sensed his discomfort, saying, 'I heard about Megan. Jennifer wasn't …. clear …. about what happened yesterday, but it's all over the village this morning, what with the ambulance and all. Though, of course, no-one else knows you and Jennifer …. saw …. something.'

Richard nodded and thought he was expected to say something but wanted to know what Jennifer had said; his guilt at being in the bunker at all was growing. He was saved by Dudek's warm welcome as he limped from the kitchen, Anika behind him. Dudek touched Elizabeth on the shoulder as he said hello, took off his suit jacket, loosened his tie and sighed as he sat next to her. 'So you know?'

'Yes Dudek, and it's a concern Jennifer and your nephew should have been so …. close to what might have happened.'

'Or might not. But yes. A concern.' He turned to Anika and there must have been some kind of signal, for she went inside. Dudek pulled his chair closer to Elizabeth's. 'But they are of an age to understand. Perhaps still children but not childish.'

Anika came back out, carrying three glasses and a bottle of Black Label. Dudek reached for the bottle but Elizabeth stopped him, saying simply, 'Dudek. We spoke.'

He sighed again, knowing she was right and Anika took it away.

'And especially not today,' said Elizabeth. 'There will be questions, surely. Is Samuel home?'

'No. He didn't come back with us. He wanted to find time to …. talk to the Father, at the church.'

'Most in the village assume Megan passed peacefully but if …. not, it won't be secret for long.'

'We don't know it wasn't peaceful. Samuel came to see us this morning. He is a torn, broken man. Megan's pain has been growing. The painkillers were not working and she was wasting and crippled and exhausted. But the worst, for him, was seeing how much she hurt, watching him.'

'Watching him?' Elizabeth asked.

'Yes, she had to watch his heart break. No matter how hard he tried to hide it, his own heart was crushed and for her to see that was even worse than her pain. Whatever strength she had left was drained by watching Samuel's heart crack more each day, with every song he played on his saxophone, every time he carried her to bed, every time she begged for more painkillers he couldn't give. Her dying was killing the one she loved.'

Anika brought a tray with a pitcher of squash and glasses and poured for all. Dudek took a sip, made a face to show he didn't like the taste. Richard caught Jennifer's eye. She was as serious as Elizabeth. Dudek continued, 'This last week, it was too much. She begged Samuel for the last favour to save them both from the pain, and to help her from this world into whatever is to follow. This way, he always has the good memories and when he thinks of her, when he plays the saxophone, when he lies in the hammock, he will bring her back to happiness just by thinking of her, happy, calm, free of pain. It needed to be done before it was too much and he hated her for destroying his heart and she hated him, having to watch it break.'

'So he …. killed her.' Elizabeth used the 'K' word they had all avoided so far.

Dudek shrugged, 'Last night he played for her, her favourite song, 'The Last Waltz', she loved to dance when she was young, and he held her so tightly she couldn't breathe but she didn't struggle and she went so easily and quickly he has to believe it was a release. As she went I'm sure she loved him more than ever.'

'And the pillow? Doesn't sound easy.'

'The pillow was behind her head, not over her face. He needed to keep her comfortable as he held her so tightly. He didn't want to hurt the back of her neck.'

'And you believe him?'

'I do.' Dudek was breathing heavily in the heat and sweating. 'And I think he was a brave man. Megan understood what it took for Young Samuel to do that and she wasn't scared of …. dying …. because he can bring her back whenever he wants.' Dudek smiled but Richard thought it more to himself than his audience. Anika looked to Richard, as if seeking to make sure he was okay. Richard nodded. He saw questions in Elizabeth's eyes but Jennifer spoke first,

'So you believe he can bring her back?' she asked in confusion.

'You are young. For sure he can.' Dudek was confident and tapped his heart and then his head.

'But what happens when Samuel forgets …. or …. or dies?'

'Ah, he will never forget such a love …. but when he dies? The real Megan will go with him. It is sad. We can store time for a short while and use it again for ourselves, re-live it, but we can't give it to others. It is the difference between a true memory and a picture.'

Richard didn't understand but didn't know what questions to ask and they sat in silence. Elizabeth was calmer and muttered something about getting back to

Maisie but had a parting concern, 'The police may want to talk to Jennifer and Richard.'

'How would they know?' Dudek asked.

Elizabeth and Jennifer left. Anika brought out the Black Label, a pint glass full of water and two empty glasses. Dudek thanked her and poured generous measures for them both before adding some of the water. Anika went to change and came back outside in a light cotton dress. She sat at the patio and waved Richard to join them, saying it was too hot to be out in the sun. She downed the Scotch in two gulps and poured water from the pint glass into her tumbler. 'So, what people will do for love eh? Take life.' She tried to lift the tension. Dudek didn't react and she said, more seriously, 'Does not get .... more .... than that?' She made it a question, unsure of the phrasing.

'No, does not get ... more.... than that,' agreed Richard, offering support.

'Ha. What do you know? Just a girl,' Dudek said to Anika, but in a kindly way, not patronizing or with criticism. 'The things people do for love? Ha. The things I have seen. The things I have done.'

'For love?' Anika.

'And hate,' he took a long swig from his Scotch, 'but mostly for love.' He raised his glass. 'To Megan. May she rest in peace and be alive in Samuel's heart, what's left of it. And to Samuel, may he survive the storm to come.'

'To Megan and Samuel,' agreed Anika.

Richard raised his glass of squash and asked, 'Will Samuel go to prison?'

'I hope not. He is a good friend. But I don't think he will care anyway. He will be strong for Megan. I saw it in his eyes. There was a deep resolve; last time I saw such resolve was in your father's face, last time I saw him ....' his voice tailed off.

'My father?'

'Anika, a refill please,' he held his up his glass and Anika obliged. He seemed to be weighing up what, or how much, he should say and sighed, possibly swayed by Richard's pleading eyes.

'Your father, Greguska, understood what it meant to do anything for love, for your mother. He loved her. They were …. drawn together by the angels and everyone was both jealous and …. happy. Jealous because who didn't want such total love and passion but happy because it was a bad time in a bad world and how had these two come together? It had to be a miracle and who doesn't like a miracle? Especially the Catholics eh? Ha, and today, I went to church. Who would have thought? After so many, many years.' Dudek started on a tangent; Richard brought it back.

'My mum and dad. This is back in Vietnam, right?'

'Yes. Kon Tum. It had a fine Catholic church.'

'Mum never says what happened. Why was he there?'

'Why? Mostly because of me, his big brother. We were both there. Why? The reasons go back many, many years. Back to the wars and how did two brothers from a small village in Czechoslovakia come to be with British Intelligence? Long story. I don't know if I even remember why, or perhaps I'd rather not. It's not a story of men being good or doing good things. Maybe we placed too high a value on freedom of others.'

'Uncle, you're rambling.'

'I know. Sorry. We came to Vietnam in late fifty eight, for British Military Intelligence, though of course intelligence was …. limited, especially in the British Military.' He paused, waiting, but there was no response. 'You're supposed to laugh. No matter. They sent us to Kon Tum, near the borders for Laos, Cambodia and South Vietnam. There was talk the Communists were building up the Ho Chi Minh trail and Greguska and I were supposed to gather information and pass it on to the Americans.

They had their own people there as well, but I guess the British owed them something. Anyway, we were there. It was a mess, but we were good in a mess. Does that make sense? It's why the British recruited us at the end of the war. Doesn't matter now. One way or another, we came to Vietnam. Diu's father, your grandfather, was wealthy, in a place and time when few were. Very few. He made his money walking a wire between right and wrong, mostly wrong. When the communists were getting organised and the government in the south were learning they should be scared, your grandfather tried to keep both sides happy, hoping to keep his wealth. Foolish. Greguska and I were pretending to run an import export business, though what in God's name we were supposed to be moving in or out of Vietnam in fifty eight I have no idea, but the British thought it good enough cover. We were to gather information on what the communists were doing and pass it to the Americans. Your grandfather was trying to keep everyone happy and we thought he could help. He was in business, moving stuff on the trail, we were in business; it was easy to pretend we were .... helping each other and even easier to .... blackmail .... him into sharing his contacts and information. It was not a good place to be in those days. Hot and dangerous and too many .... fanatics. Too many people ready to help someone die for someone else's cause. That's when it's most dangerous. People happy to die for their own causes are easy to spot and .... deal with. But when the cause is someone else's, in another place, it's not so easy; they believe no less but hide. Very dangerous ....'

Richard didn't follow his uncle. He wanted to understand and started to ask a question but Dudek waved a hand,

'.... doesn't matter now. Another day I tell more. Now, you want to know about Greguska?'

Richard nodded. 'Of course. Mum says so little, I don't know what I'm supposed to know.'

'Okay, so your grandfather was in difficult place. Between the government, the communists and your father and me, he was easy to use, even though I was …. uncomfortable. Then Greguska met your Mother. She had been studying in the north at Hanoi Conservatory and came home. She was, is, beautiful and I was even more uncomfortable …. she was younger than Greguska. He had to use all his Czech charm to win her. She was young and pretty and smart and played the piano like we never heard. The only piano in Kon Tum. She was much too good for your Father,' Dudek smiled to show it was meant kindly, 'but Greguska had much charm and the only person who could stop her was her father and by now he was scared of me and Greguska. He was in …. how the Americans used to say ….. too deep. Deep shit. Anyway, they were in love and I knew it was dangerous but what can you tell a man in love? Or a girl? And it was too late. Sometime in the heat they had seduced each other and she was pregnant. You came three weeks early as I recall. Your grandfather cried and laughed and cried. Then, days later, the communists came for him. We had to run but it was slow with a new baby. Oh how you cried to be hungry and slept so little. The British had a way out for us and we nearly made it. But Greguska made me take Diu and you while he went back to your grandfather's house to see what, if anything he had told them. Afterwards, I heard from the Americans, the house was burning and Greguska found your grandfather on a table, in the kitchen ….' Dudek drained his glass and motioned to Anika for a refill, '…. on a table. He was ….. dead and by the terrible wounds, Greguska had to believe he told them everything. I'm sorry.' He stopped to lean forward and brush Richard's hand.

Richard hadn't known his grandfather and didn't know if he should be shocked or sad or angry; in truth, he was fascinated.

'And Greguska knew he must get back to me and your mother. Although your grandfather didn't know where we were hiding we could trust no-one, there would be a trail to us. Someone always talked. Greguska's love would have made him rush and he was too eager to get back to us and too easy to follow. It was easy for them to pick him up. They wanted to know where Diu was. They did not want your grandfather's daughter still alive. I don't know if they knew of you. If not your grandfather must have been very brave not to have spoken of you. When your father didn't come back to us I knew he had been taken and the British came and moved you and your mother on to the next place for your escape. I went back for your father. I was too late.' Uncle Dudek stopped and took a deep breath. 'And so, nephew, you should hate me for not being the one who went back, first to find out about your grandfather and then more quickly for your father. He should be here, not me.'

'What do you mean, too late? What happened to him?' Richard's fascination was turning to excitement. He didn't quite believe it was his father Dudek talked of; it wasn't real to him.

'.... When Greguska was taken he understood he would not be able to stay silent. He took the pill we had both been carrying all these years and it would have ended quickly for him and I believe he would have been happy, knowing it meant you and your mother escaped ....' He stopped talking to choke back a sob. Anika slipped beside him and took away his tumbler, rubbing his back because what else was there? 'So, my little brother's special one, you see the things we will do for love.'

Richard was embarrassed his fascination had turned to excitement and then, in the silence, was overwhelmed with confusion and a deep, deep sorrow for a father he would never know and for a mother that might never understand. And it never really could be all right, after all, no matter how many times she told him.

'Lesson four,' said Anika. 'You told us. Lesson four. Don't have people so close that you love them and die for them.'

'Does my mum know all this?' Richard asked his uncle.

'Not all, just that her Greguska never came back. She is a brave, special lady. For so many years I have thought whether to tell her. Is it better for her to know he took his own life?' Dudek looked to them as if for the answer but they were silent. 'Such a brave lady. And though she may wish it was me didn't come back, not once has she said or hinted.'

'Why wasn't it you?' Richard asked and it sounded more damning than intended.

'Good question. I was hurt. My ankle was …. damaged. But I look back now and should have gone anyway. Should have crawled rather than let Greguska go.' Dudek shook his head as tears came. 'And he is a hero. Few know of such heroes and what they will do for love.'

Richard tried not to cry. Though it was the right time for his tears, he needed to understand if they were tears of anger or self-pity or grief and whether they were for his uncle or his mother or himself.

Dudek stayed in his study for the rest of the day. Anika went to find Erica, to apologise for the argument with Larry at the farm (not to mention waving a pistol at him). Richard memorised a list of questions he had for his uncle. He thought he heard noise from next door, so perhaps Samuel was back, and wanted to apologise for watching while Samuel helped Megan to …. pass on (Dudek's phrase), but knew such an apology was for his own benefit, not Samuel's, who didn't even know he was there. He tried to nap but couldn't settle and thought of ringing his mum, but what could he say? Correction; he knew what could be said, but not how. He sat in the garden but the afternoon was uncomfortably hot and though he couldn't smell a heath fire there was a grey haze on the horizon at the back that could have been smoke. He found himself by the pond, standing ankle deep in the still water, brushing away insects. The water soothed and when he cooled he sat on the grass, where he and Jennifer had lain less than a day earlier. The sky was the same cloudless blue and the pond still a private oasis and he wished Jennifer was with him. Or Carol; she would have a pragmatic answer for any of his worries. He heard light footsteps behind him, coming through the long grass under the apple trees and twisted to see Anika. She sat without speaking. Richard asked, 'How was Erica?'

'Angry. Very angry. More by the time I left. I don't think she will help to keep Larry calm. I should not have gone to her. Are you okay? After seeing Samuel and .... Megan, yesterday? What he did or did not.'

'I don't know. It doesn't seem real. I'm not sure what we saw now. And I suppose I need to be, when the police ask.'

'They may not.'

'They will. I need to check with Jennifer. Did we really see it? Did we see the same thing?'

'It will pass. Such as it is, it is.'

'Is that an old Czech saying?'

'No. I said it in English, didn't I? Sometimes I think I'm speaking English but the words are Czech. I don't know if that means I have been here too long or not long enough.'

'When will you go home?'

'I don't know. Without Dudek I wouldn't be here at all. He made the arrangements. It was not easy. I suppose I will go when people are tired of me.'

'Long time,' Richard muttered.

'Pardon?'

He looked at her and flashed his best (he hoped) smile, 'A long time. Before people are tired, of you.'

'Thank you. You are sweet,' she stroked his cheek, 'and now you must blush, just a little .... good.'

Richard didn't look away from her slightly crooked nose and slightly crooked smile; Jenny might be prettier (just) but Anika was radiant and he was sad for Jennifer (guilt?). The melancholy may have shown as Anika said, 'I'm sorry about your father. He really was hero.'

'Did you know? All that Dudek told us this morning?'

'Some. He has spoken of his work before: Paris, Estonia, Istanbul, Vietnam. I know he worked there but he didn't speak of how your father .... died. Soon you will be proud, not sad.'

'I hope.'

'But maybe stay sad for your uncle. He wishes it was him, still in Vietnam.'

'So he pays for my school, and stuff, I suppose. Why keep it secret?'

'Don't think it a secret, but a kindness to your mother and it would be selfish to ask him why if he doesn't want to say.'

Richard frowned. Anika sounded so reasonable (as always) but he wasn't so sure she made sense. He looked at her, 'You make things black and white but I'm not sure they shouldn't sometimes be left grey.'

'I don't know what that means. You are speaking that funny English again.'

'I guess.' Then he was surprised to find himself asking, 'Why do you stay so pale?'

Anika laughed and looked at her bare arms and raised a leg. 'It's good to be different, isn't it?'

'You are. You're Czech. That makes you different.'

'Not where I come from.'

'Oh.'

'And don't forget, you are half Czech. You are not so different there, though I suppose you are half Vietnamese, which makes you different everywhere.'

'Except, Vietnam.'

'Exactly. You see.'

'Er, no.'

'That's okay. But when I leave you must remember you are Czech and come to visit your uncle. You know lesson four? Don't believe it. I don't. Dudek only says it because of your father. I wonder if you look like him. Dudek has an old picture in the safe. His brother and him. We should look later. Don't look so sad.'

From two gardens along they heard Bluey bark.

'Such a beautiful afternoon. I don't like to see you so sad. And I will miss you, when you go. Would you miss me if I went home?'

'Of course. Who else knows how to shoot deer?'

'Ha, funny. But you have Jennifer. Have you and Jennifer …. made …. love? She is young. If not, wait.'

'I don't know how old she is. My age I suppose.'

'Wait anyway. For someone …. like me …. for your first.'

'How do you know it would be my first?'

'So you and Jennifer have ….?'

'Not as such.'

'Then it would be your first. Your first should be with …. someone like me, on a beautiful afternoon, in the grass, by water. That would be a first time to remember. Do you think?'

Richard nodded, speechless.

Anika moved closer to him and a thrill of excitement pulsed through him. He was breathing fast and she kissed him slowly, pushing him to lay flat on the grass. He didn't resist; this was already out of his control. She slid her body across his and kissed again, biting his bottom lip and stroking his face and neck. His arousal was quick and obvious but he was not embarrassed and she pressed to him. He smelt her perfume. Her soft cheek nestled against his face. She was beyond compare.

'Oh shit,' she said and pushed away from him but still knelt astride. 'No. You will think it is because I am sorry for you, because of how your father died and you are upset about seeing Samuel …. you know. You are too young to have seen that. So you will look back and believe this is pity. It's not, but you won't believe. It won't be perfect. I'm sorry.'

'No. Honestly, it's fine ….' He looked up at her. The cotton dress was hitched up to her hips, showing her white thighs. The top four or five buttons of the dress were undone, exposing her neck and cleavage, though her breasts were still covered. He had only to reach up to brush their fullness. 'It's not pity. I believe you. I do.'

'I'm sorry. And now you will hate me for stopping. I'm sorry. Please believe me.' She was close to tears. 'There will be another time. A better time. And Jennifer is a pretty girl, but it is better you don't …. you know. For her and you.' She bent down and pecked him on the cheek before rolling away from him. 'We should make sure your uncle is okay. He has been thinking of sad things today, like you.' She stood and smoothed her dress. Richard watched. She offered him a helping hand. He took it and held it as they went back to the house.

Under the apple trees he asked, 'We aren't cousins, are we?'

'No. Of course not.'

'And will there be …. another time?'

'Of course.' She squeezed his hand and, all things considered, Richard felt it was a good way to end the day.

Chapter 14
No Safe Place

Jennifer looked pleased to see him. She came from behind the counter in the newsagent to meet him at the door, shouting to Big Bill, 'Popping out for a few minutes. No customers!' and asking Richard, 'You okay? You look ....' tired,' once they were outside.

'I'm okay ....'

'Really?'

'Not sure. You?'

'Okay. I suppose. Happy to be working today. Elizabeth is going on and on and on about why we shouldn't have been in the bunker. She says the police will want to know what we saw. She rang your uncle last night to talk again. I guess he persuaded her, again.'

'I heard. It's what he's good at. I saw Samuel in his garden this morning, putting away the hammock. I keep thinking I should tell him we were there. But uncle says wait and see what happens over the next few days. And now I'm wondering what we did see, and it's only two days ago.'

'Weird eh?'

'Weird. More I think of it, more I wonder if I imagined any of it. Did I? We?'

Jennifer shrugged. 'Maybe your uncle was right. Did we actually see .... you know?'

'Not as such, I guess.'

'Does it matter? Megan was gonna .... go ....
anyway, right?'

'Yeah, but even so .... if Samuel .... did ....'
Richard's voice tailed off, drowned by the clatter of a
heavy diesel engine as a tractor rumbled through Oakjack
Ford. The tractor trundled clumsily, pulling a trailer with a
gang of six young men, each carrying at least one fire
beater. The men in the trailer sat in two rows opposite
each other, without speaking; the tractor's engine was so
noisy as to prevent normal conversation and the lack of
interaction increased their appearance of intent. Richard
recognised none except Larry, who looked up to see
Jennifer and Richard as the tractor passed. Richard looked
away and asked Jennifer, '.... so what did we see? What if
the police do want to talk to us? Shouldn't we be saying
the same thing? Did we see the same thing?'

'Of course we saw the same thing. We're just not
sure what we saw. But I suppose we ....' Her voice faded
as she looked past Richard to the figure walking quickly
towards them.

'What's the matter?' Richard asked while Anika
caught her breath.

'The police just rang Dudek. They are coming to
talk to him, in a short while. Dudek said you should not be
worried, but until he knows what they know, says you
should not come home. I think your uncle is .... careful. It
is his way. They won't be long though. Why don't you two
go to Jenny's den?'

'Jennifer. Or Jen. Please not Jenny.'

'Sorry. Go to Jen's den. That sounds right. Jen's
den, ha. Anyway, just for a short while,' Anika said and
turned to walk quickly back to Dudek's.

Jennifer and Richard left the village, using the track
they'd walked before to the den. As they turned off the
road the Land Rover fire engine entered the other end of
the village. An older man in full fireman's uniform climbed
from the Land Rover and went into the first shop.

Ten minutes out of the village they turned into the field where Jennifer's den lay and followed the edge until reaching the part-camouflaged shed. The smell of the heath fire was strong here. Grey smoke drifted over their field but, as they followed the tree line bordering the field, they couldn't see from where it came. They heard the crackling of burning gorse. At the den they sat on the boxes. There was no excitement in being there. Jennifer turned on the transistor radio but there was not even a hiss. 'Shit,' said Jennifer, 'I forgot a battery, again. We'll have to make our own entertainment.' She looked at Richard. 'You're not gonna have a bad head again, are you?'

'Nah,' he said with false confidence.

'Good.' She moved closer to him but he thought of Anika.

'Hey, guess what?'

He waited for Jennifer to answer, 'Okay, what?'

'My dad poisoned himself.'

Silence.

'What? When?'

'Just after I was born. I mean, not right after. A couple of weeks or so. He really was a hero.'

'For poisoning himself?'

'No. For .... saving me and my mum. I've got a picture.'

'Of your dad saving you?'

'No ....'

'Not of him taking poison?' Jennifer asked with horror.

'No, dopey. Just a picture of him.' He pulled out a small black and white picture of his father and uncle. 'This is sometime in ninety fifty-seven, uncle thinks. In Istanbul. What do you think? He was early thirties. Do I look like him?'

'Which one is he?'

'On the left.'

Richard pointed to the tall figure wearing a dark suit and tie. He had light hair and it was hard to see much detail on his face but he was smiling at the camera and looked happy.

'Your hair's black,' said Jennifer, 'but there's something in the smile …. He really …. you know …. topped himself? Why? And why poison? That's not a good way.'

'He was in Vietnam, British Military Intelligence, on some operation and got caught. Rather than tell 'em where we were, he took poison. He really is a hero.' Richard said it with pride.

'He did that?'

'Yep.'

'He didn't have a gun to shoot himself?'

'Maybe that's not as definite?'

'What? Like he might miss or something?'

'I don't know.'

'At least you know a bit more about him. I still know fuck-all about mine, but I doubt he was any kind of hero. Your dad really …. killed himself?'

'Yep. Really.'

'Shit.'

'Yep. Shit.'

'No, I mean, shit, I forgot my cigarettes.'

'Do you need them?' Richard sniffed the air. 'Smells like all the heath is burning today.'

'And close.' Jennifer looked through hole in the roof. The sky was blue as ever but wisps of grey smoke blew across, low, only just clearing the den's roof. She stood to go to the door, and they heard urgent shouts; distant so they couldn't understand the words, but with unmistakable urgency.

'The fire beaters?' said Richard.

'I guess.'

They both stood just outside the door and the wisps of smoke grew heavier and lower and the shouts closer and louder.

'Should we go? We should. My radio,' said Jennifer and went back inside the den for her transistor. Richard waited outside. He jumped at a succession of loud cracks, almost machine gun-like, above the shouting of the fire-beaters. From behind the den he saw the first lick of a tall flame and black smoke, rushing, not billowing.

'Jennifer! Jenny! Come on. We gotta go.'

'No.'

Richard turned to see Larry. He wore an over-sized black jacket, was red in face and sweating. He carried a long fire-beater, holding it in two hands like a baseball bat. 'What, no Czech bitch to look after you?'

Richard tensed. Larry took a step and feinted to hit him with the beater. Richard heard Jennifer shout from behind, 'Larry! Fuck off or I'll tell your mum.'

Richard laughed, despite, or because of, his sudden fear. Larry didn't laugh. He tried to bring the beater down on Richard's head but it was not a weapon to be moved so fast and Richard ducked to one side. Larry lost his balance as the beater swept down into empty space. Richard kicked out at his standing leg and Larry dropped heavily against the shed's wall, unable to put out his hands to break the fall. Richard grabbed Jennifer's hand and they moved as if to run back along the field's border but just fifty yards in front was a wall of flame and black smoke. They turned back to the den. There was a gap in the hedge behind it. Richard pushed Jennifer through to the open field beyond. Though most of the bordering hedgerow was ablaze, the field itself was clear. Walking towards them was Anika, shouting and pointing to their left. A gap in the hedgerow led to a bordering lane. Anika was there first and greeted them calmly, 'Not such a safe place after all?'

Richard was pale with shock but sweating. He looked to Jennifer. She shook and he thought she might cry - he thought he might but tried to sound brave. 'We're okay. It wasn't that close.'

'Good. We should go. Dudek is waiting for us at the top of the lane, they wouldn't let the car come this far. They have been through the village, warning we may have to evacuate and Dudek said we should find you.' As they started walking the black Citroen came to meet them, Dudek's wide grin challenging anyone to claim it had been any more than a just an adventure. He climbed from the car and they stood watching the beaters trying to control the hedgerows. In the next field the fires were burning high.

'My safe place,' Jennifer muttered and looked to be crying though Richard couldn't tell if from shock or sadness.

Richard realised: 'Larry. He …. fell. Where is he?'

'What do you mean?' asked Anika.

'He was there, at the den. He ….'

'…. tried to hit you. Arsehole.' Jennifer finished for Richard.

'Yes, but he fell and …. what if he's still there? What if the fire ….'

Anika shrugged her shoulders.

'Larry? He must be safe,' said Dudek.

'Must he?' asked Anika.

'If he isn't, how would we answer? Where was he?'

'No. Look at the fire Dudek. Look.' Anika was calm but firm. 'And you have a bad ankle …. still.'

'No. Not this time.' He limped across the road and into the field, calling Larry's name. Anika started after him but Richard caught her arm.

'I'll go.' He went after Dudek, leading him through the gap towards Jennifer's den. There were beaters flailing at the hedgerow and one of them shouted they should go away but Dudek shouted back they were looking for Larry and continued through to the adjoining field. They came to the back of the shed. The gorse was in flames but it was thin here and though hot they found a path round to the front of the den. Larry was laying half in the doorway, still holding the beater. There was blood seeping from a cut on his forehead. He was not unconscious but stared, dazed, as Dudek tried to help him stand. Richard took his other arm and they hoisted him to his feet to drag him from the den and back to safety. They emerged into the field with the other beaters and two of them ran to assist. Dudek offered no explanation as they handed Larry over and didn't wait to be asked, limping back to the car.

In Oakjack Ford there was a crowd in the car park of The Blue And The Gorse, waiting for news of whether they should evacuate or stay. Anika was driving and parked close to the police officers controlling the calm meeting. Jennifer slumped low in the back seat but Dudek leant back to pat her hand. 'It's okay. They came to ask a couple of questions of me and say Young Samuel told them what he did. No mention was made of you and Richard. You should go and see your grandmother and Maisie. They will be worried for you.'

Jennifer smiled at Richard and left the car.

'Can we go home?' asked Richard.

'I don't think so. Not yet. We should wait to see what is happening. I will ask.' Dudek left the car to talk to the officers. Anika looked back at Richard.

'Your eyes are dark. Is your head bad, again?'

'Yes.' The neon zig-zags were a corruption to his sight. 'But hey, at least it's not a tumour right?'

'Still not funny.' She turned on the radio. 'Blinded By The Light' was playing and Richard asked her to turn it down, but not off. She dug into her pocket and passed him the little plastic box for his tablets.

Three Weeks In The Summer

Richard, New Year 1976/77
Blinded By The Light

The rain came at the end of August. I was back home and hanging round the park with Malcolm and Julie when it started. We moved from the cover of trees and stood with outstretched arms, laughing and wishing for it to fall heavier. Okay, so it was not a monsoon, but it was rain and enough to make us wet. Julie's t-shirt was soaked through and Malcolm took off his shirt to cover her (he could get away with it, he had an athlete's body) and led her back under cover. I stayed out, enjoying the cleansing feel and smell but wishing Anika and Jennifer were with me. I hoped it was raining in Oakjack Ford and they were sharing it with someone - perhaps each other, but I doubted that. Since coming back I'd written three letters to Anika and two to Jennifer (all slowly, obviously) but sent them only one each. They were very formal letters which said little that I wanted to say, mainly because I didn't know what that was. I had a vague idea I should be thanking them for the summer. Much had happened in a short space of time and it seemed important. But when I told Malcom all that occurred in Oakjack Ford he was most interested in why I hadn't (in his words) 'shagged anyone' which I took to be an admission he had 'shagged' Julie while I was away. That's not to say Malcolm was no longer my best friend and confidant, but my story telling was in black and white and though I had the words to give them colour I baulked at revealing too much of myself -

even though he was still my best friend and confidant. Or maybe second best, after Anika? And Malcolm was more and more pre-occupied with Julie - and who wouldn't be? The summer had been kind to her and she was grown to womanhood in our eyes.

Come mid-September Malcolm went back to John Le Rugber, joining the sixth form and captaining the first XI at …. well, pretty much everything. I didn't (go to sixth form or captain a first XI). When I first said I didn't want to go, my mother was distraught in a way I hadn't seen before and in a manner so theatrical I thought it false. It was. We had many conversations about it (often umpired by Philip, my step-father) and it was clear she thought I should go to sixth form because my father would have approved. I asked her to ring uncle Dudek to see what he thought and by the time she put the phone down I'd as good as left school. My mother was relieved. Though we never spoke of it, the dyslexia was always just a misunderstood word away. Philip was the good man I'd come to know and got me a job in the Datsun dealership. Mostly I was cleaning cars but if all the salesmen were busy I was trusted to show prospective customers round them and point out features, occasionally accompanying them on a short test drive (none more enjoyable than a 260z). I enjoyed the work - I benefited from the respect the other employees accorded Philip and I was earning nearly forty quid a week. Besides, I was just treading water until prog rock fame and fortune found me. I was practising more; piano (when mum was around), Bontempi (when she wasn't), and still checking the ads in Melody Maker for a signed band needing a half-Czech (or half-Vietnamese) keyboard player who lived in Hounslow and didn't have his own transport. I think I was getting pretty good and when one of our local pubs started to show live bands on Thursdays I convinced Malcolm (and Julie) we should go catch the new talent. It was an education for me to sit and watch, especially if they had a keyboard player. On a couple of occasions a pretty girl (different ones each time) and a not so pretty girl (same one on three occasions) might join me and ask if I wanted to buy them a drink. I generally did, but they were all friends of Julie and I suspected Malcolm asked her to set me up. She didn't need to, I was happy enough watching the bands and missing Oakjack Ford. One Thursday, late October, Carol was there to watch the band and in the interval came over to offer me a cigarette, though I still wasn't smoking. So she offered me pot instead, but I politely refused on the grounds my consultant said it wasn't good for my head (I was still having 'issues' as my mum still called them). We chatted and she said sorry for missing the Colditz party back in the summer, especially now she saw how close were Malcolm and Julie these days and she apologised for walking away when I called her at the bus stop that day (I told her I hadn't been sure it was her and she was relieved). I still liked her (we were always able to talk) and she looked good in clothes which even I realised were expensive (she'd left school and was working as a receptionist in a solicitor's office that gave her a clothing allowance). I would have asked her out except she introduced me to Martin, a young (but older than me) trainee at her firm who looked a man with prospects and designs, particularly on Carol for later that evening, I thought. But that was okay. The band started their second set and we parted with a promise to meet up and yes, I'd love to come round for tea sometimes as her mum still asked after me.

In November, at tea break (we had a lot of those, even though we didn't have a union), I was excited to see an ad in New Musical Express for Rocknow Station, playing support at The Red Cow, Hammersmith. I went round Malcolm's after work and convinced him we should go by offering to pay the tube (only nine stops on the Piccadilly) and entry fee (fifty pence) for him and Julie. The band was tighter (and louder) and played as many originals as covers. We bagged a table but had to abandon it and stand when the crowd swamped the small floor. Rocknow Station did two sets and in the interval Mike (JB) came over to ask how I was. I was excited he remembered me (it was three months), though his attention wandered to Julie who was the coolest girl in the pub (again). Malcolm was impressed I knew a real, live, bass player, especially when JB asked me if I'd joined a band yet and insisted I must; I didn't make it obvious to Malcolm that JB hadn't heard me play. JB asked how was Blue Jean Jenny (I made a mental note to mention it in my next letter to her) and said after the gig we should have a drink, but we had to leave to make sure of the last train home. Even Julie was impressed and Malcolm encouraged me to tell the story of Blue Jean Jenny, paying more attention than when I first told it, back in August when I came home.

But the headaches and blinding lights were more frequent and I missed a few days off work and my GP arranged for another consultant appointment.

I still hadn't told my mother how my father died.

Christmas was good and we managed to keep the story of Santa Claus real for Tina, my little sister, but surely for the last year. Or maybe she already knew the truth and was humouring us. I received cards from both Anika and Jennifer, the latter signed Bonnie, which my mother insisted I explain - naturally I didn't. Uncle Dudek sent me a book with pictures of the Czech squadrons in the war and a note saying he hoped it helped to show where the lions should be painted. Philip and my mother bought me a new Yahama keyboard, a step up from my beloved Bontempi, and I experimented with it most of Boxing Day.

On New Year's Eve, Julie's mum and dad hosted a party. Malcolm was expected to help set up so I arrived early with him and we blew up balloons and made paper chains, which didn't impress Julie's mum but she was too polite not to hang them. By seven there were a few guests drinking quickly and smoking heavily. Malcolm, Julie and I were in the conservatory, sifting through a stack of seven inch singles for anything partyish and I offered to go home for my cassette player and tapes. Julie went upstairs for hers instead and risked offending her mother by playing her Donna Summer tape. She was not yet drunk enough to dance as she had at the Colditz party night and we laughed at her description of how boring we had been (me especially) to play an endless board game where the whole point (escape) seemed impossible. She exaggerated the irony of not being able to escape the playing of a board game, the purpose of which is to escape - but she was doing English Literature at A Level. I reminded her how, when bored of our tapes, she'd listen to her little transistor radio and how she always listened through the ear-piece on the bus and way home. I asked her what station she had been listening to and she leaned close to me to whisper,

'Mostly, none. Reception was crap or I forgot to change the battery. Wearing the ear-piece meant everyone assumed I was listening and didn't speak to me. I preferred that.'

I kept the smile on my face for a few seconds before apologising and telling them I had to go home - my vision was halved and the lights would soon be in my eyes. Malcolm and Julie were, as ever, understanding and wanted to make sure I got home okay but I insisted they stay - it was only a short walk and the air would be good. They let me go and I hated having lied to them.

Philip and my mother were watching television. It was only half seven. They were surprised I was home but not as surprised as when I insisted on going to Oakjack Ford that night, right then, on the train. It would have been a long argument if I hadn't grabbed my trench coat and made for the door. Philip bought time by offering to drive me to Waterloo if there were trains in the next hour (hoping there wouldn't be any - but we rang the station and there were). They didn't understand why I wanted to go (I didn't really tell them) but they saw my determination. My mother helped me pack a bag, slipped in two cartons of drink and a cheese roll and insisted I ring from Dudek's the second I arrived and be back the following Wednesday, for an appointment with the consultant. Philip said I could miss a couple days' work.

The train left Waterloo at just gone nine and I arrived in Hinton just over two hours later. It was three or four miles walk to Oakjack Ford in the cold and dark and I hoped to remember the route as I trudged. I had thought there'd be a taxi stand or something, but there wasn't. My trench coat (bought with first pay packet) struggled against the cold.

Dudek's house was in darkness. The bag I'd brought was heavy after an hour's walking and my shoulders hurt, hunched against the cold. The Citroen wasn't in the drive. I guessed the time was between midnight and one. Somewhere between Hinton and Oakjack Ford I'd missed New Year. I didn't mind. There had been enough in the old year to make it worth keeping. I huddled on the porch for a few minutes, working through possibilities and cursing not phoning first. It was too cold not to do something and if all else failed, I was pretty sure I could find a welcome at Jennifer's, so I left my bag by the door and walked into the village, stopping at The Blue And The Gorse. The Citroen was in the car park (I noticed the damage from hitting the deer had been repaired) and I peeped through the window to see Anika serving behind the bar; an after-hours New Year party was in swing. The door was locked. I knocked heavily but it took a while and three more knocks before I was heard above the juke-box. A young man I didn't know opened the door and I must have looked in need of help as he moved aside to let me in without question (or perhaps he was drunk). He went back to the clearing near the bar where a handful of drinkers jigged happily to 'Play That Funky Music'. Anika was collecting glasses, joking her way through and around the customers, laughing with young, old, men, women, drunk and sober alike. I enjoyed watching her, glad she hadn't seen me yet, but when she did I swear her smile broadened as she gave a shriek. She almost dropped the glasses on the bar and came over to me. We tried to cuddle but my trench coat was a barrier; I threw it off and we hugged each other hard. She kissed me. On the lips. Not full, not passionately, not like a lover, but not just a peck either - just a perfect kiss of welcome. She wore the red dress with low cut v-neck I'd admired back in the summer and I smelt stale alcohol and tobacco on her but she wasn't drunk. She found me a table in the corner, by a radiator, and took time from serving to make me a cup of hot chocolate. I sat and watched her conduct the symphony of customers, bringing the party to a measured close and easing them into the cold night, each convinced they'd had the best New Year's Eve party. She hadn't even asked why I was there (let alone how) and that was good, it seemed to imply it was the right thing.

We were almost the last to leave the pub. I put on the trench coat but held it up and open for Anika to huddle in with me. It didn't work to keep us warm but it was a short walk. She left the Citroen at the pub.

We were home in minutes and she took the key from behind the flower pot. I cursed at having forgotten it was there but remembered to ring mum and though it was now half one, she answered immediately with false calmness. I convinced her I was safe. Anika was making coffee and explained she was too tired to go to sleep. I thought I understood and sat where I could see the clocks.

'Kon Tum still running fast.'

'Yes. Dudek won't take it to be fixed.' Anika sat opposite me and we cupped mugs of coffee.

'Where is he?' I asked.

'At Elizabeth's. I expect he'll drink too much whisky and sleep on the sofa. Maisie is still there. Her cottage won't be built again for months. She and Elizabeth are making Jennifer crazy, but they let her have that puppy. Jaybee. He is beautiful, but Dudek will come back smelling of dog.'

'So he and Elizabeth are getting on okay?'

'Yes. She is bringing him under control. Until Christmas Eve he hadn't drunk in nearly a month.'

'And Jennifer?'

'I don't know if she is there tonight. I heard from Elizabeth there is a young lad in Hinton who has been .... calling on her. Is that a good thing?'

'For sure. And you? Anyone calling on you?'

'Hmmmm. Not really. The story of waving a gun at Larry has spread and many think I am a mad woman they dare not make angry. I don't mind. They are kind to me.'

'Sure that's not just because you are .... Anika?'

'Ha. You are still very sweet. And I like your new haircut. You look older.'

'So you would have shot Larry?'

'For your uncle's .... honour? Is that the word? Of course. Your uncle is a better man, whatever happened between them.'

'And you forgot the gun wasn't loaded?'

'For sure. Larry is a lucky man.'

She looked directly at me. I matched her smile and asked, 'So you've seen Larry around? Was he .... grateful? After the fire?'

'I don't think they ever spoke of it and now your uncle and him are okay and Erica is not so angry with me, though we no longer get the biggest buns from the bakery.'

I laughed.

'What? It's true.' She sipped from her coffee. 'Some people still believe Larry instead of your uncle. They think Dudek .... was .... too close to him .... or something.'

'He could have left him at the fire .... he might have .... you know.'

'And they think that's why he didn't .... because they were .... close. But Dudek knew they'd think that. It doesn't matter. Some people think less of him, not more. But he knew they would.' She looked back to her coffee.

'What happened to Samuel?'

'He is gone. Dudek rang some people .... you know .... as he does .... but I think it is too long since he .... worked. I don't think he has so many friends in London as before. We never heard Samuel's saxophone after .... after....'

I remembered uncle's phrase. 'The things we do for love.'

'Like your father?'

'I guess.'

'Don't look so sad. It is good to be loved so much. You need to live for him too now.'

I forced a smile.

'Have you told Diu yet?' she asked.

I shook my head. 'Maybe in the new year.'

Anika looked behind her to the clocks. 'Everywhere except Washington then? Don't keep it secret.'

'I don't think it will help her to feel guilt.'

Anika looked at me and I wished it was still August. 'It was a good summer, wasn't it?' I asked.

'Yes. Where were you when the rain came?'

'In the park with friends. Malcolm and Julie. We stood and soaked.'

'Ah, Julie. And did you and Julie ....?'

'No, no way. She's with Malcolm.'

'Good.'

'Where were you? When it started raining.'

'Down at the pond. To see the surface dance with ripples and feel the splashes …. it was …. perfect.'

'I wish I'd been there.'

'Me too. You know Dudek is wrong about lesson four.' She reached over the table to hold my hand.

'I think so.'

We sat in comfortable silence until Anika simply nodded and went upstairs, to bring down a couple of blankets, a cassette tape and a new portable player. 'This is yours. You left it.' She showed me the tape.

'Yep. I made to practise along with. I realised I'd left it here when I got home.'

'I told Dudek to buy a player. We listen a lot.' She held up the little mono player like a trophy. 'And now even Dudek likes some of it. Or pretends.' She slipped the cassette into the player and pressed PLAY. The guitar solo for 'Summer Breeze' was in full swing. She passed the blankets to me and motioned I should follow her. In the front sitting room she switched on the two bar electric fire. The orange glow barely lit the room and the colour promised more warmth than the old elements could deliver but I wasn't cold. Anika took the blankets from me and spread one on the rug in front of the fire before unzipping her dress, stepping out of it and removing her bra and panties. She gave an exaggerated shiver and made a 'brrrr' sound. I stared at her high breasts and caught a glimpse of the dark hair below her flat belly as she wrapped the other blanket around her. I shivered too, though not cold, and nearly said 'thank you' out loud - how uncool. This was surreal and fantastical but also immediate and vital and alive. Anika. Her presence was all. I held my breath. She stood close to me and tried to unbutton my shirt but it was awkward with her arms holding the blanket tucked under them to keep it from falling (oh God please let it fall), so I undid the buttons, not caring she saw my hands tremble. When my shirt was removed she knelt on the other blanket and indicated I should strip completely (as least I think she did, I was always going to) and as I knelt beside her she enveloped us both in her blanket and let me pull her down on top of me. I was careless and frenzied with touching and desperate pawing until she whispered 'shhhh,' and leant away from me, moving my head so I looked into her eyes instead of at her body. She removed my spectacles (I wanted to keep them on so not to miss any detail) and breathed deeply and obviously. I matched her breathing as our eyes steadied on each other. When I had calmed she lifted and tilted her hips and lowered herself so that I eased into her. I'm sure I gasped with the burning pleasure and she smiled and was fixed on my gaze, controlling my urge with her own movements until she too was ready and we rocked hard against each other and I heard her groan and moan and I pressed up as I hugged her and squeezed her down onto me and she screamed silently with her face buried into my neck.

I was breathing heavily though I was neither tired nor short of breath. Anika was half draped across me and patted my chest as it rose up and settled down. She whispered, 'No longer a watcher.'

I wanted something profound and important to say - something like 'watching takes time we don't have' - though it does sound like a bad movie line, so perhaps it's better that instead I muttered,

'Thank God we're not cousins.'

'Aren't we?' she said.

'What d'you mean? You said we weren't. In the summer. You said we weren't cousins.'

'No. I said we were.'

'What ....' I tried to sit up. She pushed me back down.

'Ha! Too easy. Of course we are not cousins. Your face .... ha. If Jennifer saw she would laugh.'

251

I reached down to slap her thigh, not hard, and repeated, 'Thank God we're not cousins. Thank God Jennifer isn't here to see.'

'Thank God.' She echoed and studied my face, difficult in the poor light from the meagre two bar fire. 'Remember the pond? I know this is not there, but for winter, this is perfect. If you come back next summer, by the pond, in the grass …. we should …. yes?'

'Oh yes. But next summer? It's a long time.'

'You think? That's because you are so young.' She tried to tease me but I was melancholy and unable to hide it.

'Is your head okay? It is …. dark around your eyes,' Anika asked.

'Yeah. Just a small headache. I have tablets in my bag.'

'I hear from Dudek your headaches have been worse. Diu told him.'

'It's not so much the headaches. It's the other stuff. The lights, sound, not being able to say words.' I shrugged but was fighting back tears.

'Richard? What's the matter?'

I took a slow breath. 'You know we used to joke …. my bad head …. at least it's not a ….tumour? …. Remember? Turns out it is. Can you believe that? What a pisser. They don't …. think …. you know ….' I started to cry and wasn't embarrassed. She held me, not tight, just …. perfect. I pulled the blankets closer around us and wanted to whisper 'I love you' but was scared it would sound ridiculous. Instead I said, 'My mother used to tell me everything would be all right and I believed her. Until ….'

'Shhhhhh. It will be all right,' she said and though we both knew it wouldn't, it was soothing to pretend.

'Remember when Dudek told us about Samuel and Megan?' I asked. 'He said we could save time, for ourselves, but can't give it away?'

Anika thought for a moment and nodded. I squeezed her and asked, 'Would you save this time? For me?'

'Of course. And for me.'

The cassette played 'Blinded By The Light'.

END

Three Weeks In The Summer

.... by Paul Marriner and available through www.bluescalepublishing.co.uk .

Sunrises And Other Stories

Love, grief, hope, sorrow and joy - the consequences of living that help us to learn and confront truths.

This is a collection of stories where impressionable boys and lovers, fathers and mothers, priests, con-men and angels come alive; stories of people and moments to care for and recognise. Told with compassion and care, these are tales of living and dying from an author who hopes you will bring them to life by knowing the people within.

The collection is linked by characters and events. At their core is 'Sunrises', in which Anthony grieves following the death of his daughter and struggles to know where to turn for his own peace and truth.

'Sunrises' is supported by stories depicting critical episodes from Anthony's life and the lives of those around him; how he is shaped by the choices and actions of others and how they influence his present and future.

Love, grief, hope, sorrow and joy - bringing truth to a life.

.... by Paul Marriner and available through www.bluescalepublishing.co.uk .

Charlotte's Cross

Loss, Forgiveness, Redemption

When Jay's father dies and she learns of his secret life as a musician, she is driven to understand more and search for Charlotte, the mother who left when she was young. Jay's search takes her to Portugal and the exclusive bordello where Charlotte lived. But Charlotte has spent the years fighting her own demons and trying to re-kindle her faith and is no longer there.

At the bordello Jay meets and falls for Jackson, one of the girls working for Alex, the manager. Alex hinders Jay's search but she is helped by Jackson, who wants to escape the controlling Alex.

Together, Jay and Jackson continue the search for Charlotte, needing to find her before Alex can track them down.